UNSUSPECTING WORLD

WATER DREAMER SERIES
BOOK TWO

DANA PRICE

Unsuspecting World

Water Dreamer series, Book 2
by Dana Price
Copyright © 2024 by Dana Price

This book is a work of fiction. Any names or scenes depicted in this book are coincidental and should not be construed as a representation of any actual person or circumstance.

Cover design by Rachelle Price

AI cover art

ISBN 978-1-950741-12-0

Published by Inky's Nest Publishing

1st edition
First printed in 2024 in the United States of America

Your Free Short Story is Waiting

Meet precocious Greta Sterling, a young character from the Water Dreamer series whose best friend is her chicken Bucky. In this delightful tale, nothing prepares Greta and her pa for a startling interruption to their meager country life. Magic and innocence clash, and Greta finds herself to be her own worst enemy. The Sterlings won't know what they've got their hands on until well into the series.

waterdreamerseries.com/greta

To Brandon

for your invaluable editing
and brainstorming prowess

1

Cristen huddled on the riverbank, shivering as mist from the river clung to his clothes and skin. Maintaining a cautious distance from the edge, he continued scanning his surroundings, hoping to discover any sign of the master.

Driven by the need to begin his quest, Cristen consulted his parchment that morning, seeking guidance on how to proceed. The master responded by telling him to follow his bird to a location where his true nature would be revealed and where he could receive the personal guidance he sought. Unaware of the day's unfolding path, Cristen didn't anticipate a return to Old Surge and its terrifying suspension bridge.

Despite the remote and inhospitable meeting place, Cristen felt a rush of excitement. This encounter meant more than finally meeting his benefactor; it marked the beginning of unraveling secrets—the tyrants to overcome and the training awaiting him.

His gaze stretched across the chasm to the far alcove, where he thought he glimpsed a figure again. However, with each investigation, it turned out to be nothing more than a subtle trick of misty light and shadow.

Cristen sprang to his feet when he spotted his bird. He thought it had disappeared after their arrival, but it perched far down on the railing. How long had it been there? The mere thought of crossing again made him anxious. But if the master intended to meet with him on the other side, what other option did he have?

With cautious steps, he edged onto the slippery planks of the bridge. He paused to steady his nerves with a few deep breaths before continuing across the yawning chasm. Though the turbulent waters far below struck him with the same fear as before, he pressed on, refusing to let the master down. The pigeon fluttered to the railing at Cristen's side as if to lend moral support.

After gaining some distance, the pigeon abruptly landed directly in front of his feet. With the wind picking up speed, Cristen hated to stop now. He carefully maneuvered around the bird, face dripping and hands clenched white-knuckled on the rail. "Come on, we're almost there!" he yelled over the river's roar.

Glancing back, he noticed the pigeon gripping a strange parchment in its beak. He retraced his steps a few planks to retrieve it. The single word scrawled filled him with icy dread:

JUMP

Cristen tossed the parchment in anger at the command. Trembling, he froze in place, wondering what to do. The wizard's demand echoed in his mind, each repetition like a hammer blow to his heart. Had the wizard planned this all along, to bring him here and force him to sacrifice himself? to what end? He stared at the frothing water, tears mingling with the mist on his cheeks. Giant boulders protruded from both lower banks, hinting at more dangers hidden beneath the surface—the apparent cause of the turbulence. Even if he avoided them by some stroke of luck, the impact with the water from such a height would be like hitting a brick wall. As he considered the impending jump more fully, panic tightened its grip on him.

After everything he'd been through, didn't he deserve a break? He had trusted the wizard, believing him a protector all this time! Did this unthinkable order constitute some twisted test? If so, the wizard had gone too far.

Cristen scrambled back across the bridge as quickly as he dared, the cables cutting into his palms. He never should have come to this wretched place.

2

One month later...

Cristen wore his hat low as he moved through the late afternoon crowd at King's Crossing's town square. He had avoided densely packed gatherings like this ever since winning the prized stallion Sunfire at the Array contests months prior, hoping to escape recognition as public enemy number one. He even resorted to cutting his wavy, chin-length hair short to disguise his appearance.

But today's promised exhibition of three newly captured water dreamers heading their way proved too tempting for Cristen. Though he felt the kidnapping and humiliation of fellow water dreamers a gross injustice, curiosity drew him out into the bustling square like everyone else.

Cristen felt another shell-like dragon scale materialize in his tunic pocket. No matter how often he emptied them, the cursed things reappeared relentlessly, sometimes multiple times daily. Once an annoyance, now his steadily growing collection of them made him feel oddly wealthy. With his current stockpile, he could likely buy anything he wanted—a bigger home, a fancy cart for Sunfire, or even a whole stable full of the finest horses. Damon's friends would be envious if they knew the sheer quantity of scales he accumulated without ever having to hunt for them.

A lone rider loped into the far side of the square on a dappled gray mare. "The wagon train is nearly here! Just needed to fix a broken wheel," he announced loudly to the whispering crowd.

Finally, Cristen thought, his anticipation building. He just wanted to catch a brief glimpse of the captives before slipping away unnoticed, back to the solitude of his house.

Moments later, the first two prison carts slowly rolled into view, with two gray messenger pigeons flitting about the wagons, confirming the identity of those locked inside. Cristen moved to a new position between heads to get a better view of the approaching procession. He scanned the area warily to ensure his own telltale pigeon didn't track him down amongst the townspeople. As the wagons approached the square, the murmuring crowd fell eerily silent, with all eyes fixed in morbid curiosity on the imprisoned water dreamers about to be paraded before them like exotic animals. Like the rest of the gawking onlookers, Cristen couldn't stop staring as the carts drew near.

Two teenage boys marked in red dreamer attire peered out despondently from behind their bars. One of the boys haplessly met Cristen's gaze as his barred cart slowly passed him, keeping his eyes locked on him, dredging up a profound sense of shame. A third cart finally rolled into view, wobbling unsteadily on a visibly damaged wheel. Cristen winced in sympathy, feeling sorry for the girl, also in red, being jostled roughly inside the rickety final wagon. Her white and brown pigeon clung miserably atop the splintered roof.

As her cart gradually approached Cristen's position, he gasped aloud in utter shock. The girl imprisoned looked identical to Hanna from his recurrent dreams! With her delicate facial features, slender build, and flowing light brown hair, Cristen's heart raced.

"Hanna?" he whispered under his breath. Impossible, he thought. Stunned, he hurried to run alongside the trundling wagon, desperate for a better look at her.

"Stay back from the wagons!" her burly driver bellowed gruffly at Cristen.

"I know her!" Cristen persisted. However, he quickly doubted his absurd claim. What were the odds? He must be losing his mind.

Yet why *couldn't* the sea grant life to the dreams she implanted in their minds? What if the sea crafted the girl directly from Cristen's dreams into a living, breathing reality to become an active part of his world? Did it also make Cristen from the fabric of Damon's dreams for Damon's real world?

Determined not to let the girl out of his sight, Cristen raced behind the wagon, using the bulky vehicle as a shield from the driver's furious gaze. Gathering his courage, he quickly hopped onto the back ledge, coming face-to-face with the padlocked door. Inside, the haunted girl observed him with melancholy eyes. She hugged her knees tightly to her chest, her ethereal features even more striking in person—her warm honey-tan skin, generous lower lip, and delicate straight nose left him breathless. Hanna, the enigmatic figure who had long inhabited his dreams, had inexplicably materialized before him, as real and tangible as the bars he grasped.

Trembling with emotion, Cristen croaked the impossible question, his voice catching: "Are...are you...Hanna?"

The girl's forlorn expression instantly vanished, replaced by startled curiosity. She scrambled to the barred door and fell to her knees in front of him. "Please...how do you know me? You have to get me out of here!" Hope glimmered in her desperate eyes.

Her simple act of confirming the name left Cristen reeling. "I'll...I'll try to explain everything later, I promise," he stammered in reply, his mind flooded with a thousand urgent questions. He frantically examined the iron padlock and thick wooden doorframe, searching for any possible way to break open the lock and set her free.

The girl gasped loudly, her frightened gaze fixed on something looming behind Cristen. Searing, explosive pain erupted through his vulnerable calves as a blow struck him from behind. He cried out in agony, knocked off balance and tumbling clumsily from the back of the moving wagon. He landed directly on his knees on the pebbly dirt road, calves and knees burning like fire from the ruthless assault.

A red-faced town constable loomed menacingly over him as he slapped a wooden baton against his meaty palm, poised and ready to deliver another crippling blow. "Got cotton in those ears, boy?" the imposing man growled threateningly.

"I need to talk to her!" Cristen said through throbbing pain, blinking back anguished tears.

"Hey, isn't that a water dreamer too?" a woman's voice called out from among the spectators.

Cristen hid his face, realizing his fall had knocked away his hat, though it was too late.

"I recognize him from the Array," another said excitedly.

"It is him, he's cut his hair!" shouted another.

Cristen locked his watering eyes onto the receding wagon as he nursed his battered calves and bleeding knees. He must get to his horse and catch up to that wagon.

"Well now, everything makes perfect sense," the constable scoffed, glaring contemptuously down at Cristen. "Looking to spawn a little shoal of fish?"

"Where are they taking her?" Cristen asked desperately, ignoring the man's vile insinuation.

"To Oakville Holding Center until they're formally introduced to the public," the constable said.

You mean until they're publicly hurt and humiliated at the Array, Cristen thought bitterly. He pressed further, "Where's Oakville?"

"Alright, folks. Shows over. Clear out!" The constable waved dismissively at the lingering crowd before mounting his decorated horse and riding off.

Hobbling homeward through town in intense pain, Cristen's mind raced as he mentally prepared to intercept Hanna's transport convoy on the road to Oakville. Pausing a moment in his yard to catch his breath, dizzying questions over Hanna flooded his weary mind. What if his dreams revealed his true home after all? Did family still search for him out there somewhere? What if Hanna came to find him when he mysteriously turned up missing?

Catching himself indulging in such destructive thoughts again, he chastised himself bitterly for being endlessly gullible. He'd chose the vulnerability of lifelong dreams by refusing the Oasis, so he'd better get a grip. Nothing in this cold reality supported the fanciful dreams he still clung to.

Despite countless searches over centuries, no water dreamer had ever located family or any evidence of a life predating their emergence from the sea. The girl was doubtless just another water dreamer birthed from the sea like all the rest, plain and simple. Sadly, like Damon, she could never fully return Cristen's affections without first building a genuine relationship like any other.

Still, he felt elated over her existence and looked forward to helping her through this challenging initial discovery period to understand her identity. He vowed to tell her everything he knew about Harmony so she didn't have to learn the hard way. He would especially warn her of the power of the dragon scales, Burning Mountain, and the deceptive, dangerous dragon.

Unlocking the door with his ornate key, he limped inside. He hoped Hanna liked his small living quarters. He planned to give her anything she needed to help get settled, even sleep in the drafty barn to accommodate her.

Cristen promptly stuffed the remainder of his bread, cheese, and fresh fruit into his knapsack, knowing Hanna would need food after her long ordeal. The food mysteriously appeared each morning, somehow left on the table before he awoke. He recognized the hand of the wizard, though he didn't understand the continued generosity after brushing him off since Old Surge. He didn't dare use the wizard's parchment for communication since that fateful day, fearing potential punishment or further impossible requests from the unpredictable entity. Not that he felt the need to communicate—he managed perfectly fine on his own.

Cristen took the orb from his top drawer and dropped it into his knapsack with the food. Growing increasingly anxious to leave, he quickly strapped on his waterskin, slung his pack over his shoulder, and went to saddle Sunfire for the urgent ride ahead.

3

Cristen followed the road out of town the prison carts took earlier that day, passing endless farmlands and the occasional crossroad, hoping the wagon train hadn't turned off onto any of them. As the sun gradually sank, the road narrowed, leading toward a vast forest up ahead.

He approached a small, weathered farmhouse where six ragged children played and gleefully chased one another around the front yard. He decided to stop and talk with them to see what they knew. Seeing Cristen riding up, they paused their game and changed course to gather around to greet him and his horse.

"Hey Mister, did you bring us some sweets?" asked the first child to arrive, steps ahead of the others. The bubbly girl of about seven wore messy curls down to her waist. Her thick country accent reminded him fondly of Greta. The children looked grimy, with tangled hair, dirty bare feet, and holes in their clothing.

"Is your father here?" Cristen asked the tallest of the group, a wiry boy of about thirteen.

"Our pa?" the boy replied, exchanging knowing glances with his siblings. "Sure, he's right over there under that big tree." He pointed behind him past a field to an ancient oak, prompting giggles from the group.

"His name is on a stick, so we can remember where we put him," added a younger boy matter-of-factly, provoking more hushed laughter from the others.

Cristen blinked in surprise. How could they speak so casually about their deceased father like that?

"Mister, whatcha got in that sack there?" called out a scrappy girl of nine or so, her tangled pigtails bouncing as she trotted up alongside his horse. Her gaze fixed eagerly on the knapsack lashed to his saddle.

"Just a little food for a friend," Cristen replied.

"We're your friends, and we're starving, ya know?" she said with an exaggerated pout, provoking more giggles from her cohorts.

Cristen admitted that, even with their off-putting manners, he found the children oddly likable and clever in their mischievousness.

"Does your friend live close by?" asked the middle boy.

"No, but did any carts happen to roll through here to-day?" Cristen asked, directing his question to the oldest.

"Just those stinky fish carts," piped up the youngest girl, no more than four or five, with a giggle. "That's what Jack calls them when they go by."

Cristen shook his head at the derogatory nickname they already knew, though them seeing the carts brought great relief.

"Jack's the courier," explained the middle boy. "He's the one that makes Mama giggle when he brings the post."

Cristen grimaced, not caring to hear it. "Anyone know how far the town Oakville is from here?"

The children answered all at once, each calling out different made-up distances.

"Could I possibly speak with your mother?" Cristen asked patiently. Any adult should know.

"Ma's busy," said a girl with a dismissive shrug.

"She said to always say she's busy!" the youngest said innocently.

"I think she's scrubbing the walls today," the oldest boy explained with a knowing grin.

Cristen didn't believe any of it. "Tell you what," he said. "If you run and bring your mother out here for a minute, I'll share some food with my new friends."

The children cheered in unison. Three scampered off toward the house while the others stayed put, entertained by petting Sunfire and asking Cristen endless unrelated questions.

After what seemed an eternity, the old farmhouse door finally creaked open. Two of the children triumphantly pulled an enormously overweight, disheveled woman by her thick wrists out onto the rickety front porch. A third child pushed ineffectively from behind, struggling to budge her ample backside. Though the combined efforts of the children finally coaxed the woman down the two uneven steps into the yard, her progress toward Cristen felt painfully slow.

Feeling a twinge of guilt for summoning the rotund woman, Cristen quickly dismounted and approached her to spare her further struggle. The children abruptly dispersed into the yard to resume playing.

"Pardon the intrusion, ma'am, but I'm trying to find the town of Oakville. Do you know how far it is?"

"Why din't you jest ask the chil'en?" the hefty woman muttered irritably, her round, red face glistening from her brief exertion.

"They didn't seem too sure when I asked," Cristen explained politely.

"It's prob'ly straight away through them woods, just a piece beyond, I reckon," the woman speculated with uncertainty.

Her knowledge of Oakville didn't fare better than her children's. "Thank you for your time, ma'am," Cristen said, disappointed to be getting nowhere.

When Cristen turned to leave, he fumed to find the children gathered around Sunfire, eating the bread and fruit straight from his open knapsack on the ground. When he noticed the oldest boy tossing his orb repeatedly into the air like a ball, Cristen rushed over to rescue his belongings. The boy didn't know what he held. Luckily, the daylight hid the glow of its beam. Initially amused by the cheeky children, Cristen now felt annoyed; the children lost their charm.

He promptly scooped up his ravaged knapsack and caught the orb midair before the boy could toss it again. The boy merely shrugged and took another bite from the pilfered apple, seemingly unfazed. Cristen mounted Sunfire and turned the stallion back toward the tree line. Despite the unhelpful encounter, Cristen couldn't be too far behind the slower-moving prison carts.

***

Deep into the forest, Cristen spotted an old log cabin obscured by trees at the end of a long drive. He would have ridden right by, except he noticed fresh wheel tracks cutting through the dense undergrowth. Sensing he needed to stop and investigate, he guided Sunfire off the main road, giving the cabin a wide berth as they looped through the trees. With his horse hidden, he dismounted and secured the stallion before cautiously proceeding the rest of the way in on foot.

Creeping toward the left side of the cabin, the rear end of a prison cart caught his eye around the far corner. His pulse quickened. Stepping lightly to avoid snapping twigs underfoot, he hurried over to make his way along the log wall. Peering around the edge, he did a double take when he saw a water dreamer still within the bars of a cart, though not Hanna.

"Hey!" Cristen called out quietly, trying to get the dreamer's attention.

The prisoner perked up when he saw Cristen and moved closer on his knees.

"Where are the other wagons?" Cristen asked in a hushed voice.

"I saw you in that last town," said the dreamer.

Cristen remembered him too, the one who had locked eyes with him. The look on his face revealed a chip on his shoulder, and for good reason.

"You okay?" Cristen asked him.

"You have to get me out of here," demanded the dreamer.

Cristen noticed the padlock and chain fastened around the rear cart door. "Where's your driver?" he asked.

"Inside. The fool's making me sleep out here," the dreamer retorted.

"Figures," Cristen said under his breath. The dreamer, clad only in red prisoner garb, knelt on the cart's hard surface, devoid of blankets or padding to provide comfort against the chilly night air. "Can he see you from there?"

"Probably not. He closed the curtains," said the dreamer.

Cristen stripped off his outer tunic to take over for him. He glanced nervously toward the cabin window, worried about the driver spotting him. He passed the tunic through the bars. "For warmth or a pillow if you want," he said.

"What about getting me out?" the dreamer pleaded again in a harsh whisper as he accepted the tunic.

"Look, unless I go in there and fight him for the key, there's nothing I can do." Cristen backed away a few steps, feeling guilty for leaving him there, but Hanna remained his priority. "Did the others stop too?"

The dreamer's face fell in angry disappointment. "You're going to leave me locked up in this thing?" he asked bitterly, gripping the bars. "My family is out there looking for me!"

He deserved to be upset. "Believe me, I know, and I'm really sorry," Cristen said earnestly. "I'll come back for you if I can, I promise." He hurried back toward the safety of the trees to retrieve Sunfire and continue his search.

4

When Cristen spotted Hanna's distinctive brown pigeon flitting around the roof of another remote cabin up ahead, he knew he must have found her. Like the previous encounter, the driver took the prison cart to the back of the property with the sleeping horse hitched to a tree. Hiding Sunfire again, he hurried toward the back.

Hearing muffled voices from within, Cristen crouched beneath a grimy, partially broken window to peek inside. Hanna's driver sat in a shredded armchair, fitting a walnut into a nutcracker. A low table sat at his knees, walnuts and cracked shells strewn across it. Cristen noted the man's muscular shoulders and thick arms, showing his formidable strength. Noticing the mismatch in their builds, Cristen reluctantly sank to the ground. As much as he needed to free Hanna, he knew realistically he didn't stand a chance of overpowering the man's physical advantage alone.

"Serves you right," the driver scolded. "I already warned you plenty to keep your mouth shut over there."

Cristen peered inside again as the man cracked open another nut, but Hanna remained hidden.

"Who knew a waifish sea creature like you could jabber on so much?" continued the man. "Frankly, I'm getting mighty sick of hearing the nonsense spewing from that trap of yours. What are you staring at? You want a blindfold to go along with that?"

Hanna let out a muffled scream, clearly gagged, and the cruel man only chuckled in amusement at her distress, relaxing back into his chair. Cristen ducked again when the man's eyes shifted toward the window.

After a brief silence, the man muttered, "There you go, mighty tasty, they are."

Something small and hard bounced across the wooden floor, likely a nut.

"Why can't you be easy like my last dreamer? Now that one behaved proper, as a good little sea rat should."

Cristen fumed as he imagined how many other helpless water dreamers this monster had already abused. He shifted to a more comfortable position and snapped a twig.

The man grunted. "Your pesky bird again," A whole walnut flew through the open section of the window, bouncing off Cristen's shoulder before rolling to a stop in the dirt. "You know they only follow your kind because you all smell like rotting fish. That scrawny bird would probably eat you alive if you didn't look so gigantic.

Cristen snuck around to the cabin's front, stepping through low shrubs to another window, this one intact. He spotted Hanna seated helplessly on the dirty floor, a gag around her mouth. Her hands were bound behind her back, and a short length of rope secured one of her ankles to the leg of a rusted cast iron stove, allowing her little mobility. Hanna's eyes flew wide open when she saw Cristen in the window, but she quickly averted her gaze to avoid giving him away.

Cristen ran back around to the back again. He hoped to catch the man by surprise and blind him long enough to grab Hanna and escape, as he'd done to Sefilar. As he contemplated the feasibility of making such an attempt, doubts about his ability to execute it smoothly began to worry him. His aim with the beam needed to be quick and precise before giving the man a chance to react.

It seemed Cristen might have to wait until the man finally slept. He would sneak inside, locate a knife to cut Hanna's bindings, then flee with her on Sunfire.

As the endless night wore on, Cristen remained hidden, stealing occasional glances. Finally, the man's rumbling snores signaled the time to make his move. To let Hanna know he was still there, Cristen cupped the orb with both hands, gently squeezing it to aim a beam of light onto the ceiling through the missing section of the window. Hanna's muffled cry of surprise confirmed that she saw his signal.

But the slumbering man must have heard her, for he snorted loudly, muttering incoherently. After a tense minute of silence, he mumbled with a yawn, "Alright, my sweet, let's see if you've learned your lesson, hmm?" The man's heavy boots clunked across the creaky floorboards. "Now hold still...that's it, there's a good angel fish. Now look at that, not a peep from those pretty lips. You sure are a fine-looking thing, ain't you? Crying shame you're only a dreamer. Well, it don't mean I can't do a little admiring now, does it?"

It took every bit of willpower not to crash through the window and gouge the vile man's eyes out of their sockets—until Hanna boldly spoke up.

"Touch me and die," she threatened, surprising Cristen with her fiery spirit.

The awful man chortled condescendingly at her warning. "Ain't you a feisty little spitfire! There now, just tucking that hair back nice and tidy for you, no need to fuss. Stop squirm ing…" The man suddenly bellowed out in rage, "Rotten water wart, and my good hand too! Why I oughta…"

When Cristen heard the crack of a hand striking flesh, followed by Hanna's pained whimper, he couldn't tolerate it any longer. But just as he rose to enter the cabin, he resisted his impulse—it didn't serve Hanna to blow his cover just yet, risking a head-on confrontation.

Instead, he took the orb back out and aimed another beam onto the ceiling, closer to the window where he hid. Based on the crashing sound of the man tripping over furniture, the show of light did its job, confusing him. By squeezing the orb tighter and covering more of its surface, Cristen managed to focus the beam into a brilliant dot. When he aimed it toward the center of the ceiling, the man cried out in bewildered shock.

"Strike me dead! What kind of evil sorcery is this?" he bellowed loudly, unaware of Cristen's presence.

The main ceiling beam began smoking where the concentrated light struck it. Startled by the unexpected effect, Cristen promptly released his hands, extinguishing the orb. But a small burst of flame sparked from the smoldering wood. He'd started a fire! The man cursed as he tried slapping out the small flame with his hat. Cristen jumped up in alarm as the fire spread inches across the beam.

"Stop, what are you doing!" he shouted through the window, then ran to the door to find it locked. After pounding relentlessly with no response, he whipped back around to the front to see ominous tendrils of smoke seeping out through chinks between the cabin's aged logs. "Open up!" he screamed, banging on the second locked door. He took two bounding steps from the porch to the window to witness tongues of flames beginning to spread across the length of the ceiling.

The man continued battling the fire, exacerbating the situation until flames engulfed his hat. Smoldering embers rained down, carpeting the floor as the fire consumed more of the ceiling. Hanna, still tied helplessly to the stove, screamed in horror, "Cut me loose! What are you waiting for?"

"Untie her!" Cristen tried shouting through the intact window as smoke filled the cabin. He bashed his fist against the window, shattering the glass. "Get her out!" He finally caught the useless man's attention.

A spark of recognition seemed to flare in the man's wide eyes. "You..." he snarled through gritted teeth. "What have you done?"

"You'll die, get out!" Cristen warned, ignoring the painful cuts, now dripping blood from his hand and wrist.

Finally, the man cut Hanna's rope, freeing her leg from the stove. He wrenched her up by the elbow with her wrists still tied, eliciting a pained cry. Cristen ran around back again to meet them as the man hauled her out the door, both coughing from the smoke they inhaled.

"Just let her go," Cristen pleaded. "I'll take her to Oakville myself," he lied in desperation.

Disregarding him, The man pushed Hanna past Cristen toward the waiting prison cart as she struggled against his iron grip. Filled with rage at seeing her mistreated so harshly, Cristen charged the man from behind, attacking him with his fists until the vile man shoved him out of the way onto the ground. Cristen quickly stumbled back to his feet.

As the man fought to stuff Hanna back into her wheeled cage, Cristen grabbed up a sizable rock and, with every ounce of adrenaline-fueled strength he could muster, smashed it into the back of the man's head. The man stumbled, then collapsed face down onto the ground, blood oozing from his scalp and matting his hair from the blow.

Cristen and Hanna stood transfixed momentarily, slowly realizing that he had triumphed over her captor. Snapping out of his stupor, Cristen snatched up the pocketknife that had dropped from the man's trousers and leaped into the back of the prison wagon. He cut through the layers of

Hanna's remaining bindings, pocketed the blade, and hopped back down to help her down too.

"I appreciate this, but why?" Hanna asked breathlessly as Cristen examined her bruised wrists. "How do you know my name?"

Flames licked the sides of the cabin as smoke seeped through every crack and crevice.

"I'll have to explain later," Cristen said, taking her arm. "Come on, let's get him away from the house."

They each took one of the unconscious man's wrists and dragged his dead weight farther away from the fire.

"Please, just tell me how you know me," Hanna persisted when they stopped to catch their breath. Despite the situation, she seemed determined to get some answers.

"Because we..." Cristen faltered when he looked to see her face so close, caught by the familiarity. He pulled himself together to continue. "Well...we share a gift. We both dream."

Hanna recoiled a step. "I'm not a dreamer. They're mistaken about me."

Cristen sighed, expecting as much, relating all too well. By the time they dragged the unconscious man to safety, the fire had engulfed the cabin. Luckily, the forest remained unscathed.

"Let's hurry before he wakes up," Cristen said, taking her hand. He led her toward where Sunfire waited under the moonlit trees.

"Please tell me you have food with you," Hanna said as Cristen mounted the golden stallion. "I'm honestly so hungry my stomach has stopped growling."

"I'm sorry," Cristen said regretfully. "I did, but...we'll have some first thing in the morning." He pulled her up behind him.

Hanna didn't reply but rested her weary head against Cristen's back. She wrapped her arms loosely around his waist as they rode through the trees toward the road, the fire crackling at their backs.

5

Beyond the fiery glow of the burning cabin, they rode for another quiet stretch through the forest until the road narrowed, and the forest seemed to close in around them. Worried that the darkness might get to Hanna, Cristen needed to distract her.

"You okay back there?" he asked.

"Yeah. I just need a couple of days rest, then I can start searching for my parents again."

Cristen's dreaded having to be the one to break the news to her. Would she even believe him? He hesitantly asked, "Have you dreamt of them yet?"

"Who...my parents?"

If she didn't know what he meant, then she hadn't. "Never mind."

"Tell me," she insisted.

How could he even begin? After some thought, he said, "I learned the hard way I'm a water dreamer."

"I swear I won't hold it against you, especially after helping me like this," Hanna said. "What happened?"

Cristen continued, wondering how much to reveal safely. "I woke up nearly drowning in the middle of a bay and couldn't understand why. Then bad men came hunting me down, wanting to lock me in one of those cages like an animal. That's when I started dreaming of a home and family—a mother, a father, a brother." After a weighty pause, he quietly added, "And a girl I guess I loved since childhood."

He paused again, allowing for Hanna's reaction. When she remained silent, he took a deep breath and continued. "My brother—or so I thought—informed me the dreams aren't real, that they come from the sea that gave me life, the nail in the coffin that confirmed me a water dreamer. I hated myself. I hated everything."

Still, Hanna offered no reply.

"Anyway, everyone thought I was a freak and a misfit and wanted nothing to do with me. So, I ran off to Burning Mountain, hoping to leave my troubles behind...but that horrible place only made things worse. I had no choice but to get out of there." Cristen kept quiet about the dragon and the wizard—the dragon because he didn't want to traumatize her further just yet, and the wizard because...well, he didn't want to sound like a coward and why bother to complicate things. "But dreamers like us don't need to escape to the mountains. We can make it on our own."

Cristen tensed when he heard a soft sniffle behind him. He never meant to make her cry, but he realized maybe she had dreamt, especially after she'd already refused to consider herself a dreamer. A vivid dream of home would feel like proof.

The forest opened up again, and the moon lit their way. Most of their ride remained silent except for the steady clip-clop of Sunfire's hooves and the occasional hoot of an owl or howl of a distant coyote. Later that night, when they finally neared his gate, Cristen needed to rouse Hanna. "We're here," he announced softly. He swung his leg over the saddle horn and dropped to the ground before assisting her down.

"Where are we exactly?" she asked groggily.

"My house. But I'll sleep in the barn after you're settled."

Hanna looked around the yard as Cristen unsaddled Sunfire and set him loose. She followed him inside, glancing curiously around the house.

"This place is yours?" she asked. "How old are you?"

"Dreamers don't get birthdays, I guess, but I emerged nearly a year ago now." He grabbed a pillow from the bed.

"There's shirts in the top drawer and a well out back for the wash basin, but I can help you with that in the morning."

"Who's that?" she asked, noticing the drawing of herself on a shelf above the bureau—his sketch that the wizard embellished before giving it to him.

"No one," he said, putting it in a boot in his bottom drawer. "Help yourself to the food in the morning if I'm not in yet."

"Alright," she said, looking puzzled at the absence of food. She would figure it out soon enough.

Sitting on the bed, she said, "What about a blanket? It's getting chilly out there."

"There's some in the barn. Try to get some sleep."

"Hey," she said before he could leave. "I really can't thank you enough for what you did back there. I didn't mean to seem ungrateful."

With moonlight filtering through the open door, Cristen observed the sincerity in her expression. "You don't owe me anything. I'm just glad you're safe."

They exchanged a warm, lingering gaze for a moment.

"Well...goodnight then," Hanna said. "Sleep well out there."

"You too. Goodnight."

***

Cristen gave Moonshine more oats and hay—food that remained magically stocked—then spread a woolen horse blanket on a pile of loose hay. The down pillow and stiff blanket quickly warded off the night's chill. Though exhausted from the day's harrowing events, sleep still eluded him. As he lay staring up at the rafters, his mind raced.

Did today actually happen? Was the girl from his dreams really here…sleeping in his house…in his bed? He hoped she learned to like him as much as he already liked her. What if she started dreaming of him too? It seemed unlikely, but the thought made Cristen's heart swell with hope and longing. How wonderful if she did share dreams with him—it would pave the way for them to build a real relationship together. As his mind wandered further, he wondered if two water dreamers could conceive and bear children, establishing real families.

But he quickly checked himself, realizing the premature timing of such romantic possibilities. After all, they were both still young and mere acquaintances, regardless of his connection to her through the recurring dreams. He needed to be patient to see where their relationship would lead naturally, if anywhere.

Worry over the fire plagued him. He could land in serious trouble if the man survived to witness against him, especially since everyone would presume the driver innocent, just doing his job. The orb's immense power to channel and unleash potent fire surprised Cristen. He needed to be more cautious with it to avoid causing unintended devastation again.

Regardless, Cristen would make the same desperate choices again to save Hanna. Standing up to Harmony's systemic injustice in his small way, though risky, felt inherently right.

As the circling thoughts finally faded, Cristen felt sleep taking over his weary mind. Not only sleep but an ocean current, the promise of a dream. He closed his eyes and allowed the current's embrace.

6

Cristen and Hanna fit side-by-side in the wide swing, but getting momentum took teamwork. Despite kicking back and forth, they couldn't get their timing right no matter how hard they tried.

"Lean back!" Cristen told her, frustrated with her lack of cooperation.

"I am!" Hanna shouted.

Managing only minimal movement, they abandoned their efforts.

"Let's just take turns again," said Hanna with a lisp, missing her front teeth.

"I'm first," Cristen said, shoving her off.

"Hey! You went first last time," Hanna complained as she brushed back her hair.

"Too bad. What are you waiting for? Get pushing already."

"You're being mean, Cristen. Be nice to the pusher, or you won't get pushed."

"Fine, you first," Cristen conceded. He thought of a trick to play on her.

Hanna beamed. "Help me up?"

Cristen lifted her onto the swing from behind, as usual, pulling up by her belly as his body held it steady. "Catch me if you can!" he shouted as he darted from their garden hideaway. He ducked through the opening they'd made through the purple-blooming vines.

"Wait for me!" Hanna cried.

Cristen ran full-tilt, knowing she nearly matched his speed. Glancing back, he saw her clear the vines. Finding nowhere to take cover, Cristen headed for the waving wheat fields, an unusual detour from their route home.

"Where are you going?" Hanna shouted, but Cristen fixated on finding a place.

The trek to the wheat took longer than expected, but he finally reached it and plunged into the tall green grain, trampling a path through the tender stalks. Hearing Hanna shout again, he dropped flat, panting for breath as he listened.

"Where are you?" she called, winded and frustrated.

He tracked her rustling movements through the grain. A blood-curdling scream pierced the air! Cristen bolted up.

"What happened?" he shouted. "I'm here, I'm right here."

He swam through the stalks toward her crying and quickly found her. She held the back of her head, shrieking again.

"What is it?" Cristen asked, panicked yet seeing nothing.

"It's stinging me!"

"What is?"

"Something's in my hair!"

She screamed again before Cristen thought to move her thick hair aside, freeing a wasp. Red welts marked her neck.

"It's gone. It got stuck," Cristen reassured her, feeling shaken. "Are you okay?"

"No, I'm not!" Hanna wailed. "Why did you come this way?"

"I just wanted to hide!" Cristen didn't understand the big deal.

"Well, now I'll be mad at you forever," she said, turning to run homeward.

"You can't, we're getting married, remember?" Cristen called after her, wanting her to remember their long-time pact. He started sniffling, hating that he'd caused her pain.

7

C risten awoke sometime in the night, overcome by profound sadness. How could the sea torment him with
such an awful dream? She could be so cruel. Sensing movement nearby, Cristen grew uneasy, fearing a rodent had
snuck into the barn. But as he sat up and glanced around,
he saw Hanna cocooned in a blanket, leaning against the wall
beside him. Her head rested on her arms, and her hair spilled
messily over the blanket. She wore one of his tunics, having
shed her red dreamer attire.

"Hanna?" Cristen whispered.

She lifted her head. "You're awake," she said softly.

"Yeah, bad dream. Is everything okay?"

"I couldn't sleep."

Cristen gathered his blanket closer. "Yeah, kind of a rough
day," he replied.

Hanna didn't speak for a while, seemingly lost in thought. Cristen waited patiently, sensing she wanted to say more.

Finally, she let out a heavy sigh. "I just don't know what I'm supposed to do now," she said wearily.

"What do you mean?" Cristen asked.

"I know what you were doing—trying to let me down easy. I guess I'm a little slow. I did dream once, with just a glimpse of my parents in the kitchen."

"Oh." He ached for her, yet relief washed over him that she'd come to terms with reality so quickly. "No, not slow. No one wants to believe it."

"I honestly don't know if I can do this," she continued. "I mean, how do I deserve to end up so completely alone in the world? It doesn't seem fair."

It hurt Cristen to hear it since he thought he'd been there for her. She must know he'd never leave her alone, but he also understood she meant family. "You don't have to feel alone," he said gently. "We're not the only ones dealing with this."

"Why can't I just be like everyone else? I don't want to be different."

"Trust me, I get it. Every day, I wish I could just fit in. Lying gets old, but I'm still careful with what I say."

"So that's it?" Resentment filled her voice. "I pretend until someone accuses me and locks me up again?"

Cristen let out a long exhale. He didn't dare tell her about Sefilar's sanctuary. But she was right—things would not be easy. "I promise...I'm here for you. We can figure this out together."

Hanna met his gaze, fresh tears in her eyes. After a long moment, she nodded, and Cristen felt the knot in his chest loosen. They sat quietly as the first hints of dawn crept into the barn.

***

Needing Hanna to see the brighter side of Harmony, Cristen took her riding into the hills each morning. A natural like him, she favored Sunfire's spirit over Moon-shine's calm. On the fourth day, they left early to watch the sunrise from a lofty hill. Side-by-side on their mounts, they faced the changing horizon.

Awestruck, Hanna gazed at the sky as it transformed into a breathtaking canvas of pinks and oranges.

Cristen landed a better view. The golden light made Hanna's lavender eyes sparkle and accentuated her tanned skin and hair—the most beautiful thing he'd ever seen. He also liked that she'd been wearing his clothes. They suited her well, even if a little baggy on her petite frame.

"Such a clear morning," Hanna added. "You can see forever. Look at those mountain peaks," she said, pointing north. Her voice held a note of wonder.

"That's where I got trapped," Cristen told her, hoping his words would dissuade her from ever venturing near there. "Burning Mountain is farther east," he said, nodding toward the northeastern horizon.

Hanna watched him for a moment, her expression thoughtful. "You never really told me what happened," she said.

Cristen thought about it for a minute, again wondering how much detail to provide. "It's where they send dreamers to get rid of us. A lot of us end up there," he said, his tone grave.

"Like a colony?"

"Pretty much."

"They just fend for themselves?" Hanna asked, looking concerned.

"There's someone who's supposed to care for them. An old hag," he said, though the word didn't feel harsh enough.

"A hag?"

"It seems like she's there to help, but if you step out of line, she's vicious. She threw me in a dungeon when I wanted to leave." He shuddered at the memory.

41

"How awful. How does she get away with that?" Hanna's voice rang with anger.

"Because no one cares," Cristen said bitterly. "So much injustice happens right under the people's noses."

"Those poor dreamers. How did you get out?"

"I blinded her with the orb that started the fire, then threatened to break her crystal ball," he answered flatly.

"She uses witchcraft?" Hanna said, alarmed. "She needs to be stopped."

Cristen agreed, but who could take down the dragon? And who would replace her to care for the dreamers already out there?

"Someone should protect them," Hanna said sharply. "I'll warn them myself if I get the chance."

Cristen smiled at her admiringly. He could understand her affinity for Sunfire, being a little feisty herself.

***

Hanna slumped in her chair, taking the last bite of her cheese wrapped in bread. In a funk, she deflected his attempts at conversation with one-word answers.

"I need a job," she finally said.

"I can come with you," Cristen offered, trying to lift her spirits. "Maybe I'll find one too." He brushed breadcrumbs from the table onto his hand and went to toss them outside.

"We don't have to do everything together." She avoided his gaze.

"Tired of me already?" he joked lightly but backed off when she didn't respond. He returned to his chair. "Okay, I get it. You need space, so take all you need," he said supportively, despite dreading separation from her. He thought they'd been doing well. But how could he stand in her way if she needed to spread her wings?

She finally sat up straight and sighed. "Who am I, Cristen? What's a water dreamer? I'm nobody."

"How can you say that?" Cristen asked. "You're Hanna. You're the prettiest, best girl I know."

"Pretty? That's what matters?" She gave him a skeptical look.

Her challenge flustered him, but he didn't mean it that way. "Of course not. You love nature. You're thoughtful and adventurous. Maybe...a little messy," he added with a grin.

Hanna repressed a smile. "Did you have to notice?"

"It's fine. You'd rather be out doing things."

"What I want is people. We're so isolated. How do you live without people?"

"I have people," he said defensively.

"Who? Where are they?"

"My brother."

"Your brother?" She raised her eyebrows.

"Okay, okay. Maybe the brother from my dreams," he admitted. "But I can't help how I feel about him."

"And where is he?"

Cristen sighed. "He went to the mountains."

"So he's gone," she said, giving him a look.

Cristen's thoughts turned to Jonas and Greta. "I do have people, though," he said. "They're not family...of course, but they treated me well. They even invited me to stay—a total stranger."

He recalled Greta's creekside goodbye. "I hope you find your parents," she said sweetly. At the time, needing to find his family consumed him, unaware they didn't exist. Jonas's goodbye hadn't been so innocent. He'd gone off on some tangent about a grandfather and his lonely life. He'd even spoken of an accident after Cristen mentioned his.

Then it sunk in. "He knew," Cristen said, surprised he had just put the pieces together.

"What?" Hanna asked, looking lost.

"Jonas must have suspected I was a water dreamer." With an ancestor as a dreamer, it meant Jonas and Greta descended from one. Cristen felt more connected to them than ever.

Best of all, it meant dreamers could reproduce and have their own families.

"The nice family you stayed with?" Hanna asked, still perplexed.

Cristen nodded. "I told him I'd been in an accident, and he put it together."

"And they didn't make you leave?"

"No, and Jonas said to come back anytime. They're good people."

"Then why leave at all? That's exactly what every dreamer needs...a family willing to take them in," Hanna said, shaking her head in disbelief. "Where are they?"

"A couple days' ride...in the highlands past Meadowbrook. How could I stay, though? I thought my family was out there looking for me. I had barely emerged back then, so I didn't know."

"But now you do, so what are you waiting for?"

Cristen fell quiet, stung by another attempt to push him away.

Hanna sighed and leaned back in her chair, arms folded across her chest. "I'm not trying to upset you. Nothing makes sense. I hate my life." She blinked hard, fighting tears.

Cristen felt crushed. "I'm sorry I'm not better company," he said, wallowing in self-pity as he shoved from the table. He stormed to the barn to brood alone.

"Don't take it so personally!" Hanna called after him from the porch. "You can't say you've never been angry about it."

"I'm angry about it all the time," Cristen said with his back to her as he flung his arms out. Turning to face her, he walked backward, continuing toward the barn. "But not this week," he shouted, not caring if neighbors heard. "It's been the best week of my life. Forgive me for saying so." He wanted to tell her the picture was of her, but then he'd have to delve into how he obtained the picture.

He continued to the barn, where he burrowed under his blanket. No sooner did he get comfortable, thinking sleep might temper things, than Hanna joined him again. He pulled the blanket over his head.

"Don't be mad," she said.

"I'm not mad."

Hanna chuckled softly. "Come on, I know you're in there." She stripped the blanket from his face, so he covered himself with the pillow instead. "Look...I like you too. But I need to figure some things out on my own before I can even consider...you know, a boyfriend."

"I know," Cristen answered.

"Do you? You've been here awhile. Maybe you forget how confusing it is."

He removed the pillow and looked her in the eye. "I don't forget any of it. It could have all happened yesterday."

"I guess so," she conceded, giving him a sympathetic look. "But...well, why don't you take some time to reconnect with your friends while I see about finding work in town? Bring a gift or something."

"So you can have my house to yourself?" he asked sullenly.

"Of course not, dimwit," she said with playful exasperation. "I'll rent a room somewhere near whatever job I find."

If Hanna only insisted on some time and space for herself, he supposed things could be worse. He didn't want to come across as too needy. Still, he didn't like it. He wanted to be the one to show her the ropes and protect her from bad-mannered townsfolk. Furthermore, he already thought of her as his girl and didn't want to share her.

Hanna perked up for the rest of the day after their talk. They planned for Cristen to leave once she found work and a place to live. In the meantime, they agreed to enjoy their remaining time together.

Upon Hanna's suggestion, they walked to Main Street to check out the shops. After an enjoyable afternoon spent window shopping and people-watching, they stopped at a small outside table down a side street to rest their aching feet.

"I can't wait to start earning money," Hanna said as she massaged her sore ankles. "I'll be able to buy some things I need."

"Those fancy dress shops will know you by name before long," Cristen teased with a grin.

Hanna chuckled, her eyes bright. "They're beautiful to look at, but I can't see myself in something so impractical. Besides, I already have a great wardrobe...thanks to you," she added with a playful smirk.

"In that case, I guess I'll be the one needing new dresses," Cristen returned.

They laughed, and Hanna grew thoughtful, tracing her finger along a groove in the table. "How did you get set up so nicely to begin with? You have this fully furnished house and everything you could need, but I've never heard you talk about a job."

Cristen hesitated, the wizard being behind it all. "Lucky, I guess," he muttered, immediately regretting it when Hanna shot him a skeptical look.

Leaning forward, she pressed, "Do I look like an idiot?"

"No, of course not," he said quickly. "I needed a place to live. Someone pitied me and wanted to help, that's all."

"That's it? What about all the food and stuff?"

"Someone delivers it, what can I say?" Cristen shifted uneasily under her intense gaze.

Hanna leaned back and crossed her arms. "Who?" she demanded. "It's there before I wake up."

Cristen sighed. She would never let this go. "What if I said a mysterious benefactor I've never met?"

She finally cracked a smile. "I know you're holding out on me, but I'd say then you're one lucky little water wart."

He agreed—he was luckier than them all. But he didn't deserve it. He'd never felt so unworthy of the wizard's continued generosity.

Cristen and Hanna had viewed a help-wanted sign in the window of the General Mercantile during their stroll downtown. The following morning, while Hanna returned to inquire about the job, Cristen worked on his own project, as Hanna suggested—a gift for Jonas and Greta. Perhaps he could even leave Moonshine with them, though a horse alone wouldn't solve their hardship. They needed a sturdy wagon, one narrow enough to navigate the path from their remote cottage to the creek, making fetching water easier and improving their lives. He figured only a dragon scale or two should be enough to hire a local builder to construct such a wagon.

He retrieved three scales from the stockpile he kept near the back fence far from the barn and set out for town with high hopes. However, finding an available cartwright or carpenter proved impossible. After inquiring all over town, Cristen learned he would encounter the same shortage everywhere. It seemed all available men had been hired and materials bought out by one wealthy man, Mr. D.

Cristen returned home feeling discouraged. Spotting Hanna through the window coming up the walk, he realized he'd left the dragon scales lying out. He hurried to stash them beneath the bureau. To feel the compelling call of the mountains could be dangerous for Hanna in her vulnerable state.

"Any luck?" he asked brightly as she entered.

"The sign's gone," she reported, looking downcast.

"Oh, sorry, that's too bad," Cristen said sympathetically.

"Because Mr. Cobb took it down after talking to me!" she squealed. "He gave me the job!"

Cristen chuckled, thrilled about her success. "Wow, congratulations! Miss Hanna, your new mercantile clerk."

"Eek! Make sure you buy something if you come to see me."

"Do they have any dolls?" Cristen asked.

"A doll? I'm thinking a slingshot might suit you better?" she teased.

He'd never seen her so cheerful and carefree, giving him hope.

"Not for me," he clarified. "Now that you're kicking me out, I need something for Greta."

"Alas," she lamented, hand to her heart, "I've been replaced by someone younger and prettier."

"Definitely younger. Prettier, though?" He pretended to consider it seriously.

Hanna slapped his arm playfully. "You're awful," she said, laughing.

"Think a five-year-old's too young for me?" Cristen deadpanned.

Hanna stared. "Wait. Greta is their daughter?"

"Just her and her father."

Hanna smiled. "You never mentioned a child, how wonderful! Yes, we have to find her a gift. I'll look tomorrow."

"You'd love her. She's precocious as they come. You have to meet her sometime."

"Of course, I'd love to."

Cristen's heart soared whenever she hinted at sticking around and that she hadn't written him off yet. Maybe a future together was possible after all.

8

The crescent moon lit the way as Cristen and Hanna raced across the cobblestone drive and the field of chirping crickets to the stables. They'd slipped off undetected after supper ended and tables were cleared. The lavish celebration for the Sallows' new baby meant everyone throughout the estate, including children, received an invitation to attend. But at thirteen and fourteen, they didn't quite fit in with the younger, rambunctious kids or the adults who talked your ear off eternally.

Tonight, Cristen seized the chance to steal some alone time with Hanna, his true motive for sneaking away. Such opportunities seldom arose. He'd used the new foal as an excuse to lure Hanna outside, and she equally wanted to escape the tedious party for a while. Confident they couldn't be spotted now, they slowed to a leisurely walk as they approached the stables. Testing the waters, Cristen took Hanna's hand in his, but she pulled it back.

"Trying to get me in trouble?" Hanna asked, glancing nervously toward the distant manor.

"We're already in trouble the minute Kimball realizes we're missing," Cristen reasoned.

"We're just going to the barn and back."

"What's wrong with holding hands?"

"I don't know... people might see," she said uncertainly.

The newborn brown foal slept soundly inside the stall, its head resting on bent legs.

"Aww, cutest thing I've ever seen in my whole life," Hanna cooed, gently stroking its nose. The foal didn't stir.

"Not me," said Cristen, unable to resist redirecting compliments to fluster her.

"Don't say it, Cristen," she warned.

"Say what?"

"He opened his eyes! Hi there, sweet baby," she said, scratching under the foal's chin as it blinked groggily. "I just want to wrap him up and take him home with me."

"Okay, I'll ask Father," Cristen replied, only half-jokingly.

"I wish. He's not going to just give me a horse." Hanna gave the sleepy newborn a few more loving pats, then rose reluctantly. "We should get back."

Halfway across the field, Cristen boldly held her hand again. When she tried pulling it back, he held on tighter this time, drawing her closer. She looked up at him in surprise. Maintaining eye contact, he slowly leaned in, waiting for a reaction. But Hanna didn't pull away. Instead, she watched him curiously as if wondering what he might dare do next. So accustomed to her rejection, this new vulnerability stirred a hint of fear in him, and his heart raced.

Feeling unsure of himself, he pulled a dance move on her, gently guiding the hand he held up past her face and around as she slowly turned back to him. Still tentative, he set her other hand on his arm and rested his lightly on her waist.

"There's no music," she whispered, instinctively swaying in time with him.

"You're sure about that? Listen again."

She smiled after a moment, catching on. "A cricket chorus doesn't count."

"Of course it does," he insisted softly.

Cristen spun her around again, drawing her nearer until he felt her heart beating rapidly to match his own. All his nervousness melted away as they lost themselves in each other's gaze. Something new and profound unfolded between them at that moment. Cristen knew then that she would forever be his.

9

Cristen kept himself busy the following morning to prevent himself from going mad. The vivid dream did a number on him, and he hated the sea for tormenting him. After brushing down his horses, he swept out the barn and restacked the hay bales into a tidier, more convenient corner. When that only occupied him until noon, he moved inside and cleaned the house from top to bottom, scrubbing every surface until it shone. By mid-afternoon, he ran out of indoor tasks, so he eventually moved back outside with a bucket of soap and water to wash the plank siding. After sweeping the long walkway, he caught himself mindlessly sweeping the grass and knew it was time to rein himself in.

Only riding could offer a true escape from his restless energy and intrusive thoughts. He took off on Sunfire bareback into the hills to gallop for miles unhindered. He rode until his legs ached and the sun lowered toward the horizon. Only then did he turn back toward home, muddy and out of breath but finally feeling some peace. He scrubbed himself clean at the well and collapsed exhausted onto his bed, emotionally and physically spent.

***

When Hanna returned home for the day, Cristen sat strumming his fingers on the table as she briefly inspected the spotless house.

"Well, someone got bit by the cleaning bug," she remarked approvingly.

Cristen remained silent, nervous to tell her he wasn't going anywhere, having made the decision just earlier.

"I brought us some dried beef," she said, setting a sack on the counter. "We can make a soup or stew or something before you leave."

Did she forget he only had a firepit? "I'm not going," he announced sullenly.

"What do you mean, what happened?" She frowned in confusion.

"I barely know them. I have everything I need right here." Cristen kept his gaze fixed on the table.

Hanna crouched down to meet his lowered eyes, resting her arm on the table. "I understand being reluctant. Expanding our social circles isn't always easy."

"You're leaving anyway, so why does it matter where I go?" He knew he sounded petty, but he couldn't help himself.

Hanna sighed patiently. "Because I want you to connect with people like I'm trying to do. I can't be your whole world. It's too much for either of us to put on the other."

Cristen finally met her earnest gaze. "You just don't get it though. You haven't dreamt about me like I have you, so you can't understand. Think of how real your parents felt at that moment. The dreams make me feel like you and I were literally made for each other."

Hanna's expression softened. "Maybe we are," she said, "and time will tell."

"But, in my mind, we've already shared a life. I started dreaming about you way before you emerged. The sea made you for me right from my very own dreams."

Hanna quickly stood, her eyebrows raised. "Excuse me...the sea did what?"

Cristen plowed ahead, desperate to make her understand. "Just think about it. Most dreamers are alone when they emerge, but we've already found each other. We can get married someday and have a family.

"Hold on, back up. Do you even hear yourself ?" Hanna interrupted, her voice rising. "The sea made me for you? To be your wife? What about me? Do I get a say?"

Stunned by her reaction, Cristen struggled to grasp how his words could have offended her. "Of course, you have a say, I didn't mean—"

"Well, you can take your dreams and shove them. And tell the sea to shove off too while you're at it. I despise the sea."

Cristen's eyes widened, still baffled by her overreaction. "Why are you being like this? Tell me what's so bad about having someone."

"I can't talk about this right now. I need some space," she said curtly, grabbing the sack of dried beef.

"Now?" Cristen asked, distressed, as she gathered a few more things from the bureau top. "You can't. Where will you sleep?" He desperately wanted to take it all back.

"I'll figure something out."

"Don't be like this, Hanna. I didn't mean it."

"You meant it," she argued, opening the door to the night, the evening breeze ruffling her hair. "See you around."

"Please don't go, I'm sorry," he implored, his face burning with hurt and embarrassment. But she already slipped away, crossing the moonlit yard and entering the street without looking back.

She'll come back once she cools off, right? he asked himself. But a nagging doubt twisted his gut as he watched her until she and her footsteps faded into the night.

***

Nearly a week passed without any word from Hanna. Cristen grew increasingly anxious, worried he had ruined things between them for good. With an abundance of time to stew over where exactly he had gone wrong, he saw his error and felt about two inches tall.

Lost in his vision of a shared destiny ordained by the sea, Cristen grasped how utterly he failed to consider her viewpoint or feelings, especially when she still struggled to understand her identity. Cristen cringed, recalling his thoughtless words, how he essentially tried to map out her future for her. No wonder she stormed off so angry and hurt.

Though tempted to visit her at the mercantile and plead his case, Cristen knew it could only worsen things. Though it pained him deeply, he understood that he must allow her space if Hanna needed distance to heal.

Cristen decided that the best course of action was to send a heartfelt letter of apology by post. Yet before he could begin drafting it, she seemed to have beaten him to the punch. That very afternoon, a courier arrived with a postcard for him. Cristen's heart leaped when he saw that she'd sent it.

Meet me in Revival Park after my shift ends today. I have some good news to share.

Nothing mentioned their argument or his idiotic behavior. Cristen felt dizzy with relief and cautiously optimistic, hoping this meant she forgave him and was willing to move past it. He preferred she just come over so they could talk, but he couldn't blame her for choosing a public meeting place. Besides, the mercantile stood just beyond the park, likely near her new lodgings.

Sundown—when her work shift ended—couldn't come soon enough. Cristen spent the afternoon mentally rehearsing his heartfelt apology. He wanted her to know that he knew why she got mad, that he expected nothing from her, and only hoped they could still be friends. As the day crawled by, his nervous excitement mounted.

✸✸✸

Cristen walked to the park, finding it deserted as usual. Besides, at this evening hour, most would be at the Rendezvous. Not like the rundown place ever drew many visitors in its condition from what he'd seen. He wondered why the town didn't put more effort into maintaining the neglected place, especially with such an attraction as the statue and fountain. Distant greenery marked its location through the trees from his current vantage.

Hanna waved from across the extensive park, passing by the dilapidated gazebo that, in its prime, might have served as a charming bandstand. Cristen smiled and waved in return, his pulse quickening. As she confidently strode toward him, he admired how stunning she looked in a new blue tunic, form-fitting leggings, and tall leather boots. Her hair was styled in a high, wavy ponytail that swished behind her. She was all smiles; clearly, any residual anger toward him vanished.

When Hanna shouted something he couldn't decipher over the distance, Cristen cupped a hand to his ear. "What's that?" he called back, quickening his pace.

A few steps closer, she tried again. "I get it! I'm a pea-brain!"

Get what exactly? Cristen wondered, thoroughly confused.

With arms spread wide, she called out, "I'm so sorry. I acted way too hard on you!"

"*She's* apologizing?" Cristen mumbled.

"You won't believe it!" Hanna shouted excitedly as the gap between them narrowed to half the park.

"What happened?" He watched her quizzically.

"You must've guessed. Come on, I've been dreaming!"

Her incredible announcement sent a chill through Cristen. "Your family?" he asked, wary of getting his hopes up.

"No, knucklehead, of you. I'm begging for another chance. Just don't make me kneel."

An angular, gliding shadow passed over the dormant grass—not a cloud, Cristen realized with confusion. An ominous feeling of dread took hold as he slowly gazed upward. Sefilar! A dragon silhouette drifted high overhead with its vast wings spread wide. Its neck craned downward, seeming to watch the park intently. Why venture out so far, especially before nightfall?

Hanna hadn't noticed yet, the trees obscuring her view. How could he subtly warn her to take cover without drawing the dragon's attention to her presence? His mind raced frantically.

Instead of merely passing by, the dragon circled lower. Cristen's panic spiked—did Sefilar somehow recognize him from this distance? Or worse...was she actively searching for him? Tracking him? As the dragon tipped into a steep dive toward the park, he immediately sprinted in the opposite direction, desperate to lure the threat away from Hanna.

"What are you doing?" Hanna shouted. "Okay, okay, I'll get on my knees!"

But it was too late. Spotting Hanna through the trees, Sefilar swiftly adjusted her trajectory to angle toward Hanna instead.

"Hanna, get down, now!" Cristen screamed in desperation.

Hanna stared around in bewilderment until she finally saw the massive dragon barreling straight toward her. Overwhelmed, she crumpled limply to the ground in a dead faint.

"No!" Cristen cried out helplessly as Sefilar closed in on her prone form. "Touch her, and I swear I'll kill you!" He grew increasingly frantic, shouting more threats. "I'll expose you and all your secrets! I'll bring armies to hunt you down!"

The dragon swooped to the ground and effortlessly snatched Hanna in one huge clawed paw. Hanna's hair hung loosely from her limp, dangling head.

"Stop!" Cristen screamed, his voice breaking. "Don't, I'm begging you!"

With tiny Hanna clutched against her belly, Sefilar turned and flew dangerously low, right toward Cristen. He ducked reflexively, covering his head as the dragon passed over him, the wind from her beating wings nearly knocking him over.

Circling back around as if to taunt him over her prize, Sefilar let out an ear-piercing, screeching cry, acrid smoke curling from her maw. Her leathery wings flapped with immense power as she ascended rapidly into the darkening sky.

"Hanna, no!" Cristen wailed hoarsely, tears of panic and despair streaming down his face as he watched the shrinking dragon carry her northward.

The initial shock and heartbreak quickly turned to rage as Cristen grasped the extent of the dragon's duplicity. Hanna remained innocent, never exposed to the dragon's scales. Yet Sefilar would still subject her to her mountain. The dragon hadn't ventured this far to capture some random dreamer. With her seer crystal providing a direct window into Harmony, Cristen now realized she could have been watching his every move from afar since he escaped her clutches. Sefilar probably witnessed Hanna enter his world, immediately recognizing her as the perfect leverage to execute a calculated act of revenge against him.

Her possession of a crystal made Sefilar far more dangerous and cunning than he'd ever thought. He should have smashed it when he had the chance. Cristen cursed himself for his foolish naivete. He should have known better than to assume the dragon forgave his escape or threat against her precious crystal.

What if Sefilar forced Hanna to shift, erasing all memories of him...changing her...taking her away forever? No choice remained but to return to Burning Mountain before he lost Hanna to the Oasis forever.

10

E xhausted and dripping sweat, Cristen finally reached the same mountainside opening he fled through when carrying the dragon's hefty seer crystal. After hours spent combing the dangerous terrain and frequently having to backtrack and reroute, he finally located it hidden behind a rock outcropping.

Before venturing into the stalagmite-infested cavern, he paused to scan the barren landscape below, hoping to spot Sunfire one last time. However, the stallion was no longer visible. Cristen hoped to return to him before Sefilar took to the skies hunting again.

Cristen stepped across the threshold into the gaping cavern entrance. In his desperate prior escape, he realized now that he hadn't fully appreciated the sheer vastness of this underground space. Countless jagged stalactites dangled ominously from the high ceiling like colossal icy daggers, while opposing stalagmites of varying heights pierced upward from the uneven and fragmented floor. The exotic, earthy scent of dragon permeated the cool air, shed scales littering every crack and crevice. Cristen felt their agitating effects amidst so many.

Doing his best to ignore the unease, Cristen carefully picked his way through the forest of rocky spikes, nearly twisting his ankle several times in the confined spaces between them. Finally clearing the last of the merciless cavern, he continued into the tunnel passageway beyond. As it wound deeper and darker underground, he withdrew the orb from his pack to light the way.

When the stench of slime hit him, he knew Sefilar's bathing cavern lay just ahead. He felt an eerie chill in the air as he cautiously stepped inside the great amphitheater. With only a single torch lit on the far wall, the dark sea of lifeless, drained waterskins and the vacant bathing pool seemed like remnants of some long-forgotten age. He shone a beam of light around to make sure he was alone. When the beam settled onto the shadowy alcove, he wondered if the dragon's seer crystal still lay in its trunk.

Of course, Sefilar would never leave it unlocked again, and Cristen didn't have time to waste. He pressed on, needing to locate the narrow breach that granted him access from these vast lower quarters up into the network of water dreamer tunnels.

However, after only a few urgent strides, a faint moan reached his ears, stopping him short. He quickly turned back to reenter the cavern, and searching with his light, he found Hanna curled motionless on the floor against the wall.

"Hanna!" Cristen cried in dismay, rushing to her side.

She should be tucked away safe in a private cave, with scales for warmth and escorts to bring her food and water.

"Hanna? Can you hear me?" Cristen said urgently as he gently shook her shoulder. She felt so cold. She stirred slightly with a soft whimper. How dare Sefilar abandon an innocent, helpless girl like this!

"You came for me," Hanna mumbled, blinking at him.

"Of course, are you okay? Cristen carefully helped her to sit upright, fuming over her neglectful treatment, though he realized it offered an easier escape.

"A little woozy," Hanna said, clinging to him for support. "That smell…" she covered her nose.

"Don't worry. We're getting out of here. Are you hurt?" Cristen briefly inspected her for visible wounds.

Hanna shook her head. "Just thirsty," she said.

Cristen untied his water and helped her drink, then left the skin with her to search for another so that she carried her own. In his hurry, he couldn't find any with even a swallow left. However, it didn't seem to matter. As he drank from an empty one sealed against his mouth, to Cristen's surprise and relief, the skin began to fill like the first time. As he drank, it steadily replenished until it matched the weight of his own water. He hurried back to Hanna with it.

"You didn't tell me your water tasted so good," she said, wiping her mouth with the back of her hand. She froze. "Oh...why do I feel so alive?"

Cristen still kept its power secret from her, wary of needing to discuss the wizard. "Did she say why she left you here?" he asked. "Is she coming back?"

Hanna seemed confused, thinking it over. "I don't... re-member."

"You sure she didn't hurt you?" Cristen pressed anxiously.

"No, she's gentle." Hanna seemed distracted, glancing around at the endless discarded waterskins.

"I'm glad you're alright, but don't be fooled—she's not your friend," Cristen warned. "Especially since she's aware of our connection. I'm sorry, I should've warned you. You must have been terrified when she came at you like that." He secured the new waterskin around her waist.

"Did you just fill this with your mouth?" she asked, hand on the waterskin.

"Sefilar steals them from us dreamers and ruins their mag-ic. She can't know we can fix them, though."

"Magic," Hanna said, her gaze distant. "How your light started the fire. How there's bundled food on your table every morning before the rooster crows."

"How my water never runs dry," Cristen added.

Hanna looked at him in surprise. "Yet you never bothered to tell me. I had to learn about the impossible from a dragon."

Cristen hesitated, feeling the sting of letting her down again. He should have been more transparent with her, even if it forced him to speak of the wizard. "I...guess I didn't feel like I deserved any of it. I swear I won't hold anything back from you anymore. You deserve better."

Hanna thought about it and nodded.

"We have to go. I'll tell you everything when we get out," Cristen said. "Can you run?"

"Yes, I'm fine now," Hanna assured him as he helped her up.

Cristen marveled at how well she seemed to handle the disorienting shock of being snatched away by a dragon. Then again, she'd already had days to process things. He took her hand in his as he led her from the cavern. By the soft light of his orb, they moved quickly through the giant tunnel, running whenever the path allowed. At last, the fresh scent of open air hit them, and the expansive sky beckoned from up ahead, promising freedom.

"That's the way out?" Hanna asked, eyeing the stalagmites anxiously.

"Don't worry, we'll make it," Cristen said, hoping he sounded more confident than he felt. The dangerous climb down still lay ahead, but at least he didn't have the seer crystal to worry about this time.

A faint yet unmistakable mournful wail echoed through the tunnel from somewhere behind them, turning Cristen's blood to ice.

"No!" he whispered under his breath, pulse instantly racing as he picked up the pace.

"Is that her?" Hanna asked wide-eyed.

"Come on, she must have found you missing."

"What will she do?"

"Let's not stick around to find out," said Cristen.

Hanna followed Cristen's lead without hesitation as he navigated the maze of stalagmites, knowing what to watch out for by now. He located the safest passages for them and assisted her in climbing or squeezing through narrow gaps, lifting her carefully over difficult obstacles before clambering over himself. A louder, closer bawl from Sefilar made Cristen fear not making it out in time.

"We have to hide," Hanna urged, glancing around for possibilities. "What about near that wall? See the big cluster?"

"She can smell us. We have to get outside so the wind can help mask our scent. We can hide in the brush until she's gone."

Hanna hesitated upon hearing another closer cry, glancing back toward the tunnel.

Cristen held her hand. "Come on, we can do this," he said. After a moment, she managed a weak smile and allowed him to lead her again.

"The climb down the mountain won't be easy," he warned her, hoping to redirect her thoughts forward. "At least while it's steep, test every step. Rocks can give way. Grab roots when possible because they run deep."

"I'll be fine."

Cristen—a step ahead of her—hurried toward the entrance to lead them outside.

11

Cristen slammed against an invisible barrier. Hanna cried out in pain and alarm as he bounced back against her, and they crashed in a battered heap on the unforgiving rocky ground.

"Hanna, the scales!" Cristen exclaimed urgently as he scrambled back to his feet. He emptied his pockets of two that found their way back in.

Still disoriented from the jarring collision, Hanna looked confused.

"Sefilar put up a wall," he quickly explained. "We can't get through with dragon scales on us. Check all your pockets."

Hanna stood and hesitantly patted herself down, finding three stacked together in a single pocket. She clutched them possessively as Cristen reached for them. He understood her instant attachment since it was her first time handling them.

In her moment of distraction, her gaze drifted over the scales scattered everywhere as if she were noticing them for the first time.

"As long as you keep them, we're trapped," Cristen said. "Let them go, and we can still escape." He gently tugged them from her rigid grasp and cast them aside. He led her through the now-opened passageway to the outside.

Cristen breathed a sigh of relief until her hand tensed in his grip, and he almost needed to tug her along. "Hanna, I need you to trust me. Please."

Hanna stopped to brush windswept hair back from her face. After an agonizing moment, she finally spoke. "You shouldn't have come," she said as softly as the rustling brush. "I never meant any harm. I didn't understand how deeply you hated all this."

Cristen scoffed in disbelief at her words. "You thought I would just let her have you? Of course, I would come!"

Hanna turned to him with a bittersweet smile. "You're right. You've always been right," she said wistfully. "My dreams showed we were truly meant to be."

"Which is all I've wanted," Cristen said, amazed that she shared the same cherished connection he felt. Yet he remained troubled by the dragon's power over her vulnerable mind and judgment. "Please, Hanna," he implored again.

"Will you love me, whatever happens?" she asked.

"You can't stay, I couldn't bear it."

"I just need a little time to sort things out."

"No!" Cristen shouted, grabbing Hanna's hand in vain as she freed herself. She turned and marched decisively several paces back into the cavern, and Cristen raced after her in a panic. "Hanna, stop, please listen to me!" he begged breathlessly, catching her arm again. "You don't understand. The dragon hates me. I'm not safe here, and neither are you!"

Hanna faced him now. With detached calmness, she said, "You're wrong, Cristen. She doesn't hate you. She wants the best for you...like I do."

"What? No!" Cristen's heart sank at hearing the frightening extent to which the dragon already poisoned her thoughts. "How could you possibly know what she..."

Sparkling dust cascaded down from the ceiling like agitated rain. Nearly indistinguishable within the ceiling's mass of stalactites, Sefilar perched stealthily on a slim outcrop, her wings fanning sporadically as she steadied herself. The shimmering particles soon coated them both—dusting hair, clothes, and the cavern floor.

Cristen backed toward the entrance, only to hit the barrier again. He rifled through his pockets but found them empty. Examining the iridescent undertones of the fragments covering his sleeves, he understood the frightful truth—Sefilar somehow pulverized her scales into dust. Terror blazed through him at the implication—he was now condemned to waste away in this isolated mountain dungeon until he could purge every last speck of the accursed dust.

He frantically shook out his hair and beat at his clothes in a futile effort to brush it away, but the damage was already done. Hanna was also dust-cloaked, yet she remained eerily calm as she combed her fingers through her hair, spellbound as the sparkling motes drifted down.

"Let me out!" Cristen shouted up at Sefilar, hands exploring every inch of the invisible wall he could reach.

Sefilar drifted nearer, massive wings sweeping slowly. "It's for your own good, my little one," the dragon purred, her syrupy speech no longer masking the venom to Cristen's ears. "Allow me to take you under my wing once again." Her deception could only be meant to appease Hanna, as any pretense of affection between him and Sefilar vanished long ago.

"Don't listen to her, Hanna!" Cristen warned urgently. "She's not what she pretends to be. She already tried to kill me!"

"I'm deeply wounded," Sefilar responded in a silken purr. "After all the care I've provided."

"You've done nothing for me! Open this up!" Cristen shouted in blind rage at the hovering dragon. He pounded both fists against the barrier that sealed his fate, the dull impacts reverberating through the cavern. "At least let Hanna go. This is between you and me."

"Search your soul, little one. I will wait for you as you prepare to embrace your destiny." Sefilar glided outside beyond their line of sight.

Enraged and distraught, Cristen brushed more scale dust from his sleeves, trying to keep it together.

"It's better this way," Hanna said. "We'll be safe now...from everyone, especially the authorities. We don't have to be on the run anymore."

"But you were already making a life for yourself! What about your new place? Your job! What about...us?"

Hanna stepped closer. "This is exactly about us. It's the only way we can be together. You said people already hate you. Our family would always be a target."

"You don't understand," he said, choking back tears. "She's dangerous. I don't trust her."

Hanna nodded, looking down at her feet. "She said you might say something like that. She's sorry for hurting your feelings but that you shouldn't let it ruin your happiness."

Sorry for hurting my feelings? Like trying to trap me in a dungeon? Tossing me around like a rag doll?

Hanna slid her fingers through his at his sides, her earnest eyes searching his. "She said her sanctuary is too amazing a place to let you pass it up. Please don't make me do this alone."

"But you *will* be alone. We won't even know each other."

"She said she can make sure we meet again."

"That's not good enough. We'll be strangers. I don't need a sanctuary. Nothing matters except us."

Hanna sighed, releasing his hands and stepping away. "You do realize I should be locked up right now. Why would you want to put me through that kind of life? And any children—what of them and the constant harassment from their peers? People don't want us around. Why is that so hard to understand?"

With her mindset, nothing could salvage this. Sefilar had won. It would be too late by the time he scrubbed himself free of the scale dust. Hanna would be shifted, and maybe he would be too if Sefilar could do it against his will.

Hanna enfolded Cristen in her arms. Overcome by despair, he broke down weeping on her shoulder.

"I hope you'll understand in time," she finally whispered. "I only did it for your good. Our good. It's the only way."

Cristen stiffened, throat clenched too tight to swallow. "Did...what exactly?" he managed.

Tortured silence followed. Cristen pried himself from Hanna's embrace to study her face. Her eyes widened in dawning alarm. Cristen retreated further, feeling the distance between them as vast and cold as the sea.

"What's the only way?" Cristen demanded. Thinking he understood, he refused to accept it until it came from her lips. "Tell me, Hanna!"

Hanna recoiled from him. "I thought you figured it out."

"What did you do?" he demanded.

"The dragon found me arriving home late from work after inventory," she finally stammered, tears spilling down her pale cheeks. "She swore this gave us the only opportunity."

And there it was—the painful, gut-wrenching confirmation of her ultimate betrayal. Everything that had transpired between them, from her fainting spell at the park to being left alone in the dank cavern just to be found, even their supposed joint escape—all nothing but an elaborate ruse to trap him.

The realization that Hanna conspired so intimately with his sworn adversary dealt Cristen a wound no balm could ever heal. He didn't know this girl at all.

"Did you even dream about me?" he spat bitterly. "Or was that just part of the grand scheme to take me down?"

"How dare you ask that!" Hanna shouted back at him through her tears. "The dreams were the only reason I listened to her! It's why I wanted to fight for this...for us. I only agreed to get you out here because I care about you and our future."

"Don't you get it? There's no future for us there!" Cristen shouted in her face.

Hanna swallowed hard as if trying to dislodge the lump of regret in her throat. She pressed her lips together and nodded, looking as vulnerable as a lost child, her betrayal seemingly wasted. Cristen desperately wanted to wrap her in his arms until all their combined hurt melted away.

"Alright...if I don't matter enough..." Hanna said.

Cristen gaped in sheer disbelief that she could reach such a twisted conclusion. Seemingly unaware of any wrongdoing, she remained oblivious to the gravity of the situation. Sefilar's toxic influence had impacted her even more than Cristen grasped.

Before he could respond, Sefilar swooped in, her massive talons gently enveloping Hanna and lifting her off the ground. Cradled protectively against the dragon's scaled belly, Hanna's pleading gaze lingered with his until Sefilar carried her away.

Cristen supposed Sefilar planned to come for him next. As the truth of Hanna's betrayal sank in, he fell to his knees. But as despair threatened to swallow him, a flicker of defiance rose from deep within. He didn't have to allow the dragon to take him.

Jaw set with new determination, Cristen stood and turned to peer back into the shadows of the tunnel beyond the stalagmites. If he were to remain trapped, it would be on his terms this time, holding on to whatever small control he still possessed.

Instead of waiting for Sefilar to return, he would find his way to the dreamers' tunnels. With any luck, Sefilar might even think he managed to escape once she saw the cavern empty. He grinned smugly as he imagined her frantically searching every passageway, desperately trying to find him again. She might even sic every escort on him, but he knew to hide from their prying eyes. Sefilar may have won this battle, but the war raged on.

12

The small pocket carved out of the tunnel wall served as a sorry excuse for a cave, yet the new location near the entrance placed Cristen amid the escorts' comings and goings. The strategic position afforded him a heads-up on Hanna's departure for the Oasis when the time came, which could be within a few weeks from what he understood. The location also provided fresh air and a better grasp of the passage of night and day.

Cristen never planned on being shifted himself. He had worked tirelessly for the past several days, scratching away the scale dust as he moved from hiding place to hiding place. Just this morning, his anger toward Hanna began to subside. After all, he couldn't lay the blame entirely on her. She too fell victim, tricked by a sweet-talking dragon, much like what had happened to him. She genuinely believed she was doing the right thing for the well-being of their shared future.

Longing for her again, he agonized over what to do, even entertaining the idea that the Oasis might offer him his best future given the circumstances. With little to go on, he wondered how completely the shift would alter their minds. Would it leave a remnant, at least enough to draw him to her? What if he could still care for and protect her there? It still offered a chance, whereas choosing not to go meant permanent separation.

Cristen sighed, finding little hope in either option. In reality, the decision might not end up being his. The longer he stayed here, the more likely he was to be shifted involuntarily. He couldn't shake the sorrow of seeing Hanna's dreams on the brink of being cruelly snatched away from her—such a heartrending tragedy.

More shuffling footsteps approached from down the tunnel, interrupting Cristen's conflicted thoughts. The familiar clang of a spear against stone signaled the approach of another escort. Cristen readjusted his position, using the light from his orb to get a clearer view since the escorts' candles provided little light. A male escort led a girl past him, still in her trance, which likely meant they only intended to relocate her. From Cristen's observation, dreamers were brought closer to the exit as they progressed through their shift. He always felt some relief each time someone besides Hanna passed by, even knowing she wouldn't be ready for a while.

Cristen drank a few sips of water to curb his nagging hunger. The last thing he'd eaten was a few pieces of the dragon's meat he stole from another dreamer when he happened upon his cave room. Cristen couldn't finish even the tiny amount of food, losing his appetite after remembering he'd left Sunfire unprotected. He missed the simple fare from home he'd grown accustomed to.

Upon hearing more shuffling feet, he directed his light down the tunnel again. Strangely, the dreamer following the female escort wore a burlap sack over her head. As they drew nearer, he quickly identified Hanna by her hands and leggings, then as she got closer, he recognized her eyes through the substantial eyeholes in the mask. Why would Sefilar disguise her, and had she earned a closer room so soon? At least he could track her now, maybe find a vacant room close to hers.

"Hanna!" Cristen called out to her in a strained whisper as she passed by his hidden alcove. He grabbed his water and fell in behind her and her escort. He noticed that Hanna no longer carried the skin he'd given her, which came as no surprise. Sefilar probably confiscated it immediately. Cristen held Hanna's arm as they walked. "I'm right here," he whispered into her ear, knowing she couldn't respond in her trance. "Everything's going to be okay." He offered the heartfelt reassurance as much for his peace of mind as hers.

Moments later, however, a feeling of dread washed over Cristen when the escort abruptly turned, leading Hanna down the passage toward the entrance cavern. It could only mean one thing—she was on her way! But how was it possible? Only days had passed, and her trance still held her captive. What if she didn't snap out of it in time? He distinctly recalled that the dreamer Caralee had emerged on the other side of her trance before leaving the mountain. She had been excited and prepared to return to the family and home she believed waited for her after being gone to boarding school. The very thought that something might go wrong chilled Cristen to the bone.

He followed Hanna and her escort for as long as he dared, stopping just before they crossed under the archway into the cavern. Cristen closed his eyes against the pulsating breeze from Sefilar's beating wings. He loathed her for causing him such misery, forcing him into such an impossible situation.

Pressing his back against the rough tunnel wall, mostly concealed by the arch, Cristen cautiously watched as Sefilar landed on two sinewy hind legs. After folding her expansive wings, she settled onto her feet, coiling her long tail around her.

As the dragon tilted her head to sniff the air, Cristen shrank farther against the wall, realizing she might have already detected his scent. When he finally gathered the nerve to peek out again, Sefilar's wing extended flush with the floor. The escort guided Hanna by the arm until she stood alongside it.

Sefilar sniffed the air again, then craned her neck down until her snout came to rest on Hanna's free arm—the same arm Cristen had touched momentarily, he realized nervously.

"It's you," Sefilar rasped quietly. "What sort of mischief have we been up to?"

Leaving Hanna alone, the escort exchanged her spear for a sack stuffed with dragon scales leaning against the wall. Returning to Hanna's side, she guided her closer by the arm until Hanna took the initiative to climb onto Sefilar's proffered wing. Though Cristen and Hanna's looming separation ate away at him, he still breathed a sigh of relief, believing she had woken.

Defeated, Cristen turned away, his spirits at an all-time low. The thought of surrendering to the nearest passing escort, letting them assign him to a cave to wait out his shift, crossed his mind. But intense anger welled up, overpowering his momentary weakness. Appalled by his naivete, he refused to surrender. Why sacrifice himself just because Hanna had? She was already lost to him. Caring for her at the Oasis was only a fanciful dream. He'd been a fool to commit so much of himself to a girl he barely knew? If she didn't value his wishes, why should he be so desperate to protect her, willing to sacrifice everything for her sake?

Clenching his fists, he wondered how it had come to this. How had everything gone so wrong? Turning abruptly, he marched back down the dim passage with renewed resolve. He would return to the dragon's tunnels and wait for the barrier to come down. Armed with his orb and water, he could survive a long time. Steeling his resolve, he vowed to flee this wretched place at all costs.

Another escort approached carrying a sack of dragon scales. As he passed, Cristen ensured the guy didn't have snake eyes before grabbing hold of his tunic front. "Sift the truth from the lies!" he yelled into his unresponsive face. "Wake up, and don't be so gullible, this isn't you." Cristen knew he only reprimanded himself.

Caw!

Cristen released his grip when the sudden strange noise sounded directly in his mind. Caw? As in a crow's call? As the escort continued toward the cavern, Cristen heard the bizarre cry again. After the third time, comprehension dawned when he recalled how much Sefilar despised his pigeon. Maybe she held the same disdain for all birds. He perceived it as a direct summons. Despite everything, he realized he still had a duty to try and rescue Hanna, personal feelings aside.

Though uncertain if his spur-of-the-moment plan had any real chance of success, Cristen didn't hesitate. He sprinted back down the tunnel, politely excusing himself as he maneuvered around the escort. Returning to the arched entrance, he drew a deep breath and cupped both hands tightly around his mouth. Mustering every ounce of strength, he crowed loudly three times.

13

B edlam erupted as Cristen's caws echoed spectacular-
ly through the cavern and branching tunnels. Sefilar's thick tail whipped around, smacking violently against
the rock face, dislodging pebbles that clattered to the
floor. Her serpentine body followed the whip-crack motion, sending Hanna and the escort sliding back to the
ground. He struggled to accept the staggering notion that
a commanding creature of such size and ferocity could be
frightened by a threat of mere crows, yet his cawing had
sent her into a panic.

Cristen sprinted toward Hanna and knelt at her crumpled
form. He pulled the sack from her, freeing her face. At the
same time, the escort staggered back onto her feet, mean-
dering about in a confused daze. Sefilar rose on two powerful

hind legs, her elongated neck arching toward the gaping fissure high above.

"Master, not the pecking crows!" the dragon roared, launching herself upward and taking flight into the fissure. Her voice trailed off as she cleared the mountain. "You promised no more curses or end it now. I'm not responsible for those boys' lives."

Master! Cristen gasped aloud at the revealing outburst. So Sefilar answered to the wizard, under the control of his powerful thumb! Additionally, if she meant the two escorts who met their untimely demise by Cristen's own hands, it seemed clear that limits had been imposed by the wizard, confining the damage Sefilar could inflict without serious repercussions. It explained why Cristen still drew breath despite the dragon's utter disdain for him.

As he cradled Hanna protectively, it dawned on him that the wizard likely disrupted things only to spare her, not to help him. After all, he had already proved his disloyalty. The sobering thought reminded Cristen that the wizard's world didn't revolve around him.

He gently shook Hanna to rouse her. Though she still breathed, her eyes were closed. "Hanna," he softly called. The side of her cheek and chin showed abrasions from the fall. Cristen's gaze briefly lifted to the night sky, but only briefly before the dragon returned.

As Sefilar landed back inside, she nearly trampled right over the still-wandering escort. Cristen was about to chastise her for her carelessness around her 'little ones,' when he was taken aback when the dragon spoke again.

"Well, what are you waiting for? We haven't got all night," she snapped, still on edge and watching the sky. She remained entirely oblivious to what had unfolded beneath her oversized snout.

Cristen froze in bewilderment. Did Sefilar believe him to be Hanna's assigned escort? What if he followed her mistaken assumption and replaced the escort for the journey ahead? Did an astonishing new option just open up? *What if I did go?* he wondered with nervous excitement. What peril might he potentially face if he traveled to the Oasis unshifted? This could be the ultimate situation! If he could go with his identity and memories intact, he could care for Hanna after all.

Cristen quickly pulled the coarse burlap sack over his head. Doing his best to mimic the escorts' slow, stiff movements, he lifted Hanna and carried her toward Sefilar. Gently, he laid her on the nearest wing. Looping an arm around her back, he carefully pulled her slack form with him as he climbed awkwardly up the bony wing webbing.

About halfway up, Cristen felt the dragon shifting impatiently. With a lurch, she tossed them the rest of the way onto her ridged upper back with the wing they attempted to scale. Cristen grabbed Hanna just in time, preventing her from slipping over the other side. She opened her eyes with a sharp gasp at the sudden impact.

"Hanna?" Cristen anxiously whispered her name, but only a glazed, vacant fog still filled her half-open eyes. She'd merely startled momentarily from her trance.

Sefilar snagged the scales from where the dazed escort had dropped them. Cristen couldn't imagine why they would even need them—unless dreamers traded them as currency at the Oasis. Were they meant for Hanna's benefit, perhaps to aid her in establishing herself in the new land?

With Cristen and Hanna finally secured within ridged neck vertebrae, Cristen held Hanna tightly from behind, and the dragon lunged skyward. Cristen clung on for dear life as they tilted back at a sharp angle, fighting against the driving thrust of mighty wings. They ascended through the rocky column to the fissure, buffeted by each sweeping downward stroke.

As they emerged outside and Sefilar gained substantial altitude, she leveled off into a smoother flight, making their journey less jarring and erratic. Cristen pulled the sack from his head and got better situated with Hanna. Every inch of him felt alive in the cold night air, free as a bird from the confines of the troubled world below.

What an incredible shame Hanna was missing out on all this. Yet, Cristen marveled at the astonishing turn of events, the tides of fortune suddenly shifting so dramatically in his favor. Never in his wildest dreams could he have hoped to join Hanna without first being shifted himself, stripped of everything that defined him.

When the air around them grew increasingly frigid, he wrapped the burlap sack around Hanna's shoulders and held her tighter, sharing his body heat to keep them warm.

Though the landscape beneath them lay shrouded in darkness, Cristen could still discern the blackness of the mountain range they followed, confirming a westward course. He found it somewhat odd since Sefilar had flown due north with Caralee. He tried not to think about Sunfire somewhere down there. And if the wizard did intervene in saving the horse again, Cristen didn't deserve it. The wizard should be looking for a worthier apprentice.

As their journey stretched on, Cristen wondered how far they would need to travel tonight, though he remembered Sefilar's assurance that distance posed no challenge with a winged escort. He also wondered what kind of reception awaited them. New possibilities began to intrigue him, and he couldn't wait for Hanna to emerge from her shift so he could start explaining things to her. He pictured her happy and carefree like Caralee.

He vowed never again to deny his deep love for the girl he held shivering in his arms and that he would faithfully do whatever it took for as long as necessary to help her fall equally in love with him again. How blissful their life could now become. Cristen contentedly pictured row upon row of charming matching houses, each with lush green grass, cheery flower beds, and quaint picket fences bordering their future street.

The smell of the sea eventually reached Cristen on the stiff breeze. Soon, its ominous dark expanse spread before them, filling him with a creeping sense of dread. He hoped they wouldn't fly over the open ocean for any distance. However, Sefilar unexpectedly dipped to the left, angling to follow the coastline in a new southern direction, leaving Cristen utterly confused. With the Oasis north, why would she choose to take them on such a detour?

A swirling kaleidoscope of butterflies suddenly trailed behind them, sparkling under the moonlight. But Cristen quickly realized they weren't butterflies but a slew of dragon scales from the sack. So they weren't meant for Hanna at all. But why would Sefilar bother to bring them only to discard them?

Damon's scale-hunting friends would be ecstatic if they happened upon such a find. He amused himself with the absurd notion that she scattered them over the land just to be found but quickly became horror-struck to think the idea held merit. King Thane once called the scales the dragon's lure. Then why *wouldn't* she spread them far and wide? Like a patient fisherman, did Sefilar deliberately scatter her bait to reel in desperate, hungry dreamers? If the notion held any truth, an even more disturbing question arose—to what end? What could Sefilar possibly stand to gain from enacting such a bizarre scheme? A renewed worry for Hanna's safety began gnawing at him as he grew suspicious of Sefilar's question-able intent. The farther south they traveled, the more his anxiety mounted.

Finally, after what felt like hours, the air grew warmer, and Cristen spotted a few pinpoints of light below—street torches. To his dismay, they had glided inland at some point and now flew across a swath of Harmony's heartland until the dragon descended directly over one of its small towns.

Sefilar circled the unsuspecting village several times, her neck craning downward as if searching for something. Grad-ually, they descended until Cristen could make out livestock in the fields and hear the occasional dog bark until something strange and unsettling unfolded. One after another, cows and horses lowered themselves into prone positions as if suddenly overcome by an urge to sleep. Even the barking tapered off into silence.

It took a moment, but the unnatural event jogged Cristen's memory. The same phenomenon happened to Sunfire that first night of his long ride to Burning Mountain alone. Cristen had traveled into the wee hours of the night before dawn broke. Without warning, the horse laid itself down to sleep. At the time, Cristen thought he was merely sick or too exhausted to continue until the horse arose about an hour later, and they continued onward as if nothing happened. But now, witnessing the pattern repeated on a larger scale, he understood. Harmony must be asleep before the dragon could infiltrate its borders, for she couldn't risk being seen.

With the cattle asleep, Sefilar stopped circling and aimed for the town's outer neighborhoods. She passed over thatched and wooden-tiled roofs, then fenced backyards and gardens until she landed gracefully in the grass between a slumbering dog, its head poking halfway out of its little house, and a towering cherry tree.

Sefilar spread her wing against the grass, signaling the time for Cristen to disembark with Hanna. Though still locked in her trance, Hanna again seemed to know what to do because Cristen was suddenly in her way. He managed to stay a little ahead of her while she awkwardly climbed from the wing without assistance. With their feet back on the ground, he squeezed her arm, wanting her to look at him, but she still didn't seem to know of his presence. The moment he released her, she headed off alone toward the house. As Sefilar craned her neck in his direction, he quickly picked up the burlap sack that fell to the ground with them and put it back over his head.

Cristen stared after Hanna in dismay through the large eyeholes. What did the dragon expect her to do—knock randomly on some sleeping family's back door in the middle of the night? Would Sefilar expect Hanna's escort to follow her? He hesitated, not knowing what to do. After only managing a few uncertain steps in Hanna's direction, Sefilar pounced on him from behind, knocking him to the ground before he could cry out in surprise.

14

Sefilar snatched Cristen up and pulled the disguise from his head, yanking him toward her face. He'd never been so close to her, close enough to see every wrinkle in her thick, leathery skin. Intricate patterns wove themselves through her ivory horns that grew backward from her giant forehead. She pulled him closer to the black pool of an eye, forcing him to squeeze his eyes shut.

"So what? It's me!" Cristen yelled. "You can't kill me, so what are you going to do about it?"

Sefilar's face twisted into a scowl. "Who says I can't, and why do you vex me so?" she growled. With a swift motion, she flung Cristen to the grass, jarring his back. In a flash, she pounced, her massive forelegs engulfing him and trapping him in an inescapable embrace. She pressed a razor-sharp claw against his arm, pinning it to the grass and rendering him immobile.

"Why did you bring her here?" Cristen shouted, desperate to wake the house and all the neighbors. "You promised her the Oasis."

"My Oasis is for the deserving. You thought I would let you two live happily ever after?" Sefilar's cold, harsh laughter cut through the air like a blade.

Still on his back, Cristen watched in astonishment as Hanna entered the house as if she lived there. Facing Sefilar again, he shouted, "She's done nothing wrong! If she doesn't deserve it, then who does? She's done everything you wanted, including betraying her only friend."

Cristen winced under the point of her claw. If only Hanna had known Sefilar wouldn't keep her promise, she would have understood why Cristen wanted nothing to do with her. Sefilar retreated a couple of steps, allowing Cristen to inch backward, putting a little distance between them.

"The truth is," Sefilar said, a touch of pleasure in her gravelly voice, "her soul has been bought and paid for."

Cristen shuddered from the coldness of her words. "What are you talking about? Bought by who?" he asked, his face heating up. He couldn't imagine a worse nightmare. And why hadn't Hanna come back out yet? Unless...had she fallen into the hands of her purchaser? He needed to get into that house.

"I owe you no explanation," answered Sefilar dismissively.

A bat darted erratically from the cherry tree's heights, and Sefilar jerked in surprise, eliciting a loud laugh from Cristen.

"Afraid of another tiny creature, are you?" Cristen mocked. "Hurry, better hide before it sucks your blood."

Seething, Sefilar crawled back to him with terrifying speed, a lick of flame escaping her fanged maw. She grabbed him by the torso, squeezing the breath out of him. Lifting him, she flew over the fence into the empty field behind the houses and gouged a deep hole in the soil with a mighty swoop of her claws. Cristen kicked and screamed as she forced him into the grave and held him down, filling it back in and silencing him as dirt pressed against his face, flooding his mouth. A final stomp from above knocked the remaining air from his lungs and nearly broke his nose. Enveloped in blackness, he couldn't breathe and felt himself on the brink of death.

But Cristen refused to let this be his grave. As he compelled himself with every bit of inner strength to move his arms, he felt a surprising wave of energy course through him, a feeling almost familiar. Vivid images flashed through his mind—of the Array and a javelin hurtling toward his throat in slow motion. Somehow, he knew time slowed for him again, even with no visual cues. Waiting patiently for the next beat of his heart, his lack of oxygen seemed only an annoyance.

With a surge of adrenaline, Cristen forced his arms upward against the crushing weight of the dirt. He clawed weakly at first but soon felt the soil start to give way. He dug his fingers into the walls around him, scraping and loosening chunks that he shoved upward and outward, gradually displacing the soil above him. As he slowly widened the space, the work became more accessible, and he finally pushed through to the surface, allowing him to gulp the fresh night air. His first breath restored his natural heartbeat, and he rose out of the grave. He spat the dirt from his mouth and brushed more from his eyes and face.

Seeing that Sefilar had left him for dead, Cristen collapsed onto his back to recover from the harrowing ordeal. Maybe she *would* end up killing him now that her patience wore thin. She only needed to drop him from the sky or engulf him in flames. Did her hatred towards him run so deep that she risked the pecking crows to be rid of him?

Cristen struggled to grasp the power he unwittingly wielded—the magic that twice stalled time to save his life. All other magic he'd witnessed had come from the wizard, but this felt as though he were drawing upon an inner reservoir of power. Too exhausted to go after Hanna, he watched the stars until he fell asleep.

Hours later, a barking dog finally jarred Cristen awake. *Hanna!* What had become of her? Cristen groaned as he forced himself up, pain radiating through his battered body. Guided by the tall cherry tree, Cristen found his way around the houses to the neighborhood street. As he approached the house's front yard, a stocky boy no older than ten burst from the house, leaving the door wide open behind him.

"What are you looking at?" he shouted at Cristen as he ran past.

A tall, dark-haired woman emerged onto the porch, calling after him: "Warren Flynn Myers, get back here this instant and finish your breakfast." But the reprimand fell on deaf ears as the boy Warren darted down the block and vanished around the corner. With a weary sigh, his mother ducked back inside.

Cristen held his breath as he lightly knocked on the door. The woman's nagging voice again rang, "Hurry up, those dishes won't wash themselves." The sizzling aroma of fried ham wafted out as the door swung open again, making Cristen's mouth water.

"Can I help you?" asked the woman, wearing a pristine white apron over a conservative black dress with cuffed sleeves. A scarf wrapped up her dark hair. Creases lined her forehead, prematurely aging her. Shadows ringed her otherwise pretty brown eyes.

Cristen hesitated, not knowing what to say exactly. "I... uh, is there a girl here? She came last night. About my age. Her name is Hanna."

"You have the wrong house," the woman replied briskly. "And the wrong block. There's no one named Hanna around here."

Cristen took an uncertain step back. "You...didn't get a visitor late last night? She came in the back door."

"I should hope not! I'm sorry, but you've caught me at a bad time." She tried to shut the door again, but another hand blocked it.

"Who've we got here?" asked a portly man with rosy cheeks and bright green eyes.

The woman ducked beneath the man's arm, retreating into the house.

"I'm looking for..." Cristen began explaining, but his heart leaped into his throat when Hanna suddenly crossed the woman's path behind the man. She now wore a dress with frilly layers on the elbow-length sleeves and hem at her calves, an outfit he felt she previously wouldn't be caught dead in. Her silky brown hair was pulled back from her temples, ringlets cascading around her shoulders, including two smaller ones framing her face. Glancing only briefly at Cristen, she disappeared down a hallway.

The woman turned to call after her. "Did you put the cutlery away, dear?" she asked sternly.

"Yes, Mother," Hanna replied from down the hall.

The exchange left Cristen dizzy—Hanna had just called this stranger her mother!

The man stared at Cristen, eyebrows raised. "You were saying, young man?"

Cristen's mind raced, struggling to make sense of it all.

"Sorry, my dear boy. We're just trying to get out the door. Perhaps we'll cross paths down at Mulberry Park for the contests," the man said amiably, moving to close the door.

"Wait, can I just have a minute to talk with her?" Cristen blurted out.

"With Evelyn?" the man asked. "I'm afraid we're running a bit behind schedule."

"No, with Hanna," Cristen insisted, assuming he meant his wife. "I swear I just need a minute."

The man's brow furrowed further. "As my wife said, no one named Hanna lives here."

Cristen might have thought they were trying to hide her from him, except that they knew he saw her. "Then who's that girl?" he demanded.

"As I said, she's our daughter, Evelyn."

Evelyn? Cristen felt lightheaded, beads of sweat forming on his forehead. "But...she just got here last night," he managed weakly.

"Pardon me?" said the man, eyebrows raised.

Cristen might have eight eyes and as many noses by the way the man studied him.

"Good luck to you, young man," the man said. "And by the way...a little...dirt." He gestured to indicate that Cristen had some in his hair, then apologetically closed the door on him.

Cristen took a few steps back in shock, tripping from the porch steps onto the walkway. Overnight, Hanna had become Evelyn, a daughter of strangers, but they fully embraced her as their own. Neither did Hanna seem to know differently. Did this innocent-seeming family somehow ruin her chances for the Oasis? Or did they serve as pawns in some deeper scheme? The implications left Cristen in awe at Sefilar's power. She could manipulate anyone, both water dreamers and townspeople alike, to suit her whims.

15

Cristen wandered aimlessly, his surroundings a blur of unfamiliar buildings and streets, oblivious to the town's name.

Still shaken by the trauma of being buried alive, he felt starkly aware of Sefilar's dangerous, unpredictable side. He shook with anger over the dragon's callous betrayal of Hanna, dumping her back in Harmony, selling her soul...whatever that meant exactly. He felt robbed of the life they might have built together, cheated out of a happiness he had started to believe possible.

A sprawling park with gently rolling hills and clusters of giant shade trees bustled with activity while horses and carts lined the crowded streets. A sign farther down read Mulberry Town Park.

"Mulberry," Cristen whispered. He wondered where it lay in relation to King's Crossing and home.

Cristen remembered the father at the house mentioning a park with contests. It looked like some festival. Hanna and her new family must have come here. He suddenly needed to find her, to privately tell her she didn't belong with these strangers or even in this unfamiliar town.

He realized Sefilar did them a favor by bringing Hanna back to Harmony. Besides having a house in King's Crossing, Cristen knew Harmony, while the Oasis always remained a mysterious unknown. Instead of a makeshift family of fellow water dreamers, Sefilar had given Hanna a traditional one to care for her. Cristen only needed to court her the old-fashioned way. He would discover where she spent her time and let her slowly get to know him again. She may not initially be romantically interested in him, but he could be patient.

The park bustled with the excitement of lumberjack games, drawing in families and spectators alike to join in the festivities and cheer on the competitors. Children raced eagerly across the grass in three-legged races, stumbling and falling in squealing heaps. Other youngsters hopped and stumbled along in potato sacks, screaming joyfully. More adventurous kids climbed the trees. It seemed a pleasant way to enjoy the weather—until Cristen stopped to observe some of the competitions.

The women's hatchet-throwing contest, in particular, turned surprisingly ugly fast. The rowdy audience behaved rudely when their favorite contestant didn't win, booing and heckling the victors. Unsettled, Cristen quickly moved on, but the next event proved just as unpleasant. Teams wielding long two-handled saws worked feverishly away at massive logs. Cristen noticed one team whose saw had nearly cut through to the bottom. When their slice of log finally tipped and fell to the ground with a thud, the spectators behaved even worse than at the previous game, with very few cheering the winners. Many expressed open displeasure and complained bitterly about the outcome.

Cristen still couldn't see Hanna anywhere.

Raucous laughter drew his attention to the lower end of the sprawling park—a large pond bustling with water activities. Perhaps Hanna had gone down there, where people seemed to be enjoying themselves. Cristen watched the pond as he descended the grassy slope through the shade trees. At the closer bank, two grinning young men at opposite ends of a floating log tried to roll the other into the water. One inevitably lost his footing and fell backward with a big splash. The winner lost control and fell in with him.

On the far bank, a man in a canoe with a single oar paddled out into the middle of the pond. Another dragged a second empty craft to the water's edge and paddled out. Once a fair distance from the bank, the boats faced off. At the shrill whistle, the two contestants paddled forward, trying to pick up speed. The energized crowd lining the banks chanted loudly, "Sink the boat! Sink the boat!"

As the dueling canoes closed in, the men held their paddles aloft like weapons about to strike. Gliding past each other, they jabbed wholeheartedly in each other's direction but ended up too far apart to make contact. Spectators crowed with laughter at the miss and dramatic antics. Circling back around, the contestants geared up for another lunge. This time, one man lost control when his opponent rammed the side of his canoe.

Now adjacent, the first man nimbly stepped onto the rim of the other's boat, attempting to overturn it. But his forceful stance only shoved the unstable craft farther away, causing him to do an awkward split. Capitalizing on this vulnerability, the second man thrust his paddle into the floundering fool's chest, pushing him into the pond.

The winner gleefully jumped into the water after the sputtering loser. Each positioned at their opponent's canoe, they endeavored to tip them until one succumbed, their canoe capsizing in defeat. The crowd erupted in wild cheers and boos. It seemed the sinking of both oarsman and their canoe decided the winner.

Things quickly escalated as one sore loser shoved a man who hooted his excitement, igniting a shouting match that soon drew more irate spectators into the fray. Yelling obscenities and shoving violently, fists started flying in all directions. Cristen backed away as the mayhem inched closer to the pond, wanting no part of the madness. What was wrong with everyone? He'd never witnessed such pandemonium and viciousness at a public event.

An adolescent boy zigzagged through the different groups, shouting through his bullhorn, "The first prizes! First round of prizes at the east side!"

Cristen couldn't be less interested, and with no sign of Hanna, he saw no reason to stay. He exited the park the opposite way from which he'd entered, leaving the frenzy behind. Wandering through neighborhoods, he found himself on Main Street in the small town, heading toward the shops. His rumbling stomach reminded him he needed food, but he hoped to use the dragon scale in his pocket to secure a ride home.

A street sign up ahead read: SION ST. Strange, Cristen thought. It bore the same name as his street. Intrigued by the possibility of others sharing his address, he trailed Sion for eleven blocks until they reached a dead-end—much like his own street. He stared in disbelief at an impossible sight. The white house looked identical to his, down to the street number, yellow trim, and window with its blue curtain to the left of the door. The large yard, surrounding fence, and brown barn looked slightly different, but the familiar sign over the door eliminated any remaining doubt:

WHEREVER YOU GO, YOU ARE KNOWN

Cristen double-checked the unfamiliar neighborhood to be sure this wasn't somehow King's Crossing. A dog from the house catty-corner barked non-stop at Cristen from its backyard, which shared a fence with this yard. No such canine neighbors existed back at his house. Down the street, not a single other home resembled those from his block. Cristen hesitantly unlatched the gate, letting himself into the yard. Most shockingly, Sunfire emerged from the barn to greet him with a welcoming whinny. He'd made it home safely, after all.

"What are you doing here, boy?" Cristen asked gently, tears threatening to spill as he rubbed the stallion's neck.

He took another skeptical look at his surroundings, questioning his perception. He followed the walkway to the front door and knocked to be sure. When no one answered, he slid his ornate key into the deadbolt and clicked open the lock. Cautiously opening the door, he stepped inside. He shook his head, still not entirely understanding. Everything around him identically mirrored his house, items sitting just as he'd left them. Had the wizard really not found a worthier apprentice after all this time? He didn't feel so much anger toward him anymore. He barely thought of him at all. But if he still waited for Cristen to jump off the bridge, he was in for a long wait.

16

Damon chewed absently on a long grass stalk, watching the busy park from his hidden hillside vantage point. He had escaped the chaos for a brief reprieve to clear his aching head. Though their greed proved the key to his dreams, he found them all rather pathetic. Their constant demands exhausted him.

Simply giving dragon scales away had failed him in the past, arousing suspicion surrounding his motives. But a little 'friendly' competition helped convince these foolish townsfolk that they earned the scales fair and square, taking pride in what they deemed accomplishments. Thanks to the unchecked greed in the last few villages, he had already distributed nearly two full sacks. Putting the scales directly into the hands of the people had never been done before.

Sefilar would surely be pleased about his success after he informed her tonight.

The thought of their impending meetup worsened his headache. Anticipating an encounter with the dragon always brought them on, especially since he'd suffered some head injury at Burning Mountain. For nearly three tedious years, he had served as her chosen right-hand man since she pulled him from the choppy waters that terrible day he learned of his tragic identity. Her endless requests had taken their toll over time. Even Moonshine suffered from their far-flung travels, scattering pieces of Sefilar herself across the countryside. He never understood the dragon's obsession with gathering every last dreamer to her Oasis. Not that he cared; it didn't affect him.

As his servitude drew to an end, his unwavering loyalty and backbreaking labor were about to pay off at last. Soon, he would claim the magnificent mansion Sefilar promised him, finally breaking free from her clutches. She had already provided him the detailed blueprints for a building far grander than anything he could have envisioned. She paid him triple the scales he managed to distribute to fund the extravagant project. Damon pictured himself gazing out over King's crossing from atop Beacon Hill like royalty, the envy of all who saw his splendor.

He slapped at a mosquito feasting on his arm, leaving it smashed in a splotch of blood. Sefilar sucked the life out of him much the same way, he mused. The setting sun reminded him to return to the festival stage to hand out the final prizes.

***

Damon raised his arm over the chattering crowd, allowing a hush to settle across the hundreds of spectators. Lifting the bullhorn, he announced loudly, "Friends! It is my great honor to host these games for your enjoyment. I'm a man abundantly blessed. To hoard such fortune would be wrong indeed. My deepest desire is to play some small part in bettering the lives of good, hardworking townsfolk like yourselves." He gave his small bag of dragon scales a rattle, eliciting cheers. He never let them see many at a time to make the scales appear rare. *Like putty in my hands*, he thought smugly.

"Please welcome Aldun Greenwhopper to the stage, overseer of today's exciting tree-climbing event."

Aldun wore an absurd plaid orange tunic paired with purple leggings. To Damon, his flat nose resembled a baboon's, made all the worse by an unkempt, bushy beard.

"Do we have our climbing victors?" Damon boomed for all to hear.

Aldun nodded eagerly, passing Damon a folded scrap of paper.

"Friends, the winner of the girls' climb is...Nelda Faramore!" Damon announced with pretended pride.

A young girl's excited scream pierced the air, and the crowd clapped politely, more envious than happy for her achievement. Nelda pushed her way through the crowd to join Damon and Aldun onstage. Damon made a grand show of handing over her promised dragon scale prize while she jumped up and down, waving it ecstatically for all to see.

Once Nelda stepped back into the audience, Damon continued, "And the boys' winner?"

Aldun passed him another scribbled note.

"Del Murphy! You are a monkey in disguise. Come on up and claim your well-deserved prize."

Del Murphy looked far too old to be a child. The crowd noticed, too, and tried to prevent the teen from taking the stage by booing his questionable victory. But Damon saw only an opportunity in the controversy.

"Good people! As I failed to set proper age divisions for this particular event, I am happy to compensate for my oversight. Mr. Greenwhopper, who do you say climbed the second fastest?"

Damon's generosity elicited raucous hooting and applause from the spectators. But the flustered Aldun drew a blank, unprepared with an answer.

"My Cory!" shouted a shrill woman's voice. "I watched from below. He climbed faster than anyone but Del up there!" She began pushing her confused son of about twelve years toward the stage.

"You're out of your mind!" bellowed an angry man. "I witnessed the entire event, and your clumsy little oaf didn't make it halfway up before bawling to come back down! It's my boy Ethan's prize—been climbing since a rug rat." He hoisted his grinning son onto his shoulders and carried him toward the stage. Inspired by the outbursts, other parents joined the heated quarrel, each insisting their child deserved to be declared the rightful runner-up.

Damon did a double take when he noticed a striking dark-haired beauty near the back of the crowd. She turned her head to speak with a tall woman beside her, offering him a better angle. She suddenly looked faintly familiar, but how? Where could he possibly have seen her before? The crowd's ongoing bickering demanded his attention again.

"My friends, all is well!" Damon shouted through the bullhorn. "If you feel your young one has rightfully won this contest, then please bring them forward so we can hear them out and make a fair decision."

A steady stream of boys and their parents headed to the front. The excited young climbers continued trickling on-stage until the last several struggled to find room to stand. Forcing a smile, Damon handed out scales to everyone, sending the pretended winners on their way with more jubilant cheers and buzzing excitement.

Damon felt the day's success thrilling for an entirely different reason. By day's end, he would have earned enough to begin the next ambitious construction phase. He'd already accepted delivery of the lumber, and first thing tomorrow, he could pay for the stacks of bricks waiting for him down at the quarry.

Peering intently into the crowd, with a few more restless children at his elbows, he located the dark-haired beauty again, unwilling to lose track of her. His chin fell slack when it suddenly dawned on him why he knew her. She looked identical to someone he'd dreamt about many times, which meant she might be a dreamer too. *Cristen's Hanna*, he thought with flared nostrils and pursed lips, huffing through his nose. Damon's worst dreams consisted of the two of them running off together, frolicking in the woods or meadows like lovestruck birds in springtime.

It didn't matter. He hardly needed the sea's help to woo a woman. With his striking good looks and natural charm, the ladies in town couldn't keep their eyes off him. His upcoming reputation guaranteed him the pick of Harmony's finest, including this siren. But secrecy became imperative—should Sefilar ever discover him courting a stray dreamer, the consequences might prove...unpleasant.

Damon knew firsthand that the sea manifested people from dreams because she'd done it with Cristen. Damon had been rattled seeing him exit Poppy's Inn and unnerved again when he appeared with Lora at the stables. Once again, Cristen had snagged the girl. Though the kid had started to grow on Damon, Cristen would only be in the way now. If he happened to have similar dreams about the same girl, he might be a nuisance. He should be long gone by now, tucked away at Sefilar's Oasis, his dreams and memories wiped clean.

The girl...she went by Hanna in his dreams...noticed him staring. With a charismatic smirk, Damon brazenly held her gaze.

A woman's voice intruded next to him, "Knock knock. Hello, anyone home?"

Damon scowled at her rude interruption.

"I have the pond winners," she said flippantly, hand on her extended hip.

"Congratulations," Damon muttered, snatching the paper from her, not trying to hide his annoyance. He finished dispensing the final few scales before looking for Hanna again, but she had slipped away. He pressed the prize bag into the rude woman's hands. "You're in charge—be generous and take a few for yourself." He needed to catch that girl.

17

Dismounting, Damon led his horse up Beacon Hill on foot in case the witching hour caught him off guard again. Sefilar's sorcery granted her nightly access into town for these private rendezvous, the townspeople trapped in an enchanted slumber.

His head still throbbed from the day's taxing activities and the long ride back to King's Crossing to meet Sefilar in time. At least the delight of Hanna's—no, he must call her by the name she introduced herself by—of Evelyn's pleasant company earlier helped offset his discomfort when he'd found her feeding the ducks by the pond. The new name didn't suit her, but he would need to get used to it or risk offending her. He'd already decided that Beacon Hill needed someone like her. How would she fancy being princess of the land?

Damon reached the hill's crest, where endless stacks of pungent lumber and their eerie shadows stretched across the vast grounds. Finally passing the last of it, he crossed a field destined to be part of his landscaped terrace. He then moved along the eastern boundary stakes outlining what would soon be Sefilar's grandiose gesture—a mansion of staggering proportions beyond his wildest imaginings.

At that moment, he resolved to name his palatial estate and all of Beacon Hill: Damon's Place. The entire land of Harmony—towns and countryside alike—would know of him and even laud his name. Indeed, whispers already circulated amongst the architects and builders about the man commanding something unheard of atop the hill.

"I take it you approve," Sefilar purred, having crept up behind him while he envisioned the completed mansion.

She startled Damon, but he kept his composure. Clasping his hands behind his back, he didn't turn to face her immediately, unwilling to appear reactive. "It far surpasses my expectations," he said, always formal with her. "Accept my deepest gratitude for such generosity."

"Consider it inadequate compensation for years of steadfast loyalty," Sefilar gently rasped.

Damon finally pivoted to face her. Finding the dragon closer than comfortable, he cautiously retreated a pace, avoiding the fathomless obsidian pools of her eyes.

"I must confess to some surprise that we needed to convene again so soon," Damon remarked boldly yet guardedly, taking care not to tempt her wrath. "With the influx of water dreamers flooding the mountain—as you have assured me—I believed we had already rounded up the last stragglers. What more can I do for you?"

"Indeed, all have come," Sefilar confirmed.

"I'm pleased to hear it," Damon responded. "The Oasis will continue to thrive under your benevolent stewardship." Navigating the dragon's vanity was delicate and perilous, yet it often succeeded in pacifying her.

"Except for one," Sefilar hissed, a hint of her true reptilian nature betraying her mild-mannered guise.

Damon tensed. Did she know about Evelyn? "I...who..." he stammered, cursing himself for the lapse of composure.

"If this one is not stopped," she interjected, "then you and I stand to lose everything."

"Because of one?" Damon managed to ask, willing his rapid heartbeat to steady, fearing he would be asked to give up the girl so soon.

"Because of one bent on exposing me," Sefilar uttered with abrupt malice, a chill permeating her husky tone that made his neck hairs stand on end. "If this rebel dreamer succeeds, the safety of every other is jeopardized. The veil protecting our enterprise will be ripped away, exposing everything that allows it to survive, and once broken, it cannot be mended. Do you grasp the danger? Your dreams for this grand hilltop will collapse into ruin alongside my own."

Damon long understood that Sefilar and her dealings must remain secret. Any exposure would surely catapult the townspeople into hysteria. Burning Mountain and its sanctuary Oasis would then face grave jeopardy, risking the safety of every shifted soul living there. He'd never considered how such a turn could affect him too. If Sefilar fell, so would he. All would be lost, his emerging mansion pried cruelly from his fingers. Far worse, scores of jilted debtors would reduce his burgeoning status and name to ridicule.

"I will find this stray and deliver them to you myself if necessary," Damon declared, his steadfast tone masking the dread within. He couldn't let a girl get in the way.

"Not so," Sefilar rattled. "He has already refused my sanctuary not once but twice."

Damon breathed a silent sigh of profound relief—a defiant boy then, not Evelyn.

"The impudent dreamer must be silenced...permanentl y," Sefilar uttered with shocking venom.

Damon shuddered. *Permanently?* He choked back the bile rising in his throat, desperately steadying his nerves before trusting himself to respond.

"I give you my solemn word that I will get this rogue to Burning Mountain one way or another," Damon asserted firmly. "I'll threaten him with serious harm if he so much as breathes a word about you or your affairs to anyone."

Sefilar sighed, exhaling a long, rattling breath into the night air. "A storm is brewing," she said ominously. "In a day or two, this exposed hilltop will become saturated with flooding rains, and your road will turn treacherous."

Damon prayed his pounding pulse didn't betray his calm façade as he struggled to comprehend what she was getting at. Heavy rains had made his road slick, making it treacherous. In some parts, the hill alongside it dropped a hundred feet. He chose his words carefully: "Then I will halt all construction until things dry out and conditions improve for the workers."

"Let them work. Demand it," Sefilar instructed with a sinister edge to her voice. "Invite the dreamer to see this place. You will ambush him on the road when he leaves...and force him off the side."

Damon's blood ran cold. So she wanted the dreamer dead and for him to carry out the vile deed himself, even going so far as devising the exact manner in which to accomplish it. A less horrific solution must exist, but he dared not argue, having learned never to question her.

"Just tell me where to find him," Damon demanded, steeling his voice to conceal his fear.

Sefilar retracted her neck and snout as she unfurled her wings in preparation for flight. "You accompanied him to my mountain not long ago," she revealed. "You will find him at the end of Sion Street."

The dragon soared into the night with a rush of air, leaving Damon's gut roiling with dread. Why, of all people, did it have to be Cristen? He should be long gone, shifted to the Oasis by now. Yet somehow, here he remained, improbably back in King's Crossing. How cruelly ironic that Cristen's rejection of the shift could potentially lead to his demise at Damon's hands. Damon's chest tightened at the unthinkable. To compound matters, he found himself again under the oppressive control of Sefilar's whims until he dealt with this inconvenient mess.

Damon whispered despairingly, "*Cristen, what have you done?*"

***

Cristen jumped to his feet the following afternoon when a knock sounded at his door amidst the torrential downpour. Opening it warily, he found a man with a ruddy complexion beneath a sopping-wet hat. Without a word, the man handed Cristen a damp, sealed envelope.

"An invitation for you," the man said. He waited expectantly for Cristen to read it.

Cristen broke the seal and scanned the letter's contents:

You are cordially invited as a special guest to tour the grounds of the new construction site tomorrow afternoon. Take the new road to the top of Beacon Hill north of King's Crossing.

With no signature indicating the sender, Cristen eyed the man skeptically. "Who sent this?"

"A...friend." The man said, shifting uneasily.

"I don't have friends," Cristen replied, realizing how pathetic it sounded as it escaped his lips. "What's there to see on Beacon Hill?"

"As it states, a large construction project is underway," the man explained.

Cristen raised an eyebrow. "You came all the way from King's Crossing in this weather to invite me to tour some construction site?"

The man's brow furrowed. "I...apologize," he stammered hesitantly. "Are we not in King's Crossing presently? I'm happy to direct you to Beacon Hill if that's your concern."

Cristen stared. So they'd sent a kook to deliver the message. "Maybe I'll consider it when the rain lets up," he replied, uninterested in traveling anywhere.

"I urge you to reconsider," the man pressed unexpectedly. "The owner is most eager for your audience."

"Who? Why me?"

The man leaned in, lowering his voice. "You may have heard of a...Mr. D?"

Cristen had heard of him. "He bought up all the lumber." He already didn't like the man for doing so.

"Indeed, the very same." The man seemed pleased. "For the project, of course."

"Maybe," Cristen replied evasively, though he couldn't deny his curiosity.

"Splendid, tomorrow afternoon then! Any time will do."

Cristen shut the door, then discreetly watched through the curtain as the drenched man limped away into the downpour. Something about the exchange struck him as odd. Cristen shot a puzzled glance around the neighborhood. Unless he'd lost his mind, he could swear he was back in King's Crossing instead of Mulberry, where a dog should be barking at the passing man. Running a hand through his hair, he tried again to make sense of the incomprehensible. Could his house travel from place to place? He shook his head in confusion, happy to still be home regardless.

After braving the rain to blanket the horses for the night, Cristen turned in early. Shedding his damp clothes, he crawled into bed to warm up while the rain continued to pour in endless sheets. Sleep evaded him as thoughts barraged him, jumping from Hanna to the intrigue of his wandering house. Had it vanished entirely from Mulberry? If so, would the neighbors there make trouble?

Another thought struck him—what if the house could transport him randomly from town to town against his will? While initially fascinating, this erratic ability could also prove problematic if he intended to be in one place but ended up elsewhere.

Cristen finally drifted off when a crack of nearby thunder jolted him awake again. The storm raged all night, preventing restful sleep. Come morning, Cristen dragged himself out of bed. Gazing through the kitchen window, he saw the damage the still-falling rain inflicted overnight. Fallen limbs and leafy debris littered the swampy ground.

Pulling on his muck boots, Cristen slogged through the mess to feed the horses who had taken refuge in the barn. He hung up their soaked blankets to dry, then distributed fresh oats and hay.

Trudging back inside, he decided to visit Beacon Hill after all, as the intrigue over Mr. D and his project pulled him in despite himself.

18

Damon's predicament plagued him as he paced the bare wooden floorboards, lost anxiously in thought and oblivious to the damp morning chill in the room. How dare Sefilar saddle him with such a treacherous task after promising freedom?

Of course, he shared her desire to prevent Cristen from further meddling in their affairs, including his interactions with Hanna...*no, Evelyn.* But why leap to the extreme of getting rid of him instead of first attempting to silence him through warning or threat, which he precisely planned to do anyway? But how could he defy the dragon's command without her discovering his own rebellion? He would need some convincing excuse ready for disobeying her.

He hoped Orvyn managed to deliver the invitation on his way home last night and wouldn't show up using the downpour as an excuse. As if on cue, the door opened. Orvyn limped inside with muddy boots, closing the door behind him against the rain.

"Well?" Damon demanded. "What news?"

"I regret to say I'm uncertain, sir," Orvyn replied. "The weather may still stop him."

"Did you tell him who sent it?"

"I divulged you as Mr. D upon his insistence."

"Very well." Damon looked forward to seeing Cristen's reaction to the face behind the name.

"Rest assured, I will promptly pay the lad another visit if he doesn't come. And apologies, sir, but the weather is also delaying some scheduled deliveries."

"I'm well aware," Damon sighed. "At least the masons haven't refused to work yet."

"Certainly not, sir, not at your generous offering of five dragon scales per day. They feel they've struck it rich. However, with the lower scaffolding completed last night, there will be little for them to do if the bricks and mortar don't arrive."

"Make sure every supplier understands—if they deliver even one day late, there will be zero payment, and they'll never work in this town again."

"Yes sir, of course, sir," Orvyn assured him.

Damon saw right through Orvyn's attempt at masking his surprise, finding satisfaction in the reaction. He would command respect from everyone in this town, even if it meant through intimidation and fear.

"See to the horses," Damon said, dismissing him. "And wipe your feet next time. This isn't the stables, in case you didn't notice."

"I apologize, sir. It won't happen again." Orvyn quickly excused himself, leaving Damon alone again.

Damon dragged a hand over his face, exhaling in weary frustration. Even with Orvyn's assistance, the immense scale of organizing such a far-reaching endeavor wore on him daily. Crippled since birth with one leg shorter, Orvyn still proved adept at managing the work crews. Damon knew the man desperately hoped to stick around since no other employer bothered retaining him for more than a few weeks.

Damon's nagging thoughts circled back to Cristen, worsening his mental exhaustion.

***

As Cristen took in the familiar sights of the capital's shops, he felt incredulous over having returned here without any effort. He steered his horse through the muddy, deeply rutted streets. Teams of horses hauled creaking carts piled with crates and barrels, their drivers hurrying to get things done before the next downpour. Pedestrians darted about, trying to dodge puddles and mud splatters as the carts rumbled past.

Cristen waited for a rider to pass, then guided Sunfire onto the back road supposedly leading northeast up to Beacon Hill. The narrower road proved surprisingly busy for such miserable weather. Two carts laden with white speckled brick lumbered past him, the heavy wheels cutting furrows through the gravel. Cristen assumed the bricks were destined for Mr. D's project.

As the road began to climb, Cristen wondered if he shouldn't have waited another day or two. The steep, occasional drop-off to his right kept him on edge each time he needed to pass a cart on that side, and moving between the lanes of opposing wagons stirred up Sunfire's anxiety. After multiple close calls, Cristen maneuvered to the inside shoulder, even up into the rising hillside when boulders didn't force him back down. Even with obstacles, he and Sunfire relaxed, away from so much cart traffic.

When Sunfire finally crested the top of Beacon Hill, Cristen stared unbelieving at the scene before them. Enormous piles of wet fresh timber littered the grounds around the site's perimeter, along with mounds of bricks and other building materials. Over a hundred workers kept busy, laying the white bricks in orderly rows to erect the walls around a monstrous gravel foundation. A maze of scaffolding encased the entire near side, about four stories high, where dozens of men had already constructed a sizeable portion of the first and second floors' walls.

Cristen thought it somewhat strange that an ornate door—though not as elaborate as a grand entrance might be—had already been installed behind the scaffolding where the men worked. Despite the awful weather, the ambitious project bustled with noisy activity as workers with their horses hauled and stacked supplies while shouting foremen directed the organized chaos.

The sprawling field was a muddy, churned-up mess from the ongoing passage of heavy wheels and hooves. Cristen paused to watch one of the several draft horses rear up and neigh defiantly after its cart became mired in the muck. A hapless worker pulled at the poor beast's reins, struggling in vain to free the entrenched wheels while the agitated horse thrashed from side to side. Within moments, the horse overturned the entire cart, spilling prepared mortar across the muddy ground and eliciting angry shouts from other laborers.

"This way, lad! Right over here!" hollered the limping man who had delivered the invitation last night. He motioned for Cristen to wind through the activity and join him at the door.

The pair soon arrived at an opening in the scaffolding. After Cristen dismounted and secured Sunfire, the man gestured for him to head through the door alone while he remained outside, then pulled the door shut behind him.

To Cristen's astonishment, Damon sat casually at the edge of a stack of pallets halfway across the sizable room. Boots crossed, with arms in short sleeves folded across his chest, he wore a finely crafted second skin of form-fitting black leather, accentuating his strapping build.

"Damon! But...I thought..." Cristen trailed off, stunned into silence.

"I could say the same about you," Damon replied evenly, rising smoothly to his full height. "You should be at the Oasis by now, yet here you stand. And look at you—I barely recognize the scrawny kid anxious to embrace a better life."

Cristen glanced around, unable to comprehend Damon's presence in this place. "I...had to get out of there," he finally muttered, distracted by the soaring ceiling and cavernous, unfinished room.

"And continue to stir up trouble, it seems," Damon replied, drawing Cristen's scattered attention back.

"Trouble?" Cristen asked guardedly.

"Let's just say our dragon isn't particularly thrilled with you these days."

Cristen scoffed in disgust. "Is that the problem? How upsetting for her," he replied, his tone thick with sarcasm.

"So you already know," Damon replied with a raised brow.

"She likes to drop hints along the way, and genius me figures it out. You know, sweet little gestures like tossing me across her cave and trying to kill my bird. Her latest hint—she straight up tried to bury me alive. Other than that, we get along famously."

Damon remained unreadable as he began slowly pacing the room, his sharp boot clicks echoing crisply off the bare floor with each methodical step.

Cristen gazed up into the crisscrossing beams spanning the ceiling. "What's your connection to this place?" he asked. "Why are you even here?"

Damon pivoted slowly to face him, clasping his hands behind his back. His piercing blue eyes locked with Cristen's. "Let's just say Sefilar likes me better than you."

Cristen laughed derisively. "No surprise there. But what are you talking about?"

Damon lifted his chin a fraction higher. "Only that this glory rising on the hill is my reward for my service to her. Trust me, I have earned it."

The truth slowly sank in, and Cristen struggled to find words. "This can't be...you're Mr. D.?"

Damon responded with a wry, subtle chuckle, a slight exhalation of breath. "I might be," he said.

Cristen gasped with a new realization. "You're not shifted. You never planned on it, did you? Then you betrayed me too. Why does she want me so bad? I can't believe it...you really had me fooled."

Damon's brow furrowed at the accusation.

When he didn't respond, Cristen continued. "So Sefilar assigned you to drag me to her lair. I doubt I would have gone otherwise.

Damon's nostrils flared as he drew in a deep breath. "That's not what happened. I had options."

Something in his sincere tone convinced Cristen that he spoke the truth, yet Cristen remained highly skeptical of how Damon had acted at the time. "You still expect me to believe that tough Damon didn't dare face her mountain alone? It would mean you didn't trust Sefilar either."

Damon shifted uncomfortably, hesitation flickering across his face. "A temporary lapse in confidence, nothing more. But, tell me...who betrayed you?"

Cristen stared at him. Why did he care? He answered anyway. "A friend who thought she knew better. She's already shifted with a new name, but she's in Mulberry now with some random family because someone..." Cristen halted, a new suspicion dawning. "Wait...was it you?"

"Was what me?" Damon asked tersely.

"Did you pay for her to come here instead of the Oasis?" Cristen asked accusingly.

"What? Don't be absurd," Damon insisted, once again coming across as genuine. "I have no say in such matters."

"Interesting, because according to Vince, Sefilar dubbed you her 'chosen one.' Who else could influence her like that?"

Damon visibly bristled at the accusation.

Sensing he might be getting somewhere, Cristen continued. "I must say, I'm quite surprised to see you here, considering I witnessed you shifting. I guess you backed out after hitting your head."

Damon's gaze sharpened. "What do you know about that?"

"Everything. I watched it happen while you worked filling water jugs. You flipped backward in some fit, and the escorts needed to come for you."

Damon's jaw clenched as he appeared to mull over this new information.

"And another thing," Cristen said, "how did you know I lived here?"

Damon's attention came back around. "I have my ways," he said evasively.

Cristen gasped at a new thought. "You have a sear crystal! Or maybe you use hers. As her chosen one, aren't you also pretty much her spy?"

Damon stiffened. "What did you say?"

"Her crystal ball egg," Cristen clarified, suddenly feeling exposed and vulnerable to serpentine eyes. "Is she watching everything we say and do right now?"

Damon's stoic expression faltered as he glanced around the room. The crack in his steely composure betrayed the instinct to search for threats. In that small slip, Cristen saw he'd been mistaken—Damon didn't know of any crystal ball or Sefilar's capability to spy from afar.

"Seems you two aren't quite bosom buddies after all if she's keeping secrets from you," Cristen quipped sarcastically. "Are you sure it's not me she likes better?"

"Enough!" Damon bellowed, interrupting him mid-sentence. "It's time for you to leave. Now!"

"What's the matter? You don't want her to witness our charming little reunion?"

Damon's piercing eyes flashed dangerously. "I won't ask twice. Leave this instant and never return!"

Cristen slowly backed away toward the door, shaking his head at Damon in disgust over his close alignment with the dragon. "Well...congratulations on all your newfound success," he spat bitterly. "I hope it's worth the price." With that, he spun on his heel and strode furiously from the room without a backward glance.

19

Damon aggressively paced the room, jaw and fists clenched tight. A crystal ball—so much finally made sense. He'd always known Sefilar could locate him whenever she wished, though her methods eluded him until now. It also explained how she'd found him in the sea in the first place. A crystal ball would allow her to spy on anyone at will. He hated that Cristen not only knew before he did but also had to be the one to inform him about it.

So Evelyn had already been shifted. Convenient—he would never be asked to round her up, though he couldn't fathom how she ended up back here. How fascinatingly disturbing that someone had arranged it. He would have to get to the bottom of who, as he disliked the notion of anyone else having ties to her. That Cristen knew her posed enough problems, making this a race for her heart. Since she wouldn't remember Cristen, it should be a breeze. It also explained why she went by Evelyn rather than Hanna, having shed her first identity.

Damon better understood Sefilar's desire to eliminate Cristen. No longer a scrawny, naïve kid, he'd developed quite the mouth on him. Just as Sefilar warned, he could jeopardize everything with his willfulness and apparent lack of fear over it. Damon refused to let anything impede his ambitions, not even the inevitable devaluation of dragon scales after his massive distribution of them. To protect himself against the day, he had been buying up available properties everywhere. Soon, he would be sitting pretty atop Beacon Hill with the girl of his dreams by his side.

Yes, he would do what had to be done. A fleeting pang of pity towards Cristen surfaced, though he immediately dismissed it. He couldn't afford to be soft now. Cristen had made his bed, and Damon had no choice but to ensure he still proved loyal to the dragon. He squeezed the bridge of his nose against another oncoming headache. Retrieving the whistle he used to summon Orvyn, Damon opened the window and blew two sharp blasts into the elements.

"On his way, sir!" called one of the nearby workers.

Damon slammed the window shut again. Losing all control, he growled like a beast toward the ceiling, with hands held as if to strangle someone, "This is my time," he cried aloud.

"No one will take from me what is mine." He would go to any length to protect his promising future and reputation.

The necessary deed to ensure it all would be the ultimate test of Orvyn's loyalty. Damon paced again as he waited, contemplating how to convince the man. Though Orvyn had proven dependable so far, this task would cross a line that gave Damon pause. But he resolved that it had to be done for the sake of his destiny.

As Cristen stepped outside, the first hints of dusk draped over the construction site. His heart quickened with alarm as he noticed Sunfire's absence, his reins still tethered to the scaffolding.

"Where's my horse?" he shouted at the workers. After retrieving the straps, he marched into the muddy field, scouring for Sunfire among the workhorses. Far across the mire, he spotted him straining against a cumbersome load that refused to budge. One man pulled at Sunfire by a rope around his neck while another smacked at his rump with a short whip, attempting to urge him forward. Cristen hurried toward them across the muck, feeling sick over leaving Sunfire so vulnerable again after his safe return home.

"Get away from him!" Cristen screamed as he approached. He yanked the whip from the man's grasp, making him cower. "Let him go before I flog you both senseless," he threatened while brandishing the whip menacingly.

The man at Sunfire's head shouted back, "What did you expect bringing him up here? We need all the help we can round up."

Already working to detach the cart straps, Cristen demanded, "Where's the saddle?"

A whistle sounded twice, its origin somewhere back near the building.

"We never laid eyes on one," the closer man claimed.

"Of course you didn't," Cristen muttered. The instant he broke Sunfire free, he seized his mane and vaulted onto his bare back. He searched the site for any trace of the saddle. Finding none, he loped Sunfire through the mud toward the road, splashing everyone he passed.

"That looks like the king's stallion," a man pushing a wheelbarrow exclaimed, attracting unwanted attention.

"There's the lucky winner," another heckled. "Hey, dreamer, I've got the perfect cart for that horse of yours, with some fetching iron bars around it."

Cristen hurried past the gawking men, ignoring their taunts.

A foreman shouted orders to the masons and haulers. "Wrap it up! Losing light! Finish up!"

Carts and horses already crowded the narrow road, forcing Cristen to guide Sunfire to the inside again. He yelled at a driver who carelessly passed too close despite ample room. Mud sprayed Cristen and Sunfire with each passing cart while Sunfire tossed his head in protest. The ride back down felt extra miserable after Cristen's icy conversation with Damon, and he found solace in knowing he didn't have to claim him as a brother.

An accident up ahead caught his attention. A flipped cart jammed into the hillside while the poor horse endured the chaos of drivers attempting to pass. The horse needed freeing, but the driver seemed to be missing. Cristen hoped the man hadn't suffered serious injury. He scouted the hillside above for an alternate passage, but the boulders prevented climbing. Making his way left, he prepared to skirt the obstruction with the others.

A spotted white cart horse charged recklessly from behind, its driver seemingly unaware of the bottleneck ahead. Cristen shook his head in disbelief—who in their right mind would drive recklessly in these conditions, putting himself and everyone else in mortal danger?

"Slow up!" Cristen shouted urgently, then recognized the driver with dismay—Damon's hire! Despite Cristen's desperate waving, the man remained heedless. "Halt!" Cristen yelled, arms flailing. But the wagon carried on without pause. "Whoa there!" he cried in disbelief.

Finally noticing Cristen, the driver did not slow down. Instead, he seemed to deliberately jerk the reins, steering the galloping horse directly toward Cristen. The man's face was contorted in a mixture of determination and something else Cristen couldn't quite place—fear, perhaps, or desperation. Had the man gone mad?

"Hyah!" Cristen cried, digging his heels into Sunfire. With the path blocked, he had no choice but to pass the obstruction before the lunatic rammed them. His anxiety spiked as he noted the road's crumbling edge. Sunfire released a panicked whinny, struggling for traction on the slick mud and loose gravel.

"Steady, boy," Cristen encouraged nervously, guiding the horse as best he could.

But a cart bumped Sunfire in the hip, spooking the horse. Sunfire reared up, his front hooves pawing the air as he whinnied frightfully. Cristen clung tightly to his mane as he attempted to steer him away from the edge. They spun to face uphill just as the reckless driver bore down, poised to knock them over the cliff.

Suddenly immersed in viscous slow motion, Cristen reached for the only hope of salvation—the white horse's bridle. Freeing his legs' grip on Sunfire, Cristen's weight wrenched the white horse's head downward, pulling its body sideways while its cart and driver careened toward the crumbling precipice.

Time abruptly resumed full speed.

Sunfire's terrified squeal made Cristen nauseous. He glanced back just in time to see the wild look in his horse's eyes before he skidded over the edge, then listened in anguish to the succession of crashes as Sunfire collided with trees and boulders to the bottom.

Cristen's attention snapped back at the realization he was still in motion. The white horse thrashed in the harness, trying to stand, but the sliding cart dragged it backward. Horror struck Cristen as the cart's rear wheel slipped over the ledge, slowly tipping the rig. Damon's man desperately tried freeing himself, but not before the cart dragged him along with it over the edge, still attached to the horse. The man screamed as he fell to his certain death. Cristen clung to the horse's bridle, pressing his body to the ground while maintaining eye contact with its panic-filled eyes mere inches away.

"I've got you, boy. I've got you."

Several men rushed over and quickly unhitched the cart. Once freed, it plunged away, liberating the horse from its burden.

"Has everyone lost their senses?" one man shouted at Cristen as Cristen crawled to the edge, desperately scanning for Sunfire.

"My horse!" Cristen cried out in despair.

"He'll be fine now," assured the man, not understanding.

Cristen spotted Sunfire's golden form, lifeless amidst the dry underbrush far below.

The man shouted again. "You mean that cart wasn't yours? What about its driver?"

But Cristen had already taken off down the road, searching for a section where the slope eased enough to descend.

"Hey, kid," another man called, catching up to press a long hunting knife into his hand. "Just in case," he murmured. The man must have witnessed what happened. Cristen hesitated, dazed, but accepted the blade with a nod.

Others also ventured down now that they knew a man had gone over. Cristen found Sunfire crumpled over a log, legs twitching sporadically. He stared at the knife, paralyzed. As if jolted awake, he rushed to Sunfire, wrapping both arms around his head.

"Forgive me," he wept, pressing his tear-streaked face against his nose, then kissed it. "I'll never forget you." He drew the blade across Sunfire's neck in one swift stroke, ending his agony as the stallion's body went slack.

The crushing weight of his losses felt insurmountable. Both Hanna and Damon had already forsaken him, and now Sunfire, his steadfast companion whose beauty, speed, and prowess outshone any horse, had left him, too. Overwhelming grief engulfed him. He'd never felt so alone.

20

G reta swung open the door, beaming brightly. "Cristen!" She wrapped her frail arms around his waist in an enthusiastic hug, noticeably thinner than he recalled.

"Wow, you've grown!" Cristen remarked, smiling to see jam on her face. The grin faded as he noticed her pale complexion and shadowed eyes.

"I'm six now," she declared proudly.

"Practically a grownup. Where's your pa?"

"In the barn. The cow is having a baby."

"Oh," Cristen responded in surprise. "Shall we go see?"

"No. I got slimy last time."

Cristen chuckled. "I thought you liked slimy things. Frogs...beetles..."

"They're not slimy!" she said adamantly.

"Maybe I should go see if I can help."

"Okay. I'm making sandwiches," Greta said. "Do you want one?"

"I would love one!"

Greta skipped back inside while Cristen headed for the barn. It felt like ages since Cristen first wandered through their humble lives. Squinting in the dim light, it took a moment to locate Jonas on the floor beside the laboring cow. He looked unchanged, except his whiskers had lengthened into a beard. Grunting, he tugged at the calf's front legs protruding from the womb.

Jonas paused to catch his breath, brow glistening. "It's been too long. We may lose it."

"Anything I can do?"

"Take a leg, will yeh?"

Cristen joined Jonas on the floor and grasped the calf's wet leg.

"When she strains, I'll pull," Jonas instructed. "Then you pull when I say. Don't pull when I do, or the shoulders won't cooperate."

Cristen nodded, bracing himself for the next contraction.

"Any luck findin' yers family?" Jonas inquired.

"No sir," he replied.

"What yeh been up to?"

"Oh, you know...running from fire-breathing dragons, I guess." Cristen expected a chuckle, but Jonas shot him a sideways glance, his red-rimmed eyes showing fatigue.

"I meant to visit sooner," Cristen said, changing the subject, "but...well, things don't usually go exactly as planned for me."

The cow twitched, and Jonas tensed, readying himself. "Okay, pull," he directed. "Harder!"

It seemed fruitless until the calf's nose abruptly emerged, followed by its head still enshrouded by the birthing membrane.

"It's a biggie," Jonas noted. "Alright, relax yer grip."

They continued working in tandem for several minutes until the torso finally breached halfway.

"Take both legs."

Cristen complied while Jonas angled the calf toward the mother's rear legs. With a final slide, it plopped onto the hay-padded floor, and its sac ruptured.

"It's a girl," Jonas declared, then began to rub down the newborn calf.

After a brief respite, the mother heaved herself upright on shaky legs and turned to sniff and lick her new offspring. Jonas slumped against the wall, releasing a weary sigh as he mopped his sweaty brow with a bloody handkerchief. They gazed in awe at the tender scene.

"I've never seen anything like it," Cristen marveled softly.

"Nothin' beats the miracle of new life," Jonas mused. "It never gets old."

And nothing beats the pain of losing a life, Cristen reflected painfully, thoughts shifting to Sunfire.

Greta never did come out with the sandwiches. After washing up, they went inside to discover Greta listless on the sofa, her cheeks rosy in stark contrast to her pale complexion. Jonas immediately rushed to her side, pressing his palm against her forehead.

"I don't feel good, Pa," Greta whimpered.

"Yeh's burnin' up," Jonas replied fretfully, brushing the matted hair from her face.

Cristen worried that he'd come at a bad time.

"Can I sleep, Pa?" Greta pleaded weakly.

"Of course, darlin'." Jonas gathered her up and carried her off to bed. Returning to the kitchen, he put water on to boil, and Cristen joined him at the wood stove.

"Is she okay?" Cristen asked. "I can come back another time."

"Leavin' won't fix her ailing any," Jonas replied wearily. He exuded an innate kindness and trust that Cristen found comforting.

"No, sir," Cristen said. "She seemed fine when I got here. She wanted to make me a sandwich."

"The sickness has plagued her on and off these past months, but she'd been well enough for a few weeks now. I thought we left the worst behind. All I can do is let her rest and pray the fever breaks by mornin'."

Jonas knocked some dried tea leaves into a tin cup. He said, "While she sleeps, why don't you tell me 'bout these dragons yeh been slayin'."

"Just a figure of speech," Cristen backtracked. He never intended to bring fear of a dragon into their tranquil home. Besides, if he told him about the dragon, he'd also have to open up about the wizard, which felt impossible.

"I'd like teh hear more about that figure o' speech then," Jonas prodded gently.

Cristen shifted to his other foot. "There's not much to tell. Not a whole lot going on."

Jonas kept his gaze lowered, fidgeting with his cup. "I see. Is that why yer eyes'r reflectin' all that pain?"

Was it that obvious? "Well...my horse just died. I came straight here after I had him buried." Cristen had chosen Jonas's place to find solace if they would have him.

"I'm deeply sorry teh hear it."

Cristen remembered the ancestor Jonas had mentioned when they last parted ways. This time, he felt confident that he understood Jonas's intention.

"Pardon my asking, but was your grandfather...a water dreamer, by chance? Is that why you told me about him, already knowing about me?"

Jonas cleared his throat but didn't meet Cristen's eyes. "Can't say for certain he was, but I do reckon so. And if yey's one yeh'self, then I got no beef with it."

Cristen smiled with relief. "Too bad everyone else does."

"Well, if I descend from one, I figure that makes me kin to yer kind in a way."

Having suspected as much, Cristen felt the stirrings of a newfound bond with Jonas. "What happened with your grandfather?" he asked. "How do you know about him?"

"I have his old journal. But most of his tellin's is missin' under the ravages of time."

How unfortunate. Cristen would have loved to know everything about him, including how a dreamer came to find love.

"I had the opportunity to restore the damaged pages," Jonas continued thoughtfully. "I just couldn't bring myself to doin' it."

Cristen's brow furrowed. "Why, what do you mean?"

When the kettle whistled, Jonas poured the steaming water over his tea leaves, releasing a waft of sweet lemon balm.

"Take a seat," said Jonas. He beckoned Cristen back to the modest living area before retrieving a small cloth pouch from a trunk in the corner by the fireplace. Settling heavily onto the sofa, Jonas upended the bag, spilling a single black stone into his palm. "Just one left now," he said.

Cristen's eyes widened in shock when he saw the familiar stone. "You're a luminary?" he blurted out before he could stop himself.

Jonas's brows rose in puzzlement. "A what now?"

Too late to backpedal now. "You know about the magic! That stone belongs to the Master of the Realm," Cristen revealed, barely able to contain the exhilaration he didn't want to feel. "To do his bidding...a wizard." He'd opened the can of worms too wide already. Thankfully, Jonas seemed oblivious to his meaning. But if Jonas wasn't a luminary, then how did he possess such a stone?

Jonas slowly rolled the misshapen stone around in his palm. "I believe it came aside the journal of the grandfather I speak of, generations past," Jonas said as if reading Cristen's mind. "He got some notion in his head that he needed to find somethin', and it seems he would have traveled to the ends of the earth searchin' fer it. It kills me not to know if or what he ever found."

Perhaps the grandfather was the luminary then, like King Thane or Simon.

Jonas stared into space toward the fireplace. "We had more, but we squandered them. This single stone allows me one final wish—two if I'm lucky."

"A wish? Like for treasure?" Cristen asked, intrigued about how a non-luminary might use it.

Jonas smiled sadly. "It's already more valuable to me than all the world's riches," he said. "I'm unsure of its limitations, but it healed me from my troublesome joints. I've been savin' it fer Greta since she took ill. I suppose...well, I might be usin' it tonight."

Cristen felt terrible to know Jonas had been that worried about his daughter and hated to think what it might mean if something happened. He couldn't imagine him carrying on without her. Suddenly inspired, he removed his waterskin from his belt. "This might help her," he offered. "It has magic of its own. Have her sip as much as she can."

Jonas eyed it curiously. "Your kindness is noted, but there's water by her bedside."

Cristen placed the skin into his work-worn hands. "Trust me, this is no ordinary water."

Jonas scrutinized his face before giving a confirming nod. "It's medicine?"

"With any luck, something much better," Cristen replied hopefully.

Taking the skin, Jonas hurried off but returned almost immediately, pale as a ghost. Cristen braced for the worst, but thankfully, it didn't unfold like he expected.

"Did you say...master of the realm?" Jonas asked hoarsely.

"She's okay then?"

"I left it by her pillow. The Master of the realm is the very entity my grandfather addresses in his journal. I only assumed him some pagan god." Jonas turned back to the trunk and reverently extracted a wrapped bundle. Settling beside Cristen, he unrolled a cracked leather journal.

"This belonged to your great-grandfather?" Cristen asked in hushed awe.

"Leopold. Leopold Sterling, as he recorded himself. The beginning of the Sterling bloodline, if he truly was a water dreamer like yeh'self." Jonas opened the back cover and pointed to the faded inscription.

Master of the Realm. Watch for me at your gates. I am Leopold.

"That's him," Cristen said, trying to sound casual. "I know it sounds crazy, but he's a wizard."

Jonas appeared to be struggling with his emotions. "Then Leopold wasn't preparing teh die," he said. "He was pledgin' himself teh a greater purpose."

"Sounds like it," Cristen said, reluctant to elaborate further.

Jonas traced the inscription with a knobby finger. "This wizard, this master...he wields power over life itself?"

Cristen hesitated. "Well, I wouldn't go that far. But the water can make you feel better, at least. I think you should wake her up and make her drink."

When Jonas left the room again, Cristen fidgeted nervously, hoping he hadn't given him false hope. But the enchanted water could be the very thing to save this family from tragedy.

With Jonas gone a while, Cristen prepared for bed. He took a folded blanket from the armchair and its cushion for a pillow. Before stowing away the journal, he couldn't resist turning a few of its brittle pages, the outer edges nearly disintegrated. Mindful not to cause more damage, he squinted at the faded script. A page fell open, its left side still partially legible. Cristen made out a few fragmented phrases:

...venison stores dwindling.

...tedious yet the last several locations...

...nights grow colder with the coming snow...

...concealed in the attic unti...

It portrayed a challenging life of mystery and adversity. Cristen's heart swelled with sympathy for this brave ancestor. Time itself had proved Leopold's most formidable enemy, erasing his remarkable story. Cristen gently closed the journal, replaced the wrapping, and tucked it safely back in the trunk. Even now, the old dreamer's voice seemed to call across the years, silenced yet longing to be heard.

21

A tickle on his nose woke Cristen late in the morning. When he cracked open his eyes, Greta's face came into focus, poised to poke him again with a feather. He snatched it from her grasp, and she erupted into giggles. He held his hands out like a monster and growled playfully, leaping up to chase after her. She ran through the cottage, squealing and laughing, stopping to brace herself behind a chair, ready to dart the opposite way Cristen might lunge at her.

Jonas shuffled into the room in a night robe, looking like he hadn't slept a wink. "What's all this ruckus so early?" he grumbled through a yawn. Despite his scolding tone, his tired eyes shone with delight at their play.

Cristen dropped to his knees, hoping to snag Greta by her ankles beneath the table. She screamed and scrambled away in time, sprinting back through the sitting room. She shoved past a chuckling Jonas blocking her escape and disappeared down the hallway.

"That's some mighty special elixir yeh got from that wizard friend of yehs," Jonas remarked.

"She's a whole new girl," Cristen agreed, skirting the issue.

Jonas nodded. "She only rallied a few hours ago after a rough night."

"Then she should keep my water," Cristen said decisively. "She needs it more than I do."

Jonas shook his head. "I could ne'er accept such a gift, nor could I take it from yeh."

Cristen had prepared for such pushback. "What if... well, what if I stayed for a while?" he proposed. "I could work for room and board."

"All's I got is this lumpy sofa," Jonas said, frowning. Already puzzling over logistics, he filled Cristen with hope. Could he finally have the family he yearned for so desperately? "Besides, yeh've already given a lifetime's worth."

"I *want* to help," Cristen insisted. "I can haul water, or...or milk the cow. I'll watch Greta while you go into town. Anything you need."

Jonas looked taken aback. "Truth is, I... I don't have much to feed yeh."

"Then we expand the garden," Cristen said eagerly. "I'll hunt and forage...take goods in to barter." He also had a few dragon scales as a backup.

Greta scampered back in, clutching the waterskin like a beloved doll.

Resigned, Jonas shook his head at Cristen. "Reckon I got no say in the matter." The crinkles around his eyes betrayed his delight at the idea.

"Looks like you're stuck with me for a while," Cristen announced to Greta with a grin.

"You're staying?" she asked, eyes wide.

Cristen frowned, confused by the sudden tremble of her lip. "If you'll have me."

Tears spilled down her cheeks, but Jonas gave Cristen a knowing look that eased his worries—happy tears then.

***

The newly formed family of three sat around the table, finishing their early morning breakfast of porridge, wild strawberries, and fresh milk. Cristen had been recounting his troubling beginnings all morning—how he'd nearly drowned in the bay and about having found the waterskin. He described the men who'd chased him with a spear, intent on caging him in their prison cart, and his harrowing escape crossing the perilous Old Surge bridge. Jonas and Greta hung on his every word, enthralled by his winding tale.

Cristen paused, distracted by the thought of their nearly empty water stores. Jonas mentioned yesterday that they needed to return to the creek soon.

"Well," Cristen said, swallowing a mouthful of porridge, "I guess we should get a move on before the day heats up too much. Sorry for talking your ears off all morning." He shoveled in one last heaping spoonful.

Jonas and Greta stared at him, mouths agape.

Cristen glanced between them in confusion. "What?" he mumbled through his full mouth.

Jonas cleared his throat. "Yeh mean to say yeh endured all that before stumblin' onto our doorstep? And you never let on a word of it?"

Greta leaned forward in awe. "Is your horse the same one you took from the bad men?" she asked.

"No, that one ran off before I crossed the bridge," Cristen explained. "Moonshine's the one that brought me here. You'll love him. He's very gentle." That reminded Cristen of an idea he'd been mulling over. "Speaking of, Jonas, I tried finding some lumber so we could build you a little cart for hauling water. But it's all been bought up. If we could find some boards, fetching water with Moonshine would be easy as pie."

Greta's eyes instantly flooded with tears. Cristen looked to Jonas to discover if they were happy tears again, but she shoved back her chair and ran toward the door. Again, Cristen tried to read Jonas for answers.

"No, Greta, yeh don't gotta do it. We're managin' just fine," Jonas called after her. He sank his head into his hands with a weary sigh.

"Did I say something wrong? Is she okay?" Cristen asked, baffled by the quick turn of events.

"She'll be frettin' over her treehouse again."

"Treehouse?" Cristen didn't know about a treehouse. And why fret about it suddenly?

"It's overgrown past the barn out there," Jonas said, looking expectantly at the open door.

Cristen felt awkward as Jonas sat listening for something.

"Should...we check on her?" Cristen finally asked.

A faint clamor sounded outside, and Jonas lurched to his feet. "It's begun already. Never a pause teh think things through," he muttered, hurrying to the door with Cristen on his heels.

Following the sound, they hurried across the yard and alongside the barn. Beyond it, Cristen gazed up at an impressive treehouse nestled within the branches of a large maple, a ladder leading up to it. A sledgehammer came crashing through a wall, sending a board tumbling to the ground.

Cristen glimpsed a tearful Greta through the new gaping hole, looking impossibly small as she wielded the massive tool.

Jonas called up to her gently, "Come down this instant, darlin'. I've already told yeh I'd never ask such a thing. Let me fix it up proper before it's too late."

Greta choked back a sob. "It's my choice, Pa," she declared, straining with effort as she swung the sledgehammer again, half dislodging another board.

"This isn't the answer," Jonas implored urgently. "Yeh've grown too attached, and I just can't allow it."

"You've let me be selfish too long!" Greta shouted. She used the strength of a grunt to send the hammer into another board.

"No, never! We can chop our trees for lumber. How does that sound?"

"You know we don't have the tools, Pa."

Cristen finally understood. Needing the boards for other things had surfaced before.

Jonas clasped his hands beseechingly. "Please stop. This house represents all the love I have for yeh."

Greta dropped to her knees, straggly blond hair appearing through the gap. "Then, let me love you back, Pa. After what you've done for me, let me do this one thing for you."

Jonas shook his head. "The cost is too high."

Greta buried her head in her hands, weeping, while Cristen glimpsed the pain in Jonas's eyes too. He'd never witnessed such fierce love.

"You have to let her do this," Cristen said, surprised at his own words.

Jonas turned to him, astounded. Greta poked her head through a hole to look at them.

Cristen continued, "With both of us working, we can have a cart by sundown."

Jonas blinked hard. "I used a stone for the wishin' of it," he rasped. "The greatest gift I imagined fer her."

Greta stated, "And this is my greatest wish for you, Pa." She disappeared into the treehouse again, and the hammer fell with a decisive crack.

Cristen looked to Jonas, silently requesting permission. Jonas stared back for a long moment before nodding wearily. Cristen climbed the ladder to help Greta complete her monumental task.

***

As the sun dipped below the horizon, Cristen and Jonas finished a crude but sturdy cart, repurposing the treehouse boards, nails, and two wheels from the wheelbarrow. All three admired their handiwork.

They would have to wait until morning to fetch water, but the bright moonlight allowed them to take the new rig out for a test run. Greta beamed as Moonshine pulled her around the yard in what she proudly dubbed their "treehouse wagon." Its limited size only permitted small loads, yet it would immensely benefit Jonas.

Greta immediately took to Moonshine. As Jonas observed how quickly she picked up riding, he allowed her free rein of the yard while he and Cristen watched from the porch steps or worked in the garden.

Cristen stayed on for five months. He couldn't fathom a more ideal life for an outcast like himself. The three did everything together, working seamlessly like a family. The garden flourished as they expanded it. Come harvest time, they took weekly trips into Meadowbrook, the treehouse wagon overflowing with produce to trade for necessities and small treats, including a doll that Cristen wanted for Greta. For the most part, Cristen didn't let the taunts affect him when people recognized him.

Jonas regained a youthful spark, and Greta blossomed into the picture of health, practically attached to her adopted waterskin. Freeing himself from the wizard's charity brought immense relief, and as sightings of the bird grew increasingly rare, his tumultuous past dissolved into a distant memory.

On a sunny afternoon with little work to be done, Cristen lay in the grass, head propped lazily in one hand. He watched Greta disappear into the cottage with an armload of wild- flowers for the table. The day felt too resplendent to follow her inside just yet. He only needed to soak up the sun a while longer. Stretching out on his back, hands laced behind his head, he gazed at the drifting clouds. A fat bumblebee droned nearby, and a gentle breeze ruffled his hair and linen shirt. He soon drifted away on a peaceful current toward another dream, knowing this time he wouldn't wake up missing a family that didn't exist. He had everything he needed.

22

Kimball, the longtime family butler, cracked open the heavy oak door to Father's stately study, where Cristen anxiously waited for whatever ominous event threatened to unfold.

Addressing Father, seated authoritatively behind his large oak desk, Kimball formally announced, "Your Lordship, Lord Whittaker has arrived."

"Thank you, Kimball. Please offer refreshment to our guest and show him in, if you would be so kind. He has endured a dreadfully long journey to reach us. And do take special care of his horses and carriage."

"Of course, your Grace, straight away," Kimball responded with a slight bow before closing the door.

"What's going on?" Cristen implored, swiveling his head between his ashen-faced mother and solemn father.

"Take a seat, son," Father directed, gesturing to an armchair.

"But who's Lord Whittaker?" Cristen asked instead.

"He has traveled from another kingdom bearing an invitation of great import. If you can't sit, at least help your mother to a chair."

"Just to be clear, I won't be leaving like Damon did. I can learn everything from home."

Cristen huffed in frustration but gently led his distracted mother to the plush armchair, settling her into its velvet cushions. He sat on the leather sofa across from her, heel bouncing anxiously against the carpet. The trio sat in tense silence, waiting for the mysterious visitor. Mother avoided his questioning looks.

After a brisk knock, Kimball reopened the door wide. "Your Lordship, may I present the esteemed Lord Archibald Whittaker."

Cristen sat up poker-straight, nerves on edge. A man of regal bearing strode in, head held high. He carried an elaborate scroll bound in gilded handles. Garbed in formal attire—a maroon tunic embroidered with golden epaulets and gleaming brass buttons—he proceeded to the open space between Father's desk and the curtains. Father joined him a few feet away.

With a respectable bow, Lord Whitaker said, "Your Grace, I humbly request permission to present His Royal Majesty's summons to your son, Cristen."

The room instantly felt charged with mingled dread and anticipation. *This will be very good or very bad*, Cristen thought warily.

"Son," Father stated, his commanding voice ensuring he held Cristen's full attention. "Listen now as you never have before, for what Lord Whittaker is about to impart could irreversibly alter the entire course of your life."

Cristen gaped at his father, then bounced wide eyes between his mother, imposing Lord Whittaker, and the ornate scroll clutched in his hands. He wanted to flee the room but steeled himself as a knot formed in his stomach. He only needed to hear the message and be done. Back rigid, he gave a single terse nod.

Unfurling the scroll edge to edge, Lord Whittaker commenced reading. Father's sharp gaze remained fixed on Cristen as each thunderous word rang out.

"By decree of his sovereign Majesty, the king of Phaeton, I hereby invite one Cristen Stronghold, second son of Gabriel and Lena Stronghold, to journey to the secluded land of Harmony. He shall train for a year's service in the Royal Battalion in His Majesty's ongoing cause to establish world peace. Cristen..."

Lord Whitaker paused to ensure Cristen still paid rapt attention before continuing.

"Cristen, if you choose to accept this prestigious invitation, you will experience loneliness, heartache, and scorn from others. You will be tried and tested in a crucible of utmost adversity."

Cristen couldn't restrain an incredulous laugh. This is what had everyone knotted up with worry? He felt done being polite. "Sounds charming," he quipped facetiously, interrupting. "How can I refuse such a tempting offer?" He hated disrespecting his father so, but what did they expect? He also doubted this Harmony place had anything to do with Damon. He couldn't fathom his brother agreeing to such nonsense since he'd always boasted of his easy life and the responsibilities he continuously avoided. While Cristen didn't consider himself lazy, neither did he intend to volunteer for a stint of suffering.

"Cristen..." Father warned.

"But why would I ever leave home for that? I'm no soldier...a messenger boy at best." He wondered if the General volunteered his name.

"Son, it is an honor to be chosen," Father said. "The king looked favorably on your character and potential."

"When? He doesn't even know me."

Father admonished more severely now, "I ask that you show Lord Whittaker the respect he merits by hearing him out."

Cristen threw his hands up. "And who exactly is this alleged king of the whole world?" he interjected. "I've never heard of someone so exalted."

He shot to his feet. "Mother, may I be dismissed? I'm not feeling well." He wasn't exaggerating—his head throbbed, and his stomach roiled.

Mother looked down at her hands folded in her lap, her lips pressed together. Why didn't she draw him into her comforting embrace, as she always did, to soothe away his troubles?

"Ma?" he pleaded softly.

Father rarely raised his voice, but now it lashed out like a whip. "Cristen, you hold the complete right to decline this proposition. However, you will hear the man out before we send him on his way."

Temper flaring, Cristen shouted back, "Fine! I'll listen, but I'm not going!"

***

Cristen jolted awake with a shout dying on his lips, heart pounding—another twisted nightmare courtesy of the

171

depths. He sat up, drew his knees in, and dropped his head into his hands. Though he knew better than to put stock in the dreams, this one clung to him more tenaciously than the rest.

King of the world? Did the wizard fit the role? Was Phaeton the name of his world?

A chilling thought occurred to him then. What if the sea wasn't tormenting him at all but attempting communication? If he were on some all-important quest, as the dragon had divulged, wouldn't he have been sent from another realm? Until now, the mission seemed like some distant opportunity since no training or army seemed to exist. But this dream screamed of a life preceding his time in Harmony, priming him for an immediate quest.

Or did it only conjure more illusions? How could he ever distinguish truth from deception?

Before he could ponder further, an irresistible current dragged him under again. Though fully awake and resisting with all his might, the insistent tug overpowered him, forcing him back into Father's study against his will.

★★★

Having delivered his message, Lord Whittaker left the study empty-handed, leaving Cristen reeling from what he'd just witnessed. Father watched him, offering a satisfied nod of approval that he'd finally come around.

Despite having to leave everything behind for a time—and the evils he might ultimately face—Cristen realized this detour to Harmony in service to the king might provide an incredible foundation for his and Hanna's future life together. He needed to find her immediately to explain his impending absence so she wouldn't feel as confused as he did at Damon's unexplained disappearance.

When he stepped into the hall, Lord Whitaker surprised him, closing the door. He seized Cristen firmly by the wrist with startling strength. Pulling Cristen uncomfortably close, he stared intensely into his eyes with an unnerving focus. "Do you feel the power of my grip? Do you hold any shred of doubt that my coming here is not imagined?" he demanded.

Cristen squirmed, deeply unsettled. "Of course, you're here. What do you mean?" he stammered in confusion.

Lord Whittaker's piercing gaze intensified. "Then do not surrender to cunning deception. Your purpose remains unfinished."

Cristen managed a baffled, nervous laugh. What could he possibly be implying?

Whitaker leaned nearer still, breath hot on Cristen's face. "The waters harbor no consciousness, merely salt and waves.

A minnow within them is more inclined to create life and memories than the lifeless sea itself. The sea is not your god."

Cristen jerked back, smile evaporating. "I don't know what you're talking about," he snapped irritably.

"You will when you must. Now open your eyes and get back to your day." Lord Whitaker snapped his fingers right next to Cristen's ear, leaving it ringing.

23

Cristen's eyes flashed open to the expansive sky, finding himself flat on his back again. He instantly rolled onto his stomach, fingers clawing at the grass, mind racing to comprehend the dream. Gut-wrenching sobs overcame him as the shocking revelations washed over him in waves, each crushing truth landing like a physical blow. What an utter fool he'd been to believe the web of lies spun around him. The magnitude of betrayal threatened to crush him. He cried out in anguish, cursing himself for trusting everyone but himself.

Soon, his tears of regret gave way to tremendous relief upon knowing his mother and father truly lived and that they waited anxiously for his return. Damon...his brother, after all. He never should have disregarded what deep down he knew to be true. It grounded him further to know they all shared the name Stronghold, binding them together as a real family. No, he wasn't alone. He'd never been alone.

Neither had Harmony ever been his home, though he couldn't fathom why young men and women would be delivered there via the coastline waters. With a bitter laugh, Cristen realized he wasn't a water dreamer at all. No such thing existed.

He only wanted home, to be enveloped in loving arms again. The estate's familiar sights, sounds, and smells filled him with nostalgia and yearning. He longed for his upstairs bedroom in the manor, his favorite foods, and the cheerful banter of the staff. Home represented safety, comfort, and unconditional love.

Cristen still couldn't grasp why he agreed to come, though a lingering wonder over something he'd witnessed nagged at him. A dream segment eluded him as if it continued without him after he woke up. Something made all the difference, finally swaying his decision. Lord Whitaker's departure without the scroll also puzzled him. Did Father keep it?

"No!" he whispered. He jumped to his feet and started pacing the grass. This changed everything! He and Hanna did share a history. She had been his childhood friend...his future wife! And, just like that, he'd let her go. He felt sick to his stomach that he hadn't done more to protect her. With her being shifted, she might be cut off from home forever. He couldn't imagine a worse nightmare. Neither of them should have come.

The dragon bore the full weight of the blame. How could Cristen or anyone else fulfill a mission if she kept shifting and sending them away? Sefilar was the terror of Harmony without ever having to hurt anyone. The dragon's manipulations ran deep. Cristen shuddered, imagining how many lives Sefilar had irrevocably damaged by her cruel deceptions.

Although King Thane had explained that Harmony was the master's game and that the secrets weren't his to tell, Cristen still felt angry about not being told everything. He blamed both King Thane and the wizard for his misery, for needing to figure things out the hard way.

It cut him deeply that his father had been the one to persuade him to come when he'd clearly understood the dangers. Once home again, he would have a sharp bone to pick with him. Yet he still yearned for his father's love and approval. How joyous the reunion promised to be between him and his parents. His heart ached to imagine telling them that Damon might never return to them, that a dragon offered him the irresistible glory of Harmony.

A startling revelation struck him. Damon looked the spitting image of their father. They shared the same deep blue eyes, strong chin, and dark hair, though his father's turned salt-and-pepper over the years. How did he not see it before? The family resemblance seemed so obvious now.

He needed to get back to Hanna, tell her everything, and convince her they didn't belong there. King Thane said that Harmony had access to the outside world, his globe showing that it could only be north since the sea encompassed the rest of the land. He decided to use his dragon scales to secure provisions and another horse, and together, he and Hanna would embark on a journey to find their way home beyond the mountains.

The thought of leaving Jonas and Greta tore at his heart. The incredible summer they shared would forever remain etched in his memory. When Cristen finally went inside, they were busy in the kitchen. Jonas pulled a pan of roasted chicken and vegetables from the wood stove and set it on the counter while Greta set plates around the table. Cristen hadn't realized the late hour.

"Sorry I didn't come in to help," he said. "I guess I lost track of time." He would miss their cozy evenings before the fire, Greta's infectious laughter, and Jonas's quiet wisdom.

"Papa said not to bother you," Greta said.

When Jonas saw Cristen, he paused as he wiped his hands on a towel. They just looked at each other for a moment. Jonas seemed to read him about not staying. A silent understanding passed between them.

"I'm Cristen Stronghold," Cristen announced.

Jonas glanced at Greta, then back at Cristen. Cristen smiled through his sadness and nodded, agreeing with how painful the goodbye would be. He wished for another way, some compromise where he could have both families in his life. But the only path led home...to reclaim the life stolen from him.

***

With supper cleared away, the three lingered at the table. Greta drank from Cristen's water, put the cork in, and set it on the table.

"Are we playing checkers again?" she asked lightheartedly.

"Greta," Jonas said, his hands clasped and resting on the table. "Remember how yeh couldn't understand why yehs ma couldn't be yehs ma?"

Greta's smile faded. "You said not everybody gets to stay even if we want them to."

"That's right," Jonas said gently. "And people are always a part of our lives fer a reason."

"To take care of me when I was a baby," Greta said. "But that awful lightning. Why can't I remember her face?" she asked innocently.

"We can't remember things when we're so young and little. But yeh's a young lady now, almost a grownup."

"Can I get the checkers now?" asked Greta, perking up again. "Pa, you can play the winner."

Cristen caught her hand against the table before she could leave. "Greta, remember some of the dreams I've been telling you and your pa about?"

Greta nodded, her brow knitted as she tried to recall them.

Cristen paused, taking her small hand in both of his. "I have to tell you something, and I just know you'll be happy for me. Greta, people have been lying to me. They aren't dreams I'm having. They're memories even though I'm sleeping. My ma and pa are as real as your ma and pa, even though your ma needed to go."

"They are?" Greta asked, her voice wavering as she started to cry. "Where are they?"

"They're at home, far away," Cristen explained patiently. "You know I love it here. I would stay forever if I could. But I also miss my ma and my pa, just like you miss your ma, even though you can't quite remember her."

Greta wiped at her eyes, sniffling. "But when are you coming back?"

"I wish I could say for sure. But I *will* promise you, with all my heart, that if I can find a way, I'll be back one day."

Greta resumed crying, and Jonas rose from his chair to pat her on the head to console her.

Cristen continued, "When I get home, I'm going to build a treehouse to remember you and our times together. I'll tell Mother and everyone on the estate all about you. You're like a little sister to me. I've never had a sister."

Greta used her sleeves to dry her eyes and nose. "But I don't want you to go," she finally said, still snuffling.

"I know. We both have to be brave. I'll never be able to thank you and your pa enough for the best summer of my life." He looked up at Jonas to make sure he understood as well.

Jonas took his seat again. "Yeh'll always be family to us," he said sincerely.

Greta slowly pushed the waterskin across the table toward Cristen. He started to push it back when Jonas stopped it. All three hands rested on the skin.

"It's meant fer you," Jonas said. "She'll be a'right now."

Cristen hoped so. He also knew that Jonas had a backup plan in the form of a black stone. He humbly nodded, accepting the returned gift. Before leaving Harmony, he planned to leave instructions to return his horse and water to them. With such undying devotion toward this family who saved him from despair, it felt the very least he could do.

24

A somber, misty morning greeted Cristen as he rode the familiar route toward Meadowbrook before dawn, the sun still struggling to penetrate the clouds. He'd departed early after a late night explaining everything to Jonas—the dragon, the mountain, and even how the wizard protected him. Jonas seemed to sense that Cristen didn't want to delve more into the wizard's involvement and didn't press the matter. Though fascinated, Jonas didn't act entirely surprised as Cristen explained the dragon's existence. Jonas said it explained why Leopold had been watching the sky for signs of the beast.

Cristen tried focusing on the incredible gift he'd been given, validation that his deepest instincts rang true. Still, leaving Jonas and Greta left him mourning, uncertain if their paths would cross again. But nothing could feel right until he reunited with family, preferably with Hanna at his side.

The people's "born of the sea" nonsense was nothing more than a ludicrous myth concocted to explain odd occurrences surrounding them. Tradition gripped them like Sefilar's vile ooze, tenaciously clinging to anything and everything within reach of its tentacles. No matter their beliefs, there was no excuse under the sun for their ingrained hatred and behavior.

Nearing the first farms, Cristen swelled with a newfound sense of worth, knowing he was no misfit or freak of nature. The revelation of his true heritage gave him a sense of belonging and purpose that he had never experienced before. It might become his place to educate people about the truth, to help them understand the dragon's reality and the role of the dreamers. But more than that, he felt the strength to stand taller and defend himself against the barrage of ridicule and prejudice that always seemed to follow him. He smiled occasionally, marveling at how different he felt simply knowing his lineage, as if a great weight had been lifted from his shoulders.

Questions still plagued him. Why did Father want this for him? Wouldn't a caring parent go to the ends of the earth to shield their child from such trauma? At least Father ensured he could ride and even found him a job that prepared him for the Array. Perhaps he'd also hired those villainous youths to bombard him with rotten fruit. It was the perfect training, winning him Sunfire.

Meadowbrook always reminded him of Lora and her dreamer-hating father. He'd also met Damon and his scale-obsessed friends in the town, never imagining that the trek into the countryside to hunt them would deliver him to the dragon. If he'd known, he would have stayed away.

As Cristen entered town, shops down Main Street started opening. He rode to Poppy's and dismounted, securing Moonshine to the hitching post. He would grab breakfast, then catch up on some much-needed sleep before continuing to King's Crossing. The door jangled as he entered.

"It's the dreamer!" a man shouted. His companion and others spun to gawk at Cristen. "Don't you have somewhere to be? I see no wet head tables here. Best you be moving along." Laughter peppered the room. Someone else shot Cristen a disapproving look, shaking their head as if admonishing him for having the audacity to show his face in public.

Cristen stayed cool, approaching their table. The man braced himself confrontationally.

"You don't know, do you?" Cristen said, messing with them.

"Know what?" the wife challenged with a scowl.

"Us water dreamers? We're sent here to build an army. Those mountains? We're gathering our forces. Wouldn't underestimate us."

The woman's eyes popped, and she traded glances with her husband.

Another man guffawed loudly. "You think a few dozen can challenge all of Harmony?" he jeered. "Head in the clouds, as expected."

"A few dozen?" Cristen challenged. "It barely scratches the surface. Have a nice day."

Amused by the tension he left in his wake, Cristen returned to the counter to await Rip, who hurried from the kitchen and halted abruptly at seeing him. His eyes bounced warily between Cristen and the other patrons.

"You smell it too?" someone called out.

Rip approached him. "Look, you aren't welcome here anymore," he said in his weak, high-pitched voice. "I don't need any trouble."

"I just want something to eat," Cristen replied evenly, holding his gaze.

"Please...just go quietly and don't come back. I have a business to run. I'll even pay you to stay somewhere else." Rip slid over a few coins, but Cristen didn't take them. He had every right to be here.

"I can pay a dragon scale again," Cristen countered. "Breakfast and a room, just a few hours."

Rip paused, surprised. "Seems you haven't heard. Your dragon scale holds about the value of a rock."

No, Cristen hadn't heard and didn't believe such a claim. "You gave me three months' room and board last time." He felt the patrons' eyes drilling into his back.

"Thank the great Mr. D and his Beacon Hill. He promised riches, and now folks can barely eat." Rip called to another man, "Right, Nate?"

"I won't justify myself to this kind," the man grumbled.

Cristen could hardly process it. Damon tanked the scales' value practically overnight. He reached for Rip's coins, but Rip quickly withdrew them. Frustrated and somewhat mortified, Cristen left the inn.

He found a secluded grassy area behind the Rendezvous fence that would provide a decent resting place before continuing home. Since the market wouldn't open until evening, he could sleep as long as needed. Settling his head atop his waterskin, he closed his eyes, ignoring the uneven ground.

A faint voice startled him upright, but finding no one, he laid back down, humming Mother's cherished lullaby and inviting every memory of her. *Don't worry, Mother, I'll be home soon.*

The voice returned, quoting his sign: *Wherever you go, you are known.* What did the wizard want now? Rejecting the intrusion, Cristen rolled to his side.

But the voice came a third time: *Wherever you go, you are known.*

Cristen sighed. Would he not be allowed to sleep? Slowly, an understanding of the message crept in. Did he have another house here? He wouldn't object to a bed. For that matter, did a house await him in every town he happened to be in? With his curiosity peaked, he mounted Moonshine and headed back to Main to discover if another Sion Street existed in Meadowbrook.

25

Cristen skeptically eyed the familiar yellow-trimmed house with its wooden sign and house number above the door. Shaking his head at the fact that this was happening again, he nudged Moonshine forward. Entering the yard, he dismounted and latched the gate behind them. Moonshine trotted toward the barn as if he belonged, sparking a melancholy pang in Cristen that Sunfire wouldn't be there to greet him.

Climbing the porch steps, he knocked softly on the door. Of course, he didn't expect an answer. He slid his ornate key into the deadbolt—another perfect fit. A startled yelp sounded within as he clicked it unlocked, followed by a loud crash. Cristen jumped back with a gasp, his heart lurching. Did someone already live in the house, and he misunderstood the situation? No, he'd clearly been led here.

He opened the door to find a plump, round-faced boy sprawled out on the floor amidst a tangle of bed sheets beneath a toppled chair he evidently collided with. A smattering of coins lay strewn across the disheveled bed, where blankets dangled halfway to the ground at its foot. The boy's wide hazel eyes filled with alarm when he saw Cristen, a mess of brown hair above his ears. He stammered, "I wasn't...I mean, I'm not...I never meant to..."

Cristen pushed the door wider, noting that the boy came alone. "You're...jumping on my bed?" he questioned.

The boy grinned guiltily as he tried freeing himself from the chair and tangled sheets.

"Do your parents know?" Cristen asked, surveying the room. Aside from dust, the tidy space remained unchanged, except for the rumpled bedding and scattered pillows, one missing a case.

"Don't worry, I'm out of here," the boy said, gathering his coins from the bed. But Cristen shut the door before he could bolt.

"You've been staying here?" Cristen asked, eyebrows raised.

The boy shifted nervously, backing toward the back door. "Uhh...only when I'm in big trouble. If my pa gets ahold of me, he'll wallop me good."

Cristen hid his smile, pretending to study the room again. He then realized the boy looked familiar. Studying his round face and messy hair, he quickly placed him. "You're Han—Evelyn's new brother. I mean, brother. Warren...Flynn...Myers, isn't it?" He recalled the kid dashing away as his frustrated mother called after him. "How did you know where I lived?"

Warren's mouth spread into a sheepish grin. "I...might've...followed you here?"

"From Mulberry?" Cristen asked incredulously. "That's like a day's ride. And where's your horse? How did you even get here?"

Warren's face clouded in confusion.

"You should get going before they send a posse out looking for you," Cristen advised.

"They won't. I'm pretty much my own man," Warren declared with the arrogance of youth.

Cristen laughed aloud. He decided to teach the boy a lesson for intruding. "You really shouldn't have come, you know. What will your ma and pa think when they hear you've been sneaking away to a water dreamer's house?"

"You're a water dreamer?" Warren asked with wide eyes.

"Afraid of me now? Wish you never came?" Cristen challenged.

Warren shrugged. "You seem normal enough to me."

"Exactly!" But Cristen quickly softened after the outburst. If only others shared the kids' attitude. "Of course, I'm normal," he said calmly.

Warren stepped closer to examine his face, poking his nose with a chubby finger before he could swat it away. "You feel normal too. Not a wet fish at all. Can you breathe underwater?"

"You can't believe everything you hear, you know. We weren't born in the sea, we got put there. Anyway, go on, get out of here. You'll be in a heap of trouble out this far." Cristen then noticed the paper wrapping his food always came in still on the table. "You ate my food too?"

"Oh, that," Warren said. "You didn't expect me to starve, did you?"

"I might! So you ate and slept here, and for how long? Don't you owe me some room and board or something?"

"I have some buried marbles I can dig up. But that's a little steep for one meal."

"The food only came today?" Cristen asked.

"Yes, but I locked the doors, so how did it get in here?"

Though Cristen found it curious that it only got delivered with him home, he wished the wizard wouldn't waste his favors on him, as they only brought guilt. At least he only needed to worry about it until he left Harmony.

"Magic," Cristen answered, not caring about secrecy.

Warren's face lit up. "Doozy, there's magic?"

"Sure, if you believe in things like wizards and talking dragons."

Warren's eyes bulged wider. "There's talking dragons?"

Cristen only stared at him. Why did people believe him every time he mentioned dragons? Also, Warren's story didn't add up, he realized. "How could you follow me here when I came from the highlands?"

"Huh? I followed you here. It's not that difficult, a few blocks max. You left your back door open."

It finally dawned on Cristen that Warren thought himself still in his hometown. His house had wandered again, apparently refusing to stay put. "Wherever I go, I'm known," Cristen whispered, coming to terms with its meaning.

"That's what your sign says," Warren said.

"You think you're in Mulberry," Cristen said.

Warren chuckled. "Is that the problem with you water dreamers? There's not a whole lot going on up top?"

Cristen brushed off the insult. "The thing is," he said, "I'm in Meadowbrook."

"So, it's true," Warren said curtly. "You might need my marbles after all."

Cristen opened the front door to check out the neighborhood.

"Doozy, where did your street go!" Warren exclaimed from behind. "These houses are...for poor folk."

"That's what I'm saying. This is Meadowbrook. I brought you here somehow."

"You can't be serious!" Warren ran out the back door. "Whew, no one stole it," he said, returning with a weathered boomerang. "The back door is still Mulberry," he said casually.

Cristen hopped over the rumpled sheets to see for himself. He led Warren outside and around to the front of the house, which remained Cristen's familiar Mulberry neighborhood. Baffled by the abrupt town change, they exchanged incredulous glances. Cristen stepped back inside and closed the door. When they opened it again moments later, Mulberry still greeted them.

"Doozy, this is the best day ever!" Warren exclaimed.

Cristen marveled again at the house that seemed to have a mind of its own. If only he could control the phenomenon and move from town to town at will. At least he'd returned Warren home.

Once he finally got Warren out of the house, he sighed wearily as he glanced around at the tumbled bedding. What an odd kid. Though his antics might be tiresome, at least he might provide access to Hanna. Cristen remade the bed, planning to sleep the day away.

26

Darkness settled over Cristen's room by the time he awoke. Groggily, he sat up, trying to get his bearings. That's right—back in Mulberry...need to get to Hanna...must prepare for the journey home.

Rubbing the sleep from his eyes, he reached into the top drawer of his bureau and took out his orb. Positioning his hands just right, he lit the candle with a precise, direct beam of light on the first try this time. It had taken a lot of practice to get the technique down. The scattered scorch marks across the top of his bureau offered proof of his previous failed attempts.

After lighting the candle, he lifted his gaze to the oval mirror set within the shelves of his bureau at its center. Each time he used the orb at night, it cast an eerie greenish glow onto its beveled edges, reflecting onto his face and making him appear ghostly. He ran a finger slowly along the bottom frame until the strange glow gradually dissipated as it always did.

As his reflection normalized again, Cristen studied his features, wondering what traits he inherited from his parents, if any, the way Damon had. Though his memory of his mother's face had faded, he figured he must take after her in looks more than his father.

A faint ticking from the mirror brought him out of his reverie. He touched the ornate mirror frame again, feeling a peculiar energy thrumming through it as he traced his fingers around the edges. "Tell me your secrets," he whispered aloud. Taking a chance, he pressed directly on the spot where his finger stopped roving and gasped in shock when the mirror flipped around to expose the strangest clock he'd ever seen.

Its single hand ticked rapidly around the perimeter, moving faster than any clock's second hand, even double speed. Instead of numbers spaced evenly around its face, tiny gold-foil disks on spindles within small chambers were scattered across its surface, a few spinning hypnotically. Small bronze gears clicked and turned at its center beneath a larger central cog. Uneasy about its purpose and moving parts, Cristen refrained from laying a finger on any part of the peculiar clock's mechanisms. He preferred to keep his distance, especially if it connected him somehow to his supposed mission.

Warren breezed cheerily through the back door just as Cristen flipped the clock to the mirror face again. "What's up!" he exclaimed, but his expression quickly shifted to surprise when he got a glimpse of the exposed clock before it could close all the way.

"You need to knock first," Cristen admonished, annoyed at another intrusion. "What are you doing here so late anyway? I already told you to go home."

"I did. Hours ago," Warren replied, though his gaze remained fixed on the mirror, inching toward it. "Well, not home, exactly. I'll just sneak back into my window after Pa falls asleep."

Cristen went to sit on his bed, hoping to steal Warren's attention from the mirror. "I thought you said you were your own man now. Doesn't that mean facing consequences like a grownup? What did you even do?"

"Evelyn ratted me out just because I tried cutting her hair," Warren explained.

"You what?"

"Hey, she wasn't supposed to wake up in the middle of the night!" Warren cried in defense.

Cristen just shook his head in disbelief. "Why would you cut her hair at all?"

"Because she makes me real mad, that's why."

"Why, what did she do?"

"Uh...nothing really," Warren replied casually. "I just don't like her."

"That's not a reason. And what's not to like? I like her quite a bit." Cristen needed to speak with her privately as soon as possible, and he hoped Warren could facilitate such a meet-up.

"You can have her, she's annoying."

"I mean, sure, siblings can be irritating sometimes," Cristen reasoned.

"She's not my sibling, she's an alien."

Cristen wondered if Warren knew he didn't have a sister. "Then why does she live in your house?" he asked, fishing for more.

"To torment me, obviously," Warren said, eyeing the mirror again.

Warren didn't know about the Hanna situation, though Cristen wouldn't be surprised if he harbored subconscious suspicions. "You know, I have a brother too," he offered. "We don't always get along either, so I understand how hard it can be. His name is Damon."

Warren's eyes lit up with interest. "Hey, that's the name of the man Evelyn's going to marry! He's real rich too."

Cristen felt the blood drain from his face. Hanna and Damon? "What...does this Damon look like?" he asked shakily. "Tall...black hair...blue eyes?"

"That's him, alright. Looks like a gremlin."

Overwhelmed, Cristen rushed back outside, needing to get away. He felt Sunfire's absence deeply, longing for his trusty horse who had always helped him escape his troubles. He paced the grass, torturing himself with visions of Damon and Hanna together, living the life that should have been his. His heart felt crushed in a vice-like grip. How could he have let this happen? How would Hanna ever agree to return home with him if she planned on marrying? He hated his brother for moving in on the girl meant for him.

Well, Hanna and Damon weren't married yet. He would spend every waking moment trying to prevent this looming catastrophe before it grew too late. When he noticed Warren watching him pace from the porch, he marched back inside. "I need to see your sister," he urgently said.

"It's best we just avoid her," Warren said.

"She's too young to be married!" Cristen said, thinking through the disaster.

"She's older than the neighbor girl who already has a baby," Warren returned.

"The thing is, I had her first, and I want her back."

"Wait, you know Evelyn?" Warren asked in surprise. "Well, good luck with that. He already told Ma that Evelyn is the girl of his dreams."

The words chilled Cristen's spine as he understood what that meant. Damon must have dreamed of Hanna too, but as Cristen's girl, not his, making Damon's intentions even worse. "You have to take me to see her," Cristen implored. "I need to talk to her now."

Warren wrinkled his nose doubtfully. "Why would you want her anyway? Hate to break it to you, but she's really not that great."

"Because I love her. We've known each other a long time."

Warren looked skeptical. "How could you know her for a long time if you're a water dreamer? When did you even get here?"

"Don't you get it? I lived somewhere else before I came from the sea," Cristen explained not so patiently. "Anyways, haven't you ever had a crush before?"

Warren's expression showed obvious disgust at such a thought.

"Well, I promised I would marry her one day, and I intend to keep my word," Cristen stated, fearing things might already have gone too far for that.

Warren's expression slowly turned mischievous. "This might be my lucky day," he mused slyly. "We have to make a plan."

"I already have a plan. I need to explain some things to her and tell her how I feel."

Warren waved a hand dismissively. "That's not a plan. But trust me, I was born for this." He rubbed his hands together. "Just stick with me, and I guarantee they'll hate each other by the end of next week."

"What...exactly did you have in mind?" Cristen asked hesitantly. He couldn't believe he was entertaining the offer, yet felt compelled to hear him out.

Warren's eyes glinted deviously. "It's time for Operation Sabotage."

Cristen turned the phrase over slowly. "Operation Sabotage?"

"Rule number one," Warren began as if Cristen had already agreed. "There's no plan without spying and pranks and all that, so don't get all scaredy-cat on me. We have to get Evelyn so upset that Ma starts telling her it's all a bad omen. Ma's all about omens. I know right where to start. I'll be back tomorrow when the coast is clear."

Cristen felt shamefully curious, but desperation made him set aside caution, at least for now. He knew that engaging in Warren's schemes might not be the most honorable path, but the thought of losing Hanna to Damon felt too much to bear. If sabotage was what it took to win her back, he perhaps needed to take the risk. He only hoped that, in the end, Hanna would understand.

27

W arren scoped out his house until every member of his family had left, his mother and Hanna off on wedding errands for the day. With the carriage out of sight, Warren signaled to Cristen with a whistle, who waited farther away with their can of worms, and they both moved in.

Cristen followed Warren straight to Hanna's room where flowing silk, lace, and velvet lay carefully across her bed in pristine whites and creams—elegant wedding fabrics that their dirt-stained hands would inevitably ruin, foiling their worm plan.

"Even better," said Warren as he surveyed the situation. "We move to plan B." He hid the can of worms under the bed.

"I'm pretty sure we didn't talk about any plan B," Cristen said uneasily.

Warren shook Hanna's pillow from its case and tossed it to Cristen. "Hold this." He then gathered up all of the delicate fabrics into a messy ball with his grubby hands and stuffed them into the pillowcase.

Cristen didn't know whether to be giddy or horrified. "What are we going to do with it?" he asked.

"You'll see, come on." Warren grabbed the stuffed pillowcase from him, and they ran from her room, out of the house, and down the street before entering the nearby woods. After picking out a suitable place, Warren dropped the bundle on the ground. He fell to his knees and started digging a hole in the dirt with a stick, just like they'd done searching for worms earlier.

Cristen wavered, having second thoughts about upsetting Hanna so much. But he steeled himself, acknowledging that he couldn't allow anything to stand in the way of bringing her back home where she belonged. He watched Warren dig earnestly, willing to fight for Cristen's cause, and Cristen shook off his moment of weakness. He found another stick to help loosen the soil while Warren continued expanding the hole with his hands. Before long, the pillowcase with its pristine fabrics lay buried under a foot of dirt. With the deed done, the two slipped back out of the woods.

"What will we say when they ask about it?" Cristen asked as they headed back down Warren's street, dreading the inevitable aftermath.

"You don't know much about these things, do you?" Warren replied matter-of-factly. "The trick is to say nothing at all. We know nothing, see? Just don't forget to scrub all the dirt from under your fingernails when we're done. Evidence could be our downfall. Now...to get the worms into her bed."

Cristen couldn't believe Warren could say such things with a straight face.

Over the following week, Warren and Cristen worked hard to disrupt the impending nuptials, sabotaging everything they could. They carried out their mischief during the short spurts of time the house lay empty. They hid away nearly half of all candles, flowers, and other decorations whenever Mrs. Myers brought them home.

On one occasion, they snuck into the kitchen and switched out the sugar for salt, ruining numerous baked goods. They spread gossip around town, whispering fabricated stories to anyone willing to listen about fights between the betrothed couple.

Only yesterday did they find a tableful of unsealed wedding invitations to which they added a drop of vinegar before sealing the envelopes themselves. After delivering them to the postmaster's office, Warren returned home on his own to proudly announce to his mother that he did her the favor of mailing them for her, to which she showed a highly mixed reaction. The ideas came easy to Warren, often leaving Cristen in a daze.

After seven straight days of orchestrating mayhem whenever the opportunity rose and sending the Myers into a tizzy trying to find the mystery vandals, Cristen was abruptly woken from a deep sleep by a thunderous banging on his front door.

"Open up, hurry!" Warren yelled from outside. "They're after me!" He continued his relentless banging.

"Go away!" Cristen shouted back. He pulled his blankets over his head and rolled onto his stomach, exhausted after being up so late the night before covering all the doorknobs in Warren's house with honey.

"They're going to murder me dead!" Warren howled dramatically. "You gotta let me in!"

Cristen groaned and forced himself up. He shuffled over to unlock the door before Warren could break it down. Warren burst inside, nearly bowling Cristen over. A gang of four other boys chased after him, now halfway across the yard.

Cristen quickly shut the door behind them while Warren turned the lock.

Gasping for breath, Warren slumped back against the door. "What took you so long?" he griped.

"What did you do this time?" Cristen demanded, though hardly one to talk.

"Why do you assume it's my fault?" Warren whined.

Cristen laughed aloud at the absurdity of the question. "Well, nice going. You've led your enemies literally right to my doorstep."

The boys started pounding loudly on the door.

"I had no choice!" Warren insisted, cringing from the noise. "Brock said they'll pummel me until my lights go out."

Cristen sighed, trying to keep his patience. "Why are they mad at you?"

"I don't know, I didn't do anything!" Warren claimed.

Cristen fixed Warren with a look. "After everything we've been through, you really want to stand there and lie to my face? What kind of friend is that?" He used the friend jab to take advantage of the fact that Warren began clinging to him as his only friend. He'd also been trying to impart occasional doses of conscience to Warren, though he felt hypocritical each time, given his own transgressions.

Warren froze in a flash of panic. "Okay, okay! I might have started a little rumor, but they deserved it."

"Spit it out," Cristen ordered

"I might have told one of their sisters I saw them catching and skinning a stray cat," Warren mumbled.

Cristen sighed heavily, consumed by guilt. While Warren's behavior preceded their first meeting, Cristen still felt culpable for not objecting and letting things get out of hand. He should have been setting a far better example. He only wanted a heart-to-heart with Hanna, not to make her miserable.

The angry boys resumed banging relentlessly on the door.

"Knock it off!" Cristen shouted, banging back. "You're trespassing on private property." Cristen moved to the vertical window beside the door, moving the curtain aside, which stopped the banging. "Go on, get out of here," he told the group sternly through the glass.

"We just want Warren," the stockiest one with a close-shaved head called back angrily. "Send him out, or we'll smash your window in."

"That's Brock," Warren whispered fearfully, staying hidden.

"Last warning," Brock shouted menacingly. The banging started up again on both the door and window. Cristen suddenly worried for their safety, seeing that the boys meant business. He considered going outside to try reasoning with them but feared they would force their way in if given the chance. However, the window pane would surely shatter under their assault.

When Cristen risked another peek, a large rock came hurtling directly at his head. He ducked, but the rock bounced harmlessly off the glass and onto one of the boy's legs, making him yelp in pain. More rocks pelted the house, but the window remained oddly unscratched.

Warren started laughing. "They can't get us in here! As if to prove his point, he boldly went to the window and stuck his tongue out at the boys.

Cristen hurried to push him aside. "Don't you ever learn?" he asked in exasperation, moving away from the window with him. He too took comfort in knowing the house's magic kept them secure. They only needed to wait out the attack.

"But they're trying to destroy your place!" Warren answered indignantly.

An unexpected polite knock brought the boys' assault to an abrupt halt. Warren rushed back to peek out the window. "It's a lady," he reported. "Oh no, she looks cross."

Cristen hurried over to see for himself. The boys and all the rocks that should have littered the porch had inexplicably disappeared. "Where did they go?" he muttered in confusion.

"I guess she scared them off."

"That sudden?" Cristen unlocked and opened the door, peering past the lady to the changed but familiar King's Crossing neighborhood.

"Good, you're home," the elderly lady declared impatiently. "That horse of yours keeps eating my tree."

Cristen stared at her blankly. "What?"

"I said your horse won't stop eating my fruit tree out back," she repeated, slower this time. "Maybe you should try feeding him now and again."

"Oh, uh...sorry about that, ma'am," Cristen said, still trying to process another town change. "I'll try to watch out for that."

The woman harrumphed loudly. "See that you do," she scolded over her shoulder as she marched toward his gate.

"I think I might know her," Cristen said as he watched her go. "I see her gardening over the back fence sometimes."

"We're not in Mulberry anymore," Warren said.

Cristen nodded, finally piecing together what happened. "We house hopped again," he said for lack of a better term. "She knocked from King's Crossing, so we needed to be here to answer the door." It also explained the abrupt shift from Mulberry to King's Crossing when Damon's messenger visited. He now believed that his house existed simultaneously in at least the three towns, if not more.

"That old lady saved us!" Warren exclaimed appreciatively.

"Now, if only we could figure out how to control it," Cristen mused. "I can't have random visitors deciding where I'll end up."

Warren's eyes lit up. "Doozy, we can get a telescope here to scope out Beacon Hill!"

"We won't need that," Cristen replied. "But didn't you say this is where they have the big candy store?"

"Sweet Treats!" Warren said excitedly. "I'll buy since you never have money. Come on, let's go!"

Outside, Warren added, "I can't believe we're here just like that. Imagine what we'll be able to do now for Operation Sabotage!"

Cristen could see he had his hands full.

28

C risten and Warren walked the short jaunt to town. Main Street bustled with activity without the chaos and stress of rain and mud. Shoppers—some with children in tow—dotted the boardwalks out on various errands. The air smelled inviting, offering tantalizing aromas of baked goods and grilling meats.

"There it is!" Warren shouted after passing a string of shops. He pointed at a sign that read: SWEET TREATS. With Cristen at his heels, Warren eagerly hurried inside. The interior smelled divine, and irresistible rows of candy were displayed across the long front counter. The lower tier held wrapped toffees, swirled lollipops, candy sticks, and roasted nuts, while the back counter showcased a mouthwatering variety of fudge squares and fruit tarts.

The man behind the counter greeted them with a friendly smile. "What can I get for you boys?" he asked.

"How am I supposed to choose?" Warren asked with awe as he looked over the offerings.

The man chuckled. "The peppermint sticks are quite popular with young gentlemen such as yourselves," he suggested helpfully. "Tell you what: you buy a piece of fudge, and I'll throw in a candy stick for free, any flavor you like."

"Doozy, how much for both of us?" Warren asked, spilling a handful of coins that always seemed to be in his pockets onto the counter.

After discovering that Rip, the owner of Poppy's, lied to him about dragon scales' worthlessness, Cristen still used one at the mercantile in Mulberry to purchase goods. While significantly reduced in value, the scales were still traded for goods and services.

The shopkeeper picked out a few of Warren's more valuable coins and returned the rest. "What's your pleasure?"

"I'll take that fudge with all the icing," Warren decided. "What's that orange-y stuff?" He pointed eagerly at a jar of wrapped candy.

"That would be lemon-ginger flavored. It's a little spicy, and I've got them on sticks if you prefer."

"How about plain lemon?" Warren asked, looking around for them.

The man offered him a small tray of bright yellow stick candy, and Warren helped himself to one.

"I'll try the fudge with nuts," said Cristen. "With a peppermint stick."

"Excellent choices," the shopkeeper said. He neatly wrapped each piece of fudge piece in a square of cheesecloth and handed them their treats.

As Cristen tucked his fudge into a tunic pocket for later, he and Warren began enjoying their candy before leaving the store. When they stepped outside, they were greeted by the gentle patter of a light rain.

"Warren Flynn Myers!" a woman carrying shopping parcels wailed from the other side of the busy road. "My baby...who brought you out here?"

"Oh no," Warren said, his eyes wide as saucers.

Cristen located the woman and recognized her from his brief visit to their house. She now wore a lace head covering over an elaborate hairdo, along with ankle-length skirts. She looked unhappy as she searched the street for a place to cross.

"Let me guess," Cristen said wryly, "You haven't been home in a while."

"You know I have!" Warren cried defensively.

Cristen shook his head. "But have they seen you?"

Warren shrugged, unconcerned. "How's that my fault? Anyway, how can they blame me for stuff if I'm not around? See? It's all part of the plan."

Cristen sighed, suspecting he would likely be blamed for Warren's truancy.

Warren's mother found a gap in traffic and hurried across toward them, hiking her skirts up while balancing her parcels. Without warning, Warren sprinted in the opposite direction down Main Street, dropping his sweets to the ground.

After another glance at Mrs. Myers, Cristen raced after Warren, who proved surprisingly quick for his stocky build. He chased him for several blocks down the busy thoroughfare, dodging shoppers and crates of wares, until Warren finally turned a corner down a narrow side street. Halfway down the block, a white-gloved hand belonging to a gentleman in tails abruptly seized Warren by the scruff of his neck.

Cristen skidded to a halt, bracing his hands against his knees to catch his breath. He froze when he noticed that the gentleman clinging to Warren was none other than Damon emerging from a tavern. Warren struggled furiously, trying to squirm and punch his way free, but Damon hoisted him higher with a fistful of Warren's tunic so that only his toes scraped the ground.

"Well, well. What do we have here...little brother?" Damon said, not having noticed Cristen yet. "You're a wanted man, you know."

"Let me go!" Warren yelled, writhing in Damon's grip, his face reddening.

Another man exited the tavern, also dressed to the nines. Cristen figured he must know Damon since he stopped to watch the scene unfolding with amusement.

"Are you going to settle down, or must I hogtie you?" Damon asked Warren with a hint of humor. "Because I could earn serious marks with the folks for returning their little runaway."

Cristen straightened up, wiping sweat from his brow with the heel of his hand, which caught Damon's attention. A shadow fell over Damon's face as he set Warren down, though he kept a firm hold of his collar. Damon studied them back and forth as if to figure out why they might be together.

"He's running from his ma," Cristen explained.

Damon's eyes narrowed. "I think I'm beginning to understand," he said slowly. "I suspected maybe Warren, but..." Damon chuckled briefly at his friend. "I must admit," he said to Cristen, "I never saw this coming. Partners in crime. Who'd have guessed you two? But it all makes sense...doesn't it? You think Evelyn deserves all this, leaving her in tears night after night. Shame on both of you."

"You have no proof!" Warren shouted up at Damon defiantly. Now that Damon had loosened his grip, he finally stopped struggling.

Cristen bristled at the accusation, knowing he deserved it. But he couldn't back down now. "What Evelyn deserves is to know the truth of why she's in Harmony," he shot back. "Born of the sea is all a big lie. You were dead wrong when you called me a freak of nature. We were invited to Harmony, though I can't fathom why either of us ever agreed to come."

Damon opened his mouth to respond, but Warren cut him off. "Wait just a minute!" he hollered. "You two know each other?"

"Damon's my brother," Cristen announced resolutely. "My actual brother."

Damon rolled his eyes, then exchanged an amused, knowing look with his friend. "Told you so," he muttered under his breath.

Warren's mouth dropped open. "What in the...?" He wriggled free of Damon's hold and hurried away from his reach.

"Come on, Warren, let's go," Cristen said, annoyed he'd been a past topic of amusement between Damon and his friend.

As they turned to leave, Damon called out to Cristen, "By the way, the wedding's in a couple of weeks, in case you have nothing better to do."

Heat flooded Cristen's cheeks as he spun back around. "Why are you doing this?" he demanded, his voice breaking. "You know Hanna's my girl because you've dreamt of her too. Only you tell yourself the dreams aren't real. Convenient, isn't it—you can swoop right in and steal her for yourself. Well, there won't be a wedding if I have anything to do with it. I'll tell her everything."

Arms folded, Damon smirked as he listened. "Don't kid yourself. You're nothing to her. Besides, what kind of life could you possibly offer?"

Cristen fumed, the callous words hitting their mark. Warren's mother marched abruptly up to her son—who still seemed preoccupied with the brother situation by comparing the two—and caught him by the ear, causing an ear-piercing wail.

Damon must have seen her coming from behind and now grinned in satisfaction. "Caught the rascal for you, ma'am," he said, taking quick credit.

"Bless you kindly," she stately firmly to Damon. "Woe is me. What am I to do with this child?"

She scowled at Cristen before redirecting her attention to Warren. "Just wait 'til your father hears about running from me," she scolded while Warren clutched at her wrist, trying to ease the painful pinching. Her nagging voice grew fainter as she led him away by the ear back toward Main Street. "I still don't understand why you're so far from home. Who in their right mind..."

Cristen shifted awkwardly, left alone with Damon and his smirking friend. However, he had more to say and might not get another chance. "You have to believe me, Damon," he pleaded. "I swear home is somewhere beyond Harmony. I'm leaving this place, so if you want to join me, we could—"

Damon's friend interrupted, "I hate to disappoint you, but how do you plan to leave Harmony when it's the only inhabited land that exists? There is no proof of other life out there."

"You're plain wrong," Cristen said. He turned back to Damon. "Mother and Father know we're here. I know you've dreamt of them. You're the spitting image of Father."

Damon smirked, though something in his expression faltered briefly.

His pompous friend stepped forward. "Better watch your tongue," he warned Cristen. "His parents died in a carriage accident years ago."

"Wrong again," Cristen argued. "What about his grandparents and their parents? Where are they?"

The friend turned to Damon, expecting an answer, but Damon's jaw only tightened as he glared at Cristen.

"Our parents are alive and well," Cristen stated confidently. "And to think there's no other life out there is absurd. Harmony is only a speck on the map."

Damon glanced up at the darkening sky. "Well, I believe I've had enough madness for one day," he declared crisply. "Come on, let's get out of here," he murmured to his friend.

"Right, before your road turns to mush again," said the friend.

Cristen winced. That road had caused him great anguish. "You do know that Sunfire died on your road," he shouted before Damon could get too far.

"Damon halted mid-step, then turned on his heel, striding purposefully toward Cristen. With a lowered, icy voice, he said, "It was supposed to be you that day. And you'll never lay eyes on Evelyn again, I'll make sure of it. Stay out of our lives unless you want a peeved fire-breather to finish you off." He walked off in anger. As he caught up with his friend, the friend fell in step with him with a final glance over his shoulder.

With dawning horror, Cristen realized that the accident hadn't been an accident at all but rather a deliberate attempt on his life! Did Damon hate him that much? The thought gutted him. And did Sefilar still mean him harm? Why couldn't she leave well enough alone? Were she and Damon working together to get rid of him? A cold fear took hold of his heart. His brother was turning dangerous, and the realization broke his heart.

Cristen's steps felt heavy as he made his way home. He found himself plagued again by traumatic memories of losing Sunfire on Damon's ill-fated hillside road. To add to his misery, he recalled Damon's messenger knocking on his door the day before the so-called accident, oblivious that the plan he'd agreed to would soon backfire most horrifically, cutting his own life tragically short. Cristen winced, unable to shake the relentless replay of the man and Sunfire tumbling over the edge.

As his thoughts returned to Hanna, Cristen released a pent-up sigh. Damon spoke the harsh truth. Cristen had only truth to offer Hanna, which she might never believe, while Damon could offer her the world on a silver platter. How could he possibly compete with that? He might be powerless to save Hanna from Harmony after all.

29

Cristen found Warren sitting on his step when he arrived home. Warren hopped up eagerly to follow him inside as he unlocked the door.

"You're going to turn your family against me," Cristen said, still in a mood and annoyed at having to deal with Warren just now.

"We never got the telescope to spy on the wedding," Warren pouted.

"Operation sabotage was a waste of time. Anyway, it's late, so why don't you go home?" Cristen told him.

Warren ignored him and plopped down on the bed. "How could you not tell me your Damon is Evelyn's Damon?"

"You seriously didn't know? I told you what he looked like. Anyway, does it matter?" Cristen asked dismissively.

"We're going to have to tell Evelyn about that other girl," Warren said.

"What other girl?"

"Hanna. I mean, wouldn't Evelyn be mad?" Warren grabbed a pillow and made himself comfortable.

It took Cristen a moment to realize he'd slipped and used Hanna's real name when talking to Damon. It surprised him to think Warren paid any attention at all. Even with his juvenile behavior, he seemed to catch everything.

"Actually...Hanna is Evelyn. It's the same girl," Cristen explained.

"Oh. Like a code name?"

"Sure, something like that," Cristen replied, not caring to elaborate.

"Okay, I won't tell anyone," Warren promised. He sat up eagerly. "Did you eat your fudge?"

"Well, I didn't throw it on the ground like someone else I know," Cristen said.

"The enemy was closing in!" Warren whined dramatically.

"She's your mother. What are you so afraid of?" Cristen tossed the fudge to him anyway.

"Doozy!" Warren declared happily and stuffed half of it into his mouth after dropping the cheesecloth wrapper onto the floor.

Cristen's stomach had been growling since the peppermint stick, but going to bed on an empty stomach was nothing new. At least his morning rations usually took care of his hunger for much of the day. He then remembered he hadn't given Moonshine his hay that morning. He should also check the water trough.

"I'll be right back," he told Warren, taking his waterskin. He preferred the ease of dumping his own water into the trough rather than bringing water up from the well bucket by bucket, and Moonshine still thrived on it.

"Okay," Warren agreed, taking another bite of fudge and spilling crumbs on the bed.

Moonshine followed Cristen from the yard into the barn. Cristen set out new hay and oats, taking a mouthful for himself as he often did. As he chewed, he uncorked his waterskin, took a drink, and upturned it to add water to the trough.

Scarcely had the water splashed out when a blood-curdling scream pierced the air from the house. "Can you not be left alone for two seconds?" he said in exasperation. He corked the water and raced back to the rear of the house.

The door felt cold and wouldn't open despite being unlocked. Bracing himself, Cristen pushed harder until it cracked open a few inches. A wall of snow blocked the entrance, while a fierce wind howled through the narrow gap, blasting him in the face. A storm in his house! Warren continued to shriek.

Leaning his shoulder into the door, Cristen shoved it open a few more inches. The force of the icy wind dislodged the compacted snow, sending chunks and powder blowing into him. Cristen glimpsed Warren trying desperately to close the front door against a raging blizzard. When the door refused to budge further, Cristen wiped snow and ice from his freezing face and neck and raced around to the front to help Warren.

But the front door was closed, and there was no sign of the storm. When he opened it, a bright flash of light nearly blinded him, and a snow-plastered Warren flew backward with another shriek into a foot of snow, shielding his eyes with an arm.

"Devil's curse, what was that?" Warren yelled, traumatized.

Once Cristen's eyes adjusted, he stared in awe at the wintry scene before him as the last flurries drifted down. "We passed through a snowstorm. What...did you do?" Cristen asked, too astonished to be mad. He then saw the snow drift preventing him from opening the back door.

"What was that light?" Warren asked through chattering teeth, blinking snow-encrusted lashes as he shivered from the cold.

Cristen gathered the snow into the top blanket. He dragged the sodden mass out the back door, dumped the snow, and spread it in a sunny spot to dry.

"Get in," Cristen ordered when he returned to the house. Cristen felt icy water seeping through his boots as he helped Warren stand on trembling legs and guide him to the bed.

"I turned the big gear," Warren confessed, teeth chattering and body trembling as he crawled under the covers.

"What big gear?"

"On the clock."

Cristen quickly looked up to see the mirror flipped to the clock side. "Why are you messing with my things?" he asked, mostly annoyed that Warren had more guts than he did to touch the strange contraption.

"Why didn't you warn me about your storm-maker?" Warren accused.

Cristen approached the clock when he saw a new disk spinning in its chamber. He might not have noticed if not for its strange position—embedded into the frame above the clock rather than on its face. His eyes dropped to the other three spinning disks.

"It's not a clock," he realized aloud. "It's a map."

"Doozy, that's no map I've ever seen," Warren exclaimed.

"Isn't King's Crossing at Harmony's center?" Cristen asked, pointing to the spinning disk nearest the central gears. "Then up here is Mulberry, and over here is Meadowbrook—places I've been. Or this house has been. This is the newest one to activate up here," he said, pointing to the frame top.

"Doozy, you might be right!"

"It has to be north of here...maybe beyond Harmony," Cristen continued. His heartbeat quickened as he considered that, once the storm passed, it could be the escape route he needed.

"You're crazy," Warren said, sitting up. "That guy said he has proof there's nothing past Harmony." Warren's shivering subsided, his wind-bitten cheeks losing their bright red tint.

"He can't have proof," Cristen argued. "There's always more beyond a place."

"Sorry about your floor," Warren said, glancing around sheepishly. With the door open, the house quickly warmed up, melting the snow into slush.

"The thing is," Cristen said, "I didn't see snow outside."

"What? Well, it didn't come from your ceiling," Warren said.

"What I mean is that King's Crossing didn't have any. But I saw you fighting the front door through the back."

"You saved me from a horrible death. I thought I'd be found as some frozen statue."

"When I opened the closed door to your open door, it must have reset the house, causing the flash," Cristen reasoned aloud.

"Come on," he said. Help me clean up this mess you made."
He grabbed his broom from the corner and pushed melting snow from the table and chairs.

Warren threw off the covers and jumped out of bed, hurrying to the back door. "Better get home. I forgot about my own chores."

"Since when do you have chores?"

Warren hurried out the door but returned a moment later a little chagrined. "Wrong town," he said.

Cristen laughed. "Here, take it," he said, offering Warren the broom.

Warren reluctantly accepted it and began sweeping the slush and water out the door while Cristen found some rags to sop up the water behind him.

"I guess we're having a sleepover tonight," Warren said cheerfully. "Good thing Ma and Pa don't know how to find me."

"We'll see about that. You can't keep turning up missing."

"Don't worry, they're used to it."

"Doesn't make it right. You'll drive them mad."

While they worked, Cristen's gaze kept wandering back to the upper spinning disk, his thoughts consumed with discovering the storm's location.

30

Warren ended up spending the night, as no one in town was heading to Mulberry. Come morning, they procured him a ride on the post carriage and sent him on his way.

Cristen spent some time getting his hair trimmed and having his best outfit laundered in exchange for a few hours of labor. When he returned home, he bathed and polished his boots with lard the butcher had given him. He didn't dare present himself to Hanna without looking his best.

When Cristen arrived in Mulberry himself the following morning, after the two-hour ride, Warren's mother opened the door, surprised to see him.

"Did Warren get home alright?" Cristen asked.

Her nose tilted into the air in a huff. "Can you truly not find friends your age?" she said in a haughty voice.

"I'm here to see Evelyn?" he asked, quickly losing confidence.

She looked at Cristen squarely. "Then you aren't responsible for her disappearance?"

"Of course not," Cristen said, taken aback. "You don't know where she is?"

"She has quite disappeared, which is not like her."

"She's not with Damon?"

"You know Damon? Never mind, I remember. At least he's not half your age," she said dryly. "Anyway, he looked horrified when he came for her and found her already gone. He's been quite beside himself with worry, just as we all are."

"When did you see her last?"

"It's been three days now."

"Three days?" Cristen asked, alarmed. "Have you reported it?"

"Of course, we reported it," she said, raising her voice. "A search party went out last night but found nothing. And seriously, how do you know Damon? Pardon me, but I don't see the likes of you running in such circles."

Cristen thought it odd that she worried about his social status at a time like this, though she was right. Damon appeared to be quickly climbing the social ladder. "We met years ago," Cristen said. "I'll let you know if I hear anything."

"I see," she said and closed the door.

Cristen intended to find Hanna himself. He wondered if Warren had something to do with it, but then again, he'd been with him most of those three days.

"Psst!"

Cristen looked around for Warren, recognizing his voice.

"Psst! Over here."

Cristen followed the sound to the right side of the house, where Warren's nose pressed through a cracked open window.

"You have to get me out of here," Warren whispered urgently.

"Get you out? What are you doing?"

"What does it look like I'm doing, running through a field of daisies? I'm locked up. Anyway, we have to go back."

"Back where?"

"To the storm. We have to see what's there."

Cristen had every intention of returning to the storm's location, but not with Warren. "You have a death wish or something?" he asked, trying to scare him off of the idea. "What about all the cold and wind? Anyway, I don't have time. I have to find Evelyn."

"Damon has her."

"No, he doesn't. He's looking for her."

"No, he's not, he's guilty," Warren said.

"How do you know?"

"I can spot a liar a mile away. You should have seen him talking to Ma yesterday. He cried without any tears. Ma fell for it, just like she does when I fake it."

"Did you tell her?"

"Forget it! She'd be onto me too."

Cristen replayed in his mind what Damon told him, how he would make sure he never saw Hanna again. Did he make good on his threat by secreting her away?

"I'm going to Beacon Hill," Cristen said.

"Take me with you," Warren pleaded.

"How long are you grounded for?"

"Ma said until I'm old and gray."

"I'm sure you've been grounded before. How long did it last?"

"I've never been locked away to rot in my cell before. Pa put a lock on the outside."

Cristen shook his head, knowing Warren deserved it. "How do you expect me to get you out?"

"Pa's crowbar is in the shed."

"Bye, Warren." Cristen turned to leave.

"Okay, okay! I'll meet you at your house. Don't go without me."

"If I'm gone when you get there, you took too long. And maybe you should apologize and stop running away."

"Fine!" Warren yelled and slammed the window shut.

***

Warren never showed up, but it didn't matter. A giant log blocked the road to Beacon Hill, and no carts came or went. Cristen glanced up the road.

"Because of the missing girl," came a low voice from behind. A weathered gentleman on horseback passed Cristen by and guided his horse around the far end of the log.

"You mean Evelyn?" Cristen asked.

The man turned in the saddle to answer, "Mr. D sent everyone home yesterday. He told them there wouldn't be any work until she's found."

Cristen doubted Warren knew what he was talking about, knowing how much the project meant to Damon. Also, Cristen couldn't imagine Damon crying about anything, fake or not.

Cristen returned home to his Mulberry house with a heavy heart. He slumped onto his front steps, doubtful he'd ever get to talk with Hanna about anything. Even if he did, why would she listen to him? He started wondering if he shouldn't just forget about Warren and his whole family, including Hanna, who barely knew he existed. As much as it hurt, he might have to accept the situation and leave her to Damon.

Assuming they found her, that is. He hoped no harm had come to her.

Another thought nagged at him. After Hanna and Damon's choices, it seemed they had cut themselves off from home and family forever. What would his parents say if he returned home, leaving them behind without a fight? If only Cristen could reverse time so that none of them had left home to begin with.

He also remembered what King Thane told him—that he wasn't to concern himself about what lay beyond Harmony yet. Still, he hated himself for agreeing to any quest and ruining his life.

Why *did* he agree to come? What grand thing did that scroll say to convince him to leave home to fight in the wizard's army that didn't even seem to exist? Feeling disheartened over the whole thing, he went inside to take a nap.

Sometime later, Warren burst through the back door wearing so many layers of clothing that he'd doubled in size. Much of his head also hid beneath tunics tied up with sleeves so that only his eyes and mouth peeked through. Wool stockings covered his hands and arms.

"What are you doing?" asked Cristen, laughing at the comical sight.

"So I don't freeze again in the storm, of course. But we have to hurry 'cause I'm roasting in here."

"I never said we were going back, so relax."

We have to do what the clock says," said Warren as he moved to the bureau and began transferring the drawers' contents onto the bed.

"The clock didn't say anything," Cristen said. "And stop, you're making a mess."

"Hurry, put them on," Warren said, throwing clothing Cristen's way.

Cristen shook his head at Warren's insistence and finally sighed. "You're not going to take no for an answer, are you."

"Finally! I'm dying in here," Warren said. "I'll control the clock since I know how it works. He dropped Cristen's muck boots at his feet from the bottom drawer. "You'll go out first in case you have to protect me from anything dangerous, like snow monsters." Warren checked both doors to make sure they were securely shut and locked.

"Just because you found the storm doesn't mean you know how to work it," Cristen told him.

He regretted listening to anything Warren had ever said. Hadn't he learned his lesson yet? Still, he had to admit that life was never dull with Warren around. He found him both exasperating and endearing. He couldn't help admiring the boy's tenacity and determination, even in the face of Cristen's reluctance. His boundless energy and quirky perspective brought an unexpected lightness to even the most trying circumstances.

Cristen sighed, finding no reason not to check if the storm had passed since it might be his exit from Harmony. He opened the kitchen curtain to monitor outdoor changes.

Warren flipped the mirror to the clock side while Cristen started layering on clothes. He didn't get bundled up to Warren's degree, but he soon began sweating, and once he covered his head and hands, he stood at the door and gave Warren the thumbs up. Warren returned the signal and turned the gear a click to the right.

Nothing happened. Another click brought the same results. At about the tenth, the kitchen view shifted instantly to another town.

"Doozy!" Warren exclaimed at the display of magic.

"Wrong place," Cristen said, seeing no snow, though wondering what new town they'd found. He could usually see the backs of houses on the neighboring street, but the place looked desolate. When Cristen checked out the front, the neighborhood vanished altogether. Only a single flat-roofed building sat at the base of a hill in the distance.

Warren clicked the gear again without luck. After another six clicks, Cristen's Meadowbrook neighborhood appeared. "This thing is broken," Warren said. He banged the clock frame with the side of his fist.

But Cristen found it all incredible. "We're getting around on our own," he said.

"Yeah, but where's the snow? I'm sweating like a hog."

Cristen studied the clock again. More than just the gears alone must be involved. "Do it again," he said.

Click. Click. Click. Nothing happened. Warren continued trying until they found themselves in yet another town with no snow. With an encouraging nod from Cristen, Warren continued. They watched out the window as more towns passed them by until their wraps began coming off layer by layer. Regardless of the location, Moonshine strangely remained in the ever-changing yard, oblivious to everything. After more tries, they still couldn't find the storm but ended up back at King's Crossing.

Paying frequent attention to the clock, Cristen noticed things changing within it. From what he could tell, a new disk spun in its chamber each time a new town appeared, confirming Cristen's hunch. "The towns start spinning once we've been there," he said. He touched one that wasn't spinning yet, then looked up at the one he felt sure to be the storm. "So, how do we get back there?" he muttered.

"That one's going the wrong way," Warren said, pointing at King's Crossing.

Sure enough, the golden disk spun in the opposite direction. "It has to be our current location," Cristen said. "Good, we'll always know where we are."

"As long as we remember which town is which," said Warren.

"We need to make an actual map," said Cristen.

"Doozy, we need ink!" Warren said excitedly. "Time to go shopping again."

31

Hours later, Cristen and Warren sat across the table from each other, absorbed in their work on the large map crafted from butcher paper and Cristen's purple quill that Simon had given him. Ink blobs denoted each town, yet learning their names proved more challenging than anticipated.

Initially, they attempted to inquire about the town's name from the first person they encountered, but the perplexed expressions and subsequent probing about their origins and lineage only complicated matters. To avoid further scrutiny, they resorted to trekking to the outskirts of each town in search of official name signs, a time-consuming endeavor.

They never found themselves lost, relying instead on the backward-spinning disk to pinpoint their current location. They couldn't control where the house transported them, but with enough gear rotations, they always eventually arrived back in a familiar town.

Cristen jotted down a note in the margins about the last town they visited while Warren drew a dotted line connecting the note to its corresponding town.

"Write about that bull that chased us when we cut across the field," said Warren as he finished the last few dashes.

Cristen drew two horns, making Warren laugh. He then noticed the line Warren drew. "Did you have to cut through the middle of the clock?"

"It's not a clock, it's a map," Warren argued. "Anyway, it looks like a road."

"But there's no road there."

"Then it's the hand of the clock," said Warren.

"I thought you said it wasn't a clock." Petty bickering was common between them, a familiar part of their relationship dynamic.

Warren examined his work again and sighed. "You're right. I should have drawn it around here. Now, the hand crosses over the wrong town."

"Don't worry about it. We can work around it," Cristen assured him. But Warren's reference to the clock hand sparked a new thought.

"The hand crosses over the towns," Cristen said as he rose from the table to study the clock again. The single hand moved steadily around the clock face as it passed each town marker.

"We can make a new map if it bothers you," Warren offered, following Cristen over.

"You're a genius," said Cristen, staring intently at the revolving hand.

"I am?" Warren asked, puzzled.

"We've been ignoring the hand this whole time."

"We have?"

"It's got to be the locator."

"But we can't control it."

"We don't have to. Watch how it never crosses two towns at the same time."

Warren observed the hand's movement. "So?"

"So we turn the gear as the hand passes over the town we want to travel to."

Warren's face lit up with comprehension. "Doozy, we have to try it!" he exclaimed. Hurry, we need to get wrapped up again."

They layered on clothing again, but before slipping on his final stocking mitten, Warren waddled to the clock in excited anticipation. He watched closely as the hand climbed the clock toward the spinning disk they suspected represented the snowstorm. Cristen waited nervously with a hand on the doorknob. Just as the hand reached the golden foil marker, Warren turned the gear.

Click. They were instantly plunged into darkness.

"It's nighttime!" Warren declared in astonishment.

Cristen opened the door but found his way blocked by a slick, cold wall of snow. He removed a stocking mitten to feel the frozen barrier. "We're buried. The snow must have been accumulating since last time." He wondered how long it would take to melt away, delaying his departure.

"Doozy, I'll get us out of here," Warren said. "Can't promise which town since I can't see anything."

"No, wait," Cristen said. Freeing his hands from the stockings, he felt his way past Warren to the bureau and retrieved his orb, lighting the room with its soft radiance to see the white wall barricading their exit.

Warren stared raptly at the magical orb instead of the snow.

"You can't tell anyone," Cristen warned. He grabbed the broom with his free hand and poked the handle end upward at the top of the doorframe. A chunk of snow broke away, letting in a beam of hazy daylight while exposing them to the frigid wind and blowing snow. Cristen shut the door before the snow inundated the house again.

Again, he wondered how far they would need to travel to find snow like this. A fun idea made him smile. How often did

Warren get to play in the snow? Perhaps never. "Ever build a snow fort before?"

"But we can't get out!" Warren exclaimed.

"We dig down under. You're good at digging, right?"

Warren beamed. "I'm an expert! Doozy, this will be the perfect secret clubhouse."

"I have a shovel in the barn," said Cristen.

"How are we supposed to get to the barn?" Warren asked.

"Let's check the back.

They went to the rear door and were greeted by Mulberry's sunny warmth, neither quite believing their eyes.

32

Each day, Cristen and Warren experienced the enchanting phenomenon of building their tunnel in the front while sunshine greeted them out back. Now that they figured out how to travel between towns, they ensured that the back door always opened to Mulberry so Warren could return home for supper each evening, which Cristen insisted on.

Their snow tunnel grew a few feet across and a good twenty feet long—leading out the door, down the porch steps, and across the overgrown lawn that they diligently kept covered. The chink above the door that Cristen knocked open in the beginning had quickly resealed itself, though they broke it open now and then to check on the storm's status. Because they weren't exposed directly to the storm and because of the hard work, they never needed more than long sleeves to stay warm. They still thawed out their hands occasionally since their makeshift mittens could be cumbersome.

After a while, Cristen thought using the orb might work to melt the snow, but its light alone didn't radiate heat. The moment he focused the beam tightly enough to burn, it instantly melted through to the outside, sizzling and steaming away the snow no matter how thick. After a few accidental crisscrossing burns that exposed them to the frigid storm, he put the orb away before the tunnel collapsed altogether. Together, they patched up the melted seams in the walls.

Good old manual labor with tools, bowls, and utensils got the job done. After carving out sections of the dense snow, they heaped it into a tin wash bin and skated it back down the icy tunnel floor and up the porch steps. They then pushed it across the floor—now clear of table, chairs, and rug—and back outside to dump it where it quickly melted.

Cristen felt relief over the distraction the project provided. Surprisingly, Warren turned out to be a good companion. The fort seemed to give him purpose, and he worked as tirelessly as Cristen did. Warren also seemed generally more content these days, and Cristen wondered if things were improving at home.

"Aren't you hungry?" Warren asked late one morning after they dumped their latest load onto the slushy grass in the backyard.

"Starving," Cristen admitted.

They knew the routine. Cristen retrieved the bundle of food left that morning while Warren fetched the wool blanket they used for their picnics. Their snow tunnel quickly transformed into a cozy dining spot, always a celebration of how far they had tunneled.

As soon as they settled, facing each other against the tunnel walls and their mouths stuffed with bread and cheese, Warren said, "You left your light on."

Cristen found the bright spot, about the size of a plum, glowing beside his elbow. "That's not the orb, it's in the house. Besides, it only shines when I'm holding it anyway." This light also emanated a warmer hue than the orb's cool glow. He searched for another small hole they might have accidentally poked through to the outside, letting in sunlight, but he couldn't find any breach. He scraped at the illuminated patch with his fingernail, but the light remained steady behind the snow he chiseled away.

"Doozy!" Warren dropped his food and scrambled closer to inspect it, but he couldn't scrape the persistent glow away either.

"Get the bowl," Cristen directed, and Warren passed it to him. They burrowed in a foot, then two, expanding the width of the hole as they dug deeper, chasing the light.

"Where do you think it's leading us?" Warren asked curiously.

"No idea," Cristen admitted.

A few feet later, the light angled downward until it hit dirt.

"Well, that was pointless," Warren complained.

"I feel like we're over a walkway leading to a front gate," Cristen reasoned, noting the absence of grass. "Maybe we're supposed to follow it."

Something metallic clinked against their digging bowl, seizing their full attention. After a quick search, Cristen extracted a tarnished ornate key from the snow and dirt, identical to his house key, including his house number. "1208 Sion Street," they read aloud simultaneously.

"Hey, that's your address," Warren said. "Doozy, that means I can have my own copy!" Warren tried snatching it from Cristen's hand, but Cristen kept it out of reach.

"Nice try," Cristen said. He would never let Warren have free access to his house.

Cristen double-checked that he still had his original key and held the two side-by-side for comparison. Except for tarnished silver, the keys matched perfectly. When Warren reached for it again, Cristen slid both keys into his boot for safekeeping.

"Aw, come on," Warren complained.

Cristen sank into troubled thoughts as they finished eating, barely hearing Warren's endless chatter. Why did a duplicate of his key exist? Did someone live in the house before him? And how did the key end up buried out here, possibly king-doms away from Harmony? It bothered him that the wizard seemed intent on him finding it. Why couldn't he just be left alone?

***

Digging didn't offer their only pastime, as they still pro-gressed with their map. After cleaning up from their picnic, they prepared to explore again.

The clock brought them to a town they only glimpsed before. At the base of a distant hill sat a flat-roofed, gray building without any other structures visible within the trees and hills. Eager to investigate the area, they left the house.

They hiked across a broad valley, eventually climbing a hill's gentle slope. Finally, they arrived at a high chain-link fence surrounding the isolated building. Following the perime-ter, they soon found a gate with a weathered sign reading: Oakville Sanitarium.

"It's the holding center," Cristen said quietly, a chill running through him. So this was the place that held captured water dreamers...where Hanna should have been taken. The very idea made him feel ill. How could Harmony allow such cruelty? A downy white pigeon flitted across the building's roof. A gray one perched in the shadowy entrance, and a third paced along the rooftop ledge.

"Is this where they lock up the crazies?" Warren asked.

"Not crazies," Cristen corrected. "Just people they fear."

"People they fear? How does that make sense?"

"It doesn't."

Finding the main gate unlatched, they entered the fenced yard and approached the silent building's metal door, scaring away the pigeon.

"Uh, are you sure this is smart?" Warren asked nervously. "This place is messing with my head."

"You'll be fine. You're not a water dreamer," Cristen assured him.

"What's that got to do with it?" Warren asked.

Faced with a bolted entrance, Cristen rapped his knuckles against the door. He had to see it with his own eyes—to discover how many dreamers were trapped inside and witness firsthand the conditions they endured.

The lock turned from the inside, and the heavy door groaned open. A uniformed warden appeared, a baton strapped to his belt. After briefly eying Cristen, the man focused on Warren, seeming to size him up. Before Cristen could stop him, the warden grabbed Warren's arm and hauled him into the dim foyer.

"Hey, let me go!" Warren yelled, wildly struggling to free himself from the man's grip, just like when Damon accosted him. He continued shouting, "You don't have to be afraid of me. I'm just a dumb kid."

Cristen cautiously followed them inside, ready to explain Warren's innocence but also seeing the opportunity to investigate. He scanned the shadowy interior but couldn't see any other prisoners, though a cough echoed somewhere down a distant hall.

"Close the door, hunter," the warden ordered Cristen. "Never seen one so young. You should restrain them properly in transport, though, as they tend to bolt."

"Yes, sir," Cristen said.

"What are you doing?" Warren shrieked.

Cristen felt it risky to allow the misunderstanding any longer. He reached to take Warren's arm, but the warden wrenched the boy away and forced him into an open cell, slamming it shut. Cristen felt a swell of panic.

"He's not a water dreamer, sir," Cristen asserted. "He's from Mulberry. We were curious about this building and wanted to check it out."

After clicking the padlock closed, the warden turned on Cristen, looking furious. "You don't have the grit to be a hunter if you've gone and befriended one. I won't have any-one's soft heart or cold feet cost me my wages. Never."

"You have to believe me, sir!" Cristen pleaded as he fol-lowed the warden to a corner where he sat at his desk. "His parents will kill me if I don't get him home. He's not a water dreamer, I swear."

Warren shrieked about an injured leg and that he needed a doctor before gangrene set in.

The warden ignored him as he filled out a form. Keeping his eyes on his work, he told Cristen, "As commissioned by the overseer, your only duty is to keep Harmony safe. The fact you brought him out to these remote parts already confirms he's your capture. How else would you know to bring him here?"

"I have a house down there," Cristen insisted. "You can see it from here...that small place across the valley."

"A comedian too," the warden scoffed. "That's my house."

"We didn't bring horses," Warren shouted. "We walked."

"You're lying," Cristen argued to the warden. "It's my house, and we came up here on foot like he said."

The warden handed him a sealed envelope. "Just take your bounty and scram. And find yourself a suitable career for spineless cowards."

Cristen could never leave without Warren. He saw no other way but to offer himself up instead. But first, he needed answers. "What will happen to him?" he asked, ignoring Warren's horrified expression.

The warden paused, silently considering Cristen before replying. "We detain them until the Array, as you know. After that, if they refuse relocation to the mountains, they might be caught again and end up right back here. Townsfolk always fuss if a dreamer's on the loose."

"You deliver them to the mountains?" Cristen asked, dismayed at the revelation of such a service.

"Not us wardens personally," the warden clarified, "but arrangements are made, backed by the council. Only so far, though. We can't risk bringing the curse of the mountains back home. But you would have been told all this when you got licensed."

"But why the Array? Why not just get them out there as soon as they're found?" Cristen pressed, desperate to uncover every detail of their cruel practice.

The warden leaned forward, resting his arms on the desk. "The good townsfolk need to know who the pond suckers are before they try to blend in. Furthermore, they always need a little humbling." He raised a brow at Cristen. "Wouldn't you agree?"

Cristen bristled at the 'humbling' part. "You mean they need a little humiliating?" He took a steadying breath. "Never mind, I'm the water dreamer here. Take me prisoner instead and let my friend go." Cristen felt confident he could get out of any scrape he found himself in, having escaped before.

The warden laughed. "Ready to martyr yourself for a little guppy?"

"Psst!" Warren frantically gestured to get Cristen's attention. Cristen glanced his way, trying to reassure him, but Warren urgently directed his gaze to the opposite side of the cell, beyond Cristen's line of sight.

Cristen turned back to the warden. "I emerged in the bay east of the suspension bridge at Big Surge," Cristen confessed plainly, ignoring Warren. "They forced me into the Array, and I won the king's stallion, Sunfire."

The warden scrutinized him for a moment before standing abruptly, the legs of his chair scraping backward. "I know who you are. You've grown some...Cristen of Meadowbrook. It will be my pleasure to detain you."

Cristen exhaled in relief. He followed the warden back toward Warren, ready to take his place. But they passed his cell, continuing around it instead. Cristen froze in dismay at the sight of cement floors, walls, and iron bars—the sanitarium's prison block...with water dreamers trapped inside.

"It's what I've been trying to tell you!" Warren whispered loudly, having already seen them from his corner cell.

Four youths, two girls and two boys, languished in individual cages, their red clothes tattered and soiled. One boy leaned against the bars, staring vacantly while the others lay curled up on strewn hay in the corners, a single wool blanket for warmth. Cristen shuddered as a wave of fear hit him. The pitiful scene felt hauntingly reminiscent of his captivity at Burning Mountain, the moldering hay piles evoking memories of dragon scale nests.

Cristen felt so shaken by their plight that he instantly regretted his impulsive confession. Why would he risk his freedom again so foolishly?

33

Cristen grabbed at the bars of the first open cell to stop his entry, but the warden deftly broke his grip and forced him inside with a hard shove that sent Cristen sprawling to the cement floor. With a grin resembling more of a snarl, the warden padlocked the door.

"I've caught me a trophy," he boasted. "Won't the boys be proud?" He chuckled and disappeared back around Warren's cell.

"You can't keep Warren!" Cristen shouted after him, holding his throbbing elbow. "If you don't get him home by supper, his father will come looking for him."

"Well...it might take him a few days to notice," Warren whispered harshly to Cristen.

"Your father!" Cristen replied quietly. "Doesn't he have an important job or something?"

Warren's face brightened with realization. "Why didn't I think of that?"

Cristen couldn't help grinning, anxious to see Warren put on a show.

"Pa is going to have a fit when I don't come home," Warren said, loud enough for the warden to hear. With no response, he continued, "I sure don't envy the warden when he loses his job over ignoring simple safety rules. I mean, what do you think the council will do to him? Do they still skin people alive? Or maybe they'll drown him in the river. What's the punishment around here for kidnapping?"

Cristen gestured for Warren to tone it down a notch just before the warden reappeared.

"Hello there, officer," Warren greeted him brightly. "Sorry if I sound a little excited, but whew, Pa is going to bring the hammer down on you, and it won't be pretty."

"Tell me their names," the warden offered gruffly.

"If you mean my adoring parents, that would be Fred and Luinda Myers of Mulberry."

The warden swallowed. "Frederick Myers of the Council?"

"That's him, alright. He's got to be going bonkers about now. You're looking a little pale yourself, sir."

The warden wasted no time unlocking Warren's cell. "Be sure to let your parents know it was all a misunderstanding."

"I'll try, but I'm not too good at faking it. Pa will want to know every detail of what happened here. Even I know you didn't follow proper screening protocols. You can't just lock up every poor lost boy that wanders by. And Ma will be distraught for days knowing her only son got scared for his life."

The warden wiped sweaty palms on his hips. "I might have acted somewhat rashly. You really shouldn't have come around these parts," the warden said, attempting to justify himself.

"You better invent a whopper of a cover story, mister. We'll leave as soon as you let my friend out."

"We?" the warden asked as he walked Warren toward the exit. "There's no we. I know who he is, and I have his confession. Councilman Myers knows they pay us for new recruits. Unless notified otherwise by the authorities, I can't release him until we know he's isolated himself from the good people."

"I'm not a new recruit!" Cristen shouted after them. "I've already been through the Array. You want to throw me in the arena again?"

"I'm not leaving without him," Warren insisted, sitting on the floor defiantly.

"I'll get you home tonight like I promised," the warden said. "But only you. My hands are tied."

"Your hands are going to be tied, alright," Warren threatened, voice quivering. "Pa will see to it personally."

"Do your parents even know you're friends with one of them? Come on, let's go," the warden ordered, waiting impatiently for Warren to rise.

Cristen gestured for Warren to go, knowing at least his friend was safe. Warren finally stood and allowed the warden to corral him out the door. Cristen then noticed his fellow inmates watching everything.

The boy with short-cropped hair spoke up, across and over from Cristen. "We need to talk with that council right away," he said to Cristen. We aren't water dreamers, but no one believes us. By the way, I'm Cooper."

The girl past Cooper said, "Me too. I'm Rosie. My family probably assumes I got kidnapped. Or worse." She sounded near tears. "I've been so worried, but why won't anyone help me find them?"

Cristen sighed, empathizing with their distress. Yet, did they really entertain the notion that they all suffered the same memory loss from an accident? "But you all woke up in the sea, I'm guessing," he said, his tone attempting sympathy while gently nudging them toward acceptance.

An awkward silence followed as they exchanged uneasy looks.

Cristen noticed movement in the corner cell adjacent to his. A waif of a girl with brown skin lay curled up on the strewn hay, barely visible. She lay awake but seemed listless in her own world. She didn't wear red prisoner garb but a knee-length tunic, her bare legs and calloused feet exposed. Her arms looked chafed, and her long black hair somewhat matted.

"That's Mirabel," someone offered. "She doesn't talk."

Cristen nodded, revising his count to five captives, not four.

He turned back to the others. "Don't worry about the sea. It doesn't mean it birthed you. It's all a lie."

"I knew it!" Cooper nearly shouted. "Tell us what you know."

"Tell that to the warden," the inmate farthest down the block spoke up with an attitude. When he stood, Cristen recognized him as the dreamer from the prison wagon the night he found Hanna.

"What's your name? I'm Cristen," he offered, hoping to make amends, assuming the boy remembered him.

"Benedict," he answered. "But tell anyone it's a lie, and they laugh in your face."

"Because they don't understand," Cristen said. "They don't want to."

"There has to be a way to get them to listen to us," said Cooper. "If we can just get in front of that council."

"Unfortunately, even the council will say we come from the sea, but I'm telling you—we came from our parents first. We dream of home because we have homes. We're called dreamers because of those dreams."

The others glanced around at each other, looking miserable but nodding like things finally made sense.

"We all thought we were going crazy," said the girl down the row across from Benedict.

"That's Ann," Rosie informed Cristen.

Cristen couldn't see much of Ann through all the bars except for her thick, dark hair. "That's how they win," he said. "We quickly doubt ourselves and our sanity."

"How can you possibly know about having parents?" Benedict challenged.

Cristen opened his mouth, about to explain his dream about Lord Whitaker's warning, but shut it again. How could he convince them of the truth of his dreams by using another dream for evidence, even though he could practically feel Lord Whitaker's hand still on his arm? "I just know," he said, making Benedict eye him suspiciously.

"So you've all been dreaming?" Cristen asked, redirecting the conversation.

"Twice now," said Cooper. "That's how I learned I couldn't be one of them dreamers. Or...so I thought. Her too," he said, motioning to Ann. "She's been dreaming a lot."

"Like I said, I thought I was losing my mind," Ann said. She shifted forward into Cristen's view. "My father got killed in battle. My mother raised three of us with our grandparents' help. She needs me, so why am I so far from home?"

"I wish I could tell you," said Cristen sadly. He noticed Mirabel watching him now with mournful dark brown eyes.

"What about the birds?" asked Rosie. "Why do they follow us?"

Cristen hesitated, not wanting to explain about the wizard's parchment. "They're just birds. Eventually, they'll leave you alone," he said, parroting Damon's words. He felt guilty dismissing his faithful little friend so easily. With a resigned sigh, he conceded, "If you care for them, they'll stick around." He nodded toward the barred window. "A few are waiting outside, by the way, including a pretty white one."

"Not mine," said Benedict coldly. Rosie shrugged, and neither did the others know about the white bird.

Cristen looked down at Mirabel, but she quickly averted her gaze. A moment later, a tear trailed down her cheek, leaving a streak. "It's yours," Cristen said gently. "You chased it off before you understood. Well, I promise...it's not too late."

She hid her face in her hands and turned away from them, shoulders quaking with quiet sobs.

Removing the attention from Mirabel, Rosie said, "The warden said there's help for us in the mountains."

Cristen couldn't restrain a bitter laugh. "Sure, if you like hostile talking dragons." His response caused a ripple of murmurs.

"What...what are you saying?" Cooper demanded.

Cristen shrugged. "Just that Burning Mountain is her lair. If you want eternal captivity, then be my guest."

Benedict laughed scornfully. "We'd see dragons flying around if that nonsense was true."

Cristen didn't reply. He didn't care if they believed him.

"But we've all witnessed the magic of our water," Ann reasoned. "So why doubt his talking dragon?"

Cristen gave her an appreciative smile. "You have yours then?"

"We all have them," she nodded. "They're being kept safe for us in the back room."

"Safe?" Cristen scowled. "You mean they were stolen from you." Cristen wanted to scream. Did Sefilar have her feelers in this place too? "Did you ask why? What could they possibly need them for?"

"We get them back after the Array," Cooper said. "It's okay. They bring us water whenever we ask."

Cristen shook his head in disgust. "None of this is remotely okay. There's no justice or mercy anywhere." His anger swelled as he thought of Harmony's injustices, which felt just as confining as Burning Mountain at times. He couldn't wait to leave this place behind.

Outside the small window, the light steadily faded, and the warden hadn't returned to light candles in the dimming cell block. A bleak mood settled over the group, and no one spoke again. One by one, they lay on their hay beds and fell asleep.

Sometime in the depth of night, the heavy entrance door creaked open. Cristen's inmates stirred around him.

"This one's not so bad," Cooper whispered as a new warden approached them carrying a lantern. "Strange, though. None of them are usually here at night.

"Rise and shine! It's your lucky day," the warden bellowed.

34

The warden banged his baton loudly against the cell bars, the deafening racket continuing down the entire row. At the far wall, he turned to face them, slipping the baton back into its loop. "Listen up. I'll release you one by one. You'll promptly exit the building to your waiting driver," he instructed.

Cristen stood, uneasy about this unexpected change.

"You'll be taken north to the quarry where the road ends," the warden continued. "From there, you will continue on foot toward the mountain range. Return to Harmony, and you'll live out your days here in this picturesque paradise of gray and steel."

"What's happening?" Cristen asked. "We're supposed to stay until the Array." As much as he despised the spectacle they termed the Array, banishing the others to Burning

Mountain without choice seemed outrageous. They needed time and information to decide their fate.

"Someone has paid for your early release, so I suspect the games will have to go on without you. Questions? Alright, then. Any funny business, and you'll wish you still swam with the sharks." He retrieved a key ring from his belt and unlocked Benedict's cell.

"Who paid?" Cristen demanded.

"I need my water bag," Benedict interjected, resisting the warden's hold on him.

"Unfortunately, that key rests with the warden you scared off," the warden said flippantly.

"I said, I need my water!" Benedict repeated emphatically.

Cristen tried again, "Who wanted us gone?" He suspected Warren's father, not knowing what Warren possibly told him, but why the drastic response?

The warden ignored them both, forcefully escorting Benedict down the aisle. Before reaching the end of the cell block, Cristen's hunter, Mick, swaggered in.

"Where's your partner in crime?" the warden asked him.

"I operate solo now," Mick stated. "Chet's a hothead."

"I won't leave without my water," Benedict insisted as he grabbed hold of one of the bars to Warren's corner cell.

Mick approached the warden and Benedict directly. Together, they seized Benedict's arms and tied his hands behind his back.

"Consider that your first and final warning," the warden threatened.

"Landed another feisty one, I see," Mick said with a chuckle.

"Too bad he won't make it to the Array," the warden said.

Cooper murmured to Cristen, "I take back what I said. He's worse than the other one."

"No sweat off my back," Mick said. "As long as my pockets are lined with silver, I don't care what happens to them."

"Can't say I'm sorry this batch is going," the warden replied.

They carried on as if no one heard them. Noticing Cristen, Mick remarked snidely, "Well, well. The winner of the stallion—the dead stallion. Who has the last laugh now?"

Cristen glared after Mick as Mick dragged a struggling Benedict outside. The warden then moved to Mirabel's cell.

"Not her," Cristen said firmly. "She's not strong enough and won't make it out there alone."

"Not my problem," said the warden. "I just follow orders."

"At least give her back her water. You had no right taking it."

"I said I don't have the key and watch your attitude. Anyway, your kind are easier to handle without your brine."

So they knew the water offered dreamers something unique, even strengthening them. But if others tasted it and found it salty, how could Greta drink so much of it?

The warden slowly sank to his knees, head drooping drowsily. He sprawled across the floor, snoring loudly. Cooper laughed, finding the sight amusing. Cristen thought it strange too, until he realized they had entered the early morning hours when he believed Sefilar roamed free.

"They're all a bunch of drunks," Cooper said. "This isn't the first time."

"It's the witching hour," Cristen explained. "I've seen it plenty. People and animals fall asleep."

"I think I've heard of that," Ann said, rising to her feet. "When witches cast their spells."

"Or dragons," Cristen added. He observed the warden's prone form and contemplated how he might reach his keys.

"But he's the only one sleeping," Cooper pointed out.

"Us dreamers might be immune?" Rosie reasoned.

"What about the people outside?" asked Ann.

Cristen wondered the same thing. If those waiting for them also succumbed, Cristen and his fellow inmates would have about an hour before the effect wore off. But first, they needed the key—easier said than done.

The warden had collapsed nearest Cristen's cell, but only his head lay within reach, with little hair for grasping. His chin proved more accessible, so holding his head and prickly chin, Cristen pulled at him, dragging his heavy frame an inch closer.

"You're going to take off his head," said Ann.

"Got another idea?" Cristen asked, grunting with effort.

Mirabel surprised them, gingerly crawling from her hay nest to the bars. Reaching through with her bird-like legs, she managed to snag the warden's sleeve between her toes. The rest watched in fascination as she struggled to tug the arm closer until she finally grabbed it. Rosie cheered excitedly.

"You've got this, Mirabel!" Cooper urged.

"Good girl, just a little more," Ann encouraged.

With great effort, Mirabel pulled the arm up and outward until Cristen could reach the hand. Her exertion left her glistening with sweat.

Cristen paused to meet her eyes, which now burned with fiery determination. He nodded gratefully. Bracing his feet against the bars, he dragged the warden until Mirabel reached his belt. She unclipped the key ring and passed it to Cristen through their shared bars. After reaching through to the outside lock and freeing himself, Cristen unlocked Mirabel's cell before releasing the others. The five hurriedly followed him toward the exit.

Under the moonlight, the escapees found a line of five prison carts right outside with sleeping drivers—two slumped in their seats, three on the ground after toppling off. Even the horses slept, one resting on its haunches. Mick and Benedict had already left.

"I'm out of here," Cooper announced, sprinting off with Ann and Rosie.

"You don't want to go with them?" Cristen asked Mirabel. She shrugged indifferently. Her petite frame made her seem no older than thirteen.

"Well, we need to find Benedict and free him," Cristen said. "He's trapped in his wagon somewhere along the road."

Mirabel nodded shyly.

"Can you ride?" Cristen asked her.

She shook her head no. Cristen took one of the horses, unhitching it from its cart. Once mounted, he extended an arm to Mirabel and pulled her up carefully behind him by her frail arms.

He took the road north at a swift lope, anxiously aware their magical reprieve wouldn't last. After a time, they needed to retrace their steps, knowing they should have passed the cart long ago. Eventually, Cristen spotted the cart over a rise, having passed it again. It had veered off the road into the trees.

Benedict seemed to be studying every inch of his portable cell, looking for weaknesses in its structure. Cristen observed from a distance, not daring to intervene as time must be nearly up. Within minutes, the cart lurched forward, found the road again, and disappeared into the night. Cristen breathed a sigh of relief at the close call. He felt guilty over failing to free Benedict again but refused to risk his and Mirabel's freedom for another's. He turned the horse around and set off for home.

The following morning, Cristen and Mirabel ate breakfast in silence. Painfully shy, Mirabel kept her eyes downcast, barely glancing up from her plate even when addressed. She ate delicately, not like someone missing days of food. Cristen had given up his bed to her like he'd done for Hanna.

"You saved us back at the sanitarium," Cristen said, not expecting a response. "And surprised us."

Mirabel's face flushed a little as she kept her eyes on her food.

"I Hope Benedict's alright. And the others...I wonder where they're at."

Mirabel lifted her gaze to glance at him before looking out the window.

"If they don't listen to my warning about the dragon scales, they might take the bait and head out to the mountains. Best not to mess with those things."

Unexpectedly, Mirabel drew a dragon scale from her pocket and placed it gingerly on the table.

"Oh. So you know already."

She returned her half-eaten bread to her plate and spoke softly. "The first one made me dream. I didn't like it and threw it away."

Cristen hadn't considered that acquiring his first scale must have triggered his first dreams of home.

"I found another one and wanted to see more, even though I didn't like touching it," she said.

"Once the dreaming starts, it continues," Cristen clarified. "You don't need the scales anymore."

She seemed to ponder this as she gazed thoughtfully at the scale, then brushed it off onto the floor. "How do I turn off the dreams, though?"

"Mirabel, they're not just dreams. They're real memories. You don't have to be afraid to love them anymore."

"Maybe if you're not me," she said. She pulled her collar down, exposing a mottled bruise on her shoulder. "A gift from my father," she said, adjusting her clothes to hide the mark again. "I never doubted the dreams because of what he did to me."

Cristen sat stunned, struck by the revelation that the dreamed memories felt far from secure for some. He was glad she'd opened up to him to help him understand. His heart ached for Mirabel and the pain she had endured. He was glad she'd opened up to him, helping him understand her perspective and the weight she carried.

35

As Cristen and Mirabel walked down the street toward Warren's house, he ran out to meet them.

"You're out!" he shouted long before reaching them.

"Thanks to Mirabel," Cristen called back.

Warren fell in step beside Cristen as they continued walking.

"This is Warren," Cristen introduced. "Warren, meet Mirabel."

"Hi there, I'm Warren," Warren said with a mischievous grin.

Cristen shook his head. "Remember the part where I introduced you?"

Mirabel smiled shyly, the first glimpse of a smile Cristen had seen.

"I saw you at the sanitarium across from me," Warren said. "Anyway, wait until you guys see the skunk family I found. They're down past my house. Oh, and you can't be seen around here dressed in that filthy old thing," he said to Mirabel rather indelicately. "We'll raid Evelyn's closet for some options."

Mirabel glanced down self-consciously at her tattered tunic and bare feet, her cheeks flushing in embarrassment.

"Actually," Cristen redirected, "I wanted to ask if your folks know of an orphanage around here, maybe at King's Crossing? We need to find Mirabel a proper place to stay."

"An orphanage just for water dreamers?" Warren asked obliviously.

"I wish," Cristen mused. Harmony could greatly benefit from such a place. "We were hoping," he clarified carefully, "that you wouldn't mention to anyone that she's a dreamer. At least not until we get things sorted out."

"Sure, okay. But why'd they set you free already?"

"We didn't exactly get set free. We got ahold of the warden's key." Cristen paused before asking, "What exactly did you tell your father when the warden brought you home? A bunch of drivers came to haul us away."

"My pa? I didn't say nothin' to him."

"Your mother then? You must have mentioned something."

"I told the warden I'd let him off easy for being so nice to me along the way. I couldn't have an officer showing up at my house with me, now could I? Pa would be mortified if the neighbors saw that spectacle.

"So you were just going to leave me there to rot?" Cristen joked wryly.

"I was brewing a rescue plan, I swear! But it got complicated real fast. Doozy, was I glad to see you strolling up the lane."

Cristen studied Warren's guileless face. "So you said nothing to anyone about the sanitarium?"

"Not a soul. Well, except for Damon, I guess. But he's already wise to your secret."

Cristen stopped short. "You talked to Damon?" How did Warren not think it relevant?

Warren shrugged. "We passed him on the road. The warden bragged about capturing the infamous water dreamer who stole the stallion from Damon, its rightful winner. I told him you and Damon were brothers, so it didn't matter. But Damon said if I'm talking, I'm lying. That's when they went off to talk privately."

The revelation felt like a dagger to Cristen's heart all over again. So Damon orchestrated everything to haul away the dreamers, fully aware that Cristen accompanied them. He shouldn't be surprised by now, yet he refused to give up on his estranged brother. Damon had to come around eventually. Cristen longed for the old Damon, the one he'd come to know and love through his dreams and their time together at Burning Mountain. He wondered again if Warren knew more than all of them, that Hanna hadn't gone missing.

As they neared the house, Warren said, "We'll have to sneak around back since Ma's in bed with another headache. She'll raise the roof if she hears a peep."

Mirabel immediately offered, "We can come another day."

"She talks!" Warren exclaimed, eliciting a fresh blush from Mirabel.

Cristen hesitated, uneasy about disturbing Warren's unwell mother. But he also lacked any plan for Mirabel.

Warren led them around the neighborhood, where they hopped the fence to his backyard. His dog charged over, barking wildly until Warren raised a threatening fist. The chastened dog slunk away to his doghouse.

"This way," Warren whispered, cutting across the yard. "My room's real close."

They crept up the porch steps, entered the house, and skirted the dining table. Taking the few stairs up into a hallway, Warren opened a door. "Wait in my room. I'll be right back," he whispered and snuck further down the hall.

When they entered Warren's room, Mirabel cried out in distress and sank to her knees. Cristen felt it too. He helped

Mirabel back to her feet and into the hall, closing the door behind him.

"He's got dragon scales," he explained with annoyance. "You okay?"

Catching her breath, Mirabel nodded.

Warren hurried back. "I said keep quiet!" he whisper-shouted.

"Why do you have dragon scales in your room?" Cristen demanded, incensed by the discovery.

"What're you talking about? Where would I get those things?" Warren scoffed. "Pa would kill me. He wants nothing to do with them."

"Even if we can't see them, we can sometimes feel them," Cristen said. "So I know they're in there." After being exposed to them numerous times, Cristen found the effects mild, yet Mirabel's reaction suggested the presence of an excessive amount.

Puzzled, Warren opened the door, stepped into his room, and glanced around. "Only possible place is the attic," he said.

Cristen stepped cautiously back inside with him, peering upward while Mirabel hovered nervously in the hall.

"Then we have to go straight to Evelyn's room," Warren said. "Stay behind me until I say the coast is clear."

The three raced down the hallway and descended more stairs opposite. They hurried through the main living quarters and into another hallway. Warren led them to a bedroom, ushering them inside before shutting the door. Cristen mentally scanned for scales but detected nothing. Together, they wedged a chair under the doorknob, barricading themselves inside.

Warren went straight to the wardrobe, opened the doors wide, and stared blankly at the assortment of dresses and tunics. "I don't know nothin' about girl stuff," he confessed. He glanced helplessly at Cristen.

"Don't look at me," Cristen said, equally at a loss.

"Your mother won't mind?" Mirabel asked quietly.

"Take whatever you want," Warren said. "Just say it's a loan for your auntie's birthday celebration if we get caught, then forget to return it."

Mirabel selected a simple dress-length tunic from the back and glanced uncertainly at Cristen again. Taking the hint, Warren and Cristen removed the chair and stepped back into the hallway to allow her privacy.

"Heard anything about Hanna yet?" Cristen asked Warren.

"They don't tell me squat," Warren said, unconcerned.

A door creaked from somewhere, freezing them in place.

"Time to fly," Warren breathed.

"We can't ditch Mirabel," Cristen whispered.

"Ma hates visitors, especially when she's ill." Warren glanced behind him toward another door. "The closet!"

Too late. Mrs. Myers shuffled around the corner in slippers, looking haggard with dark circles beneath her eyes. Black hair stuck out from its hair wrap. She barely glanced at Cristen, zeroing in on her son. "Warren?"

"Ma!" Warren yelped in surprise.

As Hanna's door started to open, Warren grabbed the knob to keep it shut. Adopting an unnaturally chipper tone, Warren prattled, "Ma, you're looking so refreshed! Why, you must be feeling miles better."

Snorting in disbelief, Mrs. Myers muscled past him and forced open the door. "Good heavens, child," she exclaimed at the sight of Mirabel. "Does your mother not feed you?"

"Ma, we were...we just needed to..."

Mrs. Myers barreled on, "What does she have to say for such neglect?"

"Ma'am, we'll just be going," Cristen said, trying to intervene.

"Certainly not. Give me your address at once," she demanded of Mirabel. "I intend to set her straight immediately."

Mirabel watched Cristen in helpless dismay, her cheeks growing rosier by the moment.

"Ma, she's an orphan!" Warren blurted out.

Cristen stared at Warren in shock over the hasty fabrication. But then again, it was close enough.

Collecting herself, Mrs. Myers replied mildly, "Please accept my apologies, dear. Still, we must get some nourishment in you, I insist."

Warren seized the idea. "Your biscuits, Ma! Those will plump her right up."

"Precisely right, dear," she replied approvingly, tired face lighting up. "I'll start a fresh batch this instant."

"We have a quick errand first," Warren said, eyeing Cristen as if looking for help escaping. "We'll be back when they're hot and ready."

"Certainly not," Mrs. Myers said. "I'll not chance losing sight of this child again. She'll stay put until I speak with her caregivers." She led Mirabel over to the bed. "You'll rest here in Hanna's room until your health returns," she decreed, briskly turning down the quilt and urging Mirabel in.

Mirabel watched Cristen helplessly, but to Cristen, this seemed like an extraordinary solution to his dilemma. Mirabel would have a place to stay, at least until they learned of her identity and reported or kicked her out. Or until Hanna returned home.

36

Warren arrived at Cristen's house, lugging a bulging pillowcase full of dragon scales.

"Where'd you find them?" Cristen asked in surprise.

"In my room, like you said," Warren reported. "Not the attic, though. I used Pa's crowbar to rip up some floorboards and found the crawlspace stuffed with them. I'd never seen one before, but I knew it had to be them. So, I busted out more boards to climb inside. This isn't even half of them. We've hit the motherlode!"

"How did scales end up in your room? Did you ask your father about it?"

"Are you nuts? He'll think I planted them myself. I figured you'd be thrilled. With this big a stash, we can buy whatever we want."

Cristen shook his head. "They're hazardous for us dreamers." Mirabel didn't like them now, but she could easily change her mind if Sefilar's incessant call got to her. If he couldn't save Hanna from losing her way, he could at least try to protect Mirabel. "We have to get rid of them," he insisted.

"Get rid of them? What a waste," Warren grumbled.

"It's either the scales or us," Cristen said firmly. "You can't have both because I have to keep me and Mirabel safe."

"Okay, fine," Warren conceded. "We can bury them out in the field behind my place."

But Cristen didn't trust Warren not to dig them up again later. He wanted the scales permanently destroyed before they fell into the wrong hands. "We need to incinerate them," he proposed.

"Pa keeps the fire kit locked up tight."

No surprise there. "Don't worry, I have something better." Cristen would use his orb to torch every last scale. "How many pillowcases can you get?"

"Not *that* many!" Warren said as if Cristen had asked an unreasonable question. "But Pa gets free potato sacks from Mr. Creed at the general store. As many as we want."

"In Mulberry?"

Warren nodded. "Next to the gift shop."

"Alright, we can start with the scales you brought. Nice work finding them." Cristen retrieved his orb from a drawer.

Settled in the backyard, Cristen directed the orb's beam at the bulging pillowcase. Although the beam itself couldn't be seen in the bright daylight, the point where it touched the fabric glowed intensely. As Cristen tightened the focus, the beam's end grew brighter until it was as brilliant as the sun, making them squint. The concentrated light instantly seared a hole through the fabric, igniting the entire sack in seconds—but only briefly. The freed dragon scales cascaded out as the pillowcase burned away, smothering the remaining embers beneath their shimmering mass.

Cristen tried again, training the beam on a single scale. Yet no matter how long he held the light fixed on any given spot, it refused to catch fire. It neither burned nor melted under the intensely focused heat. Cristen stared, dumbfounded by their indestructible nature. He could almost hear the dragon's mocking laughter.

***

"My arms are going to fall off," Warren groaned as they neared his house

"Then why did we get so many?" Cristen asked, bearing the brunt of the heavy stack of a hundred potato sacks they had split between them.

"You'll see."

After dropping most of their load on the porch, they carried the rest to Warren's room. Cristen's jaw dropped at the sight. Dragon scales were strewn everywhere amidst torn-up floorboards scattered haphazardly around the room and nails jutting up dangerously. Cristen stepped over a board to peer into the gaping crawlspace and couldn't believe the sheer volume of scales filling it. Warren hadn't exaggerated.

"I guess we should get busy then," Cristen said with a sigh, bracing himself for the impact.

"Hopefully before Pa gets home," Warren said. "He thinks they're vulgar."

Cristen cautiously slipped into the crawlspace with a sack, while Warren, with all the finesse of a charging rhinoceros, cannonballed in, narrowly missing Cristen. Cristen waded through dragon scales up to his knees while Warren, unfazed, pretended to do the breaststroke through the sea of scales. Being surrounded by so many scales didn't bother him as much as he'd feared. However, their overwhelming presence still made him uneasy as he began filling his sack.

Warren finally found his footing and turned to watch Cristen for a moment. "I need to show you something first," he announced before climbing back out of the crawlspace and exiting the room.

"Now?" Cristen asked. He hoped Warren didn't expect him to do all the work. Puzzled, he followed him down the hall to the master suite by the stairs. He waited uncertainly in the doorway as Warren grabbed a framed child's drawing from his parents' bureau.

"Notice anything missing here?" Warren asked him.

"Should we be in there?" Cristen asked, looking over his shoulder before entering.

Warren met him halfway to show him the crayon portrait of a family.

"You with your parents?"

"Bingo. When I was a kid. Where's Evelyn? She's older." Warren tapped the blank space insistently.

"It's just a drawing," Cristen dismissed. He felt increasingly unsettled that he could still feel the effects of the scales from this far away. "I need some air." But he felt fine the moment he reentered the hallway. He spun to face Warren.

"What kid doesn't include their whole family?" Warren argued. "It's proof she's not my sister."

"That's ridiculous," Cristen countered, unwilling to get into it just then. "But bad news...your room's not the only one," he revealed.

Warren's brow furrowed. "Huh?"

"We can't keep it from your parents anymore. Their room is compromised too." Cristen's gaze dropped to the floor in front of the queen-size bed.

Warren's eyes widened in realization. He returned the picture, ran to his room, and returned with the crowbar and hammer.

"We can't," Cristen warned. "They have to be involved, or it's vandalism."

"So is what I did to the carriage. But sometimes you gotta do what you gotta do."

"What did you do to the carriage?" Cristen asked, afraid of the answer.

But Warren had already gone to work, drowning out his question. With his sharp crowbar claw, he banged the floor, splintering the first board. Once he had created enough space, he twisted the crowbar and popped the board out. They sank to their knees at the first glimmer of dragon scales. The cache looked as deep as Warren's, but the crawlspace seemed double the length.

Cristen jolted when a holler disrupted them from behind, sending his heart racing when he saw Warren's father. He jumped to his feet, ready to apologize.

"What in the name of a thousand fiery stars are you doing?"

"Why, Pa, why?" Warren cried melodramatically, still on his knees. "You, of all people."

"What are you going on about? Out of here at once."

"This!" Warren swept his arm across the broken floor, directing his pa to see. "You've done this," he accused.

Mr. Myers paused in confusion, then hurried over. He knelt and gasped at what he witnessed. "I am not responsible for this," he insisted. "How is it even possible?"

"Who else, Pa?" Warren cried. "Ma could never."

"And neither could I," said Mr. Myers. "I despise them."

"But I don't understand," Warren said. "They're in my floor too."

"You cannot be serious," said Mr. Myers, getting back on his feet. "I will get to the bottom of this immediately. You swear you didn't plant these foul objects yourself?" he asked Cristen severely.

"No sir, I swear!" Cristen said vehemently, holding his hands in surrender. "We were trying to remove them."

"It wasn't him, Pa, honest!" Warren insisted.

Mr. Myers raked a hand through his hair in agitation. "It will take far too long. What will your mother say? She will assume my guilt. It will seem the worst hypocrisy! I won't stand to be so maligned. Cursed things, shrouded in secrecy. What are they? Whence do they come? Some say remnants of fallen stars. Others claim they spawn from water dreamers. They infect a home, and only misfortune follows. Someone means us grievous harm, mark my words. We will surely pay for this."

His eyes widened with greater horror. "What would the council say? To think I've hoarded *anything* would be scandalous, never mind dragon scales." He seemed on the verge of collapse.

"Don't worry, Pa. The three of us can banish them quick before Ma finds out," Warren said reassuringly.

Mr. Myers wrung his hands. "There's not a moment to waste. We'll hide them in the carriage for now. Under cover of night, I'll spirit them away so no busybody is the wiser."

The three worked tirelessly through the afternoon, stuffing sack after sack and shuttling them out to the carriage house. Each time Mrs. Myers wearily visited the kitchen, they froze, but she seemed to intentionally ignore their suspicious activities as they trooped in and out the back door. The unspoken matter was apparently too much for her sensibilities to bear.

They filled seventy-nine sacks to bulging, cramming about half into the carriage. With their energy spent, the trio collapsed after depositing the last sack outside. Come nightfall, Mr. Myers would ferry them to a remote mine shaft and discard them into the depths.

37

Days later, Cristen sat on the back porch steps, stabbing away in frustration at a dragon scale with the sharp tip of his pocketknife.

"Thought you were sick," Cristen remarked when he spotted Warren rounding the corner of his house.

"I was. For a few days," Warren said with a casual shrug.

He watched with curiosity as Cristen hacked away at the stubborn scale. Each time he hit the thing, it simply flattened temporarily before popping right back into shape, completely unharmed. Every destructive effort failed miserably.

"Well, you've been missing all the drama at my place," Warren commented after a minute. "Pa's gone completely bonkers. And Ma too."

Cristen gave an indifferent shrug in reply, not really listening. In a fit of anger, he aimed a particularly vicious stab with the knife, nearly impaling Warren's hand resting on the porch step.

"Whoa, watch it, Buster!" Warren exclaimed, snatching his hand away.

Utterly fed up, Cristen hurled the useless knife at a nearby tree. It struck, quivering in the bark.

"Doozy, someone woke up on the wrong side of the bed," Warren remarked warily.

"Got any acid at your house?" Cristen asked abruptly.

"Acid?" Warren repeated in surprise. "Thought we retired from Operation Sabotage."

Cristen held up the pristine dragon scale. "Look. Not even a mark."

Warren took it from him, gnawed on its edge, and handed it back. "Eh, who cares? They all end up down the mine shaft anyway. Pa took them all away before he started losing it. He hasn't gone to work in days. He sleeps or mopes around, mumbling nonsense to himself. At least he's not nagging, 'Mind your mother,' every five minutes."

Cristen glowered at the scale in his hand, wracking his brain to think of anything that might damage it.

"Ma's even worse," Warren continued. "I tell you, things are seriously off there. She cries 'woe is me' all day long. At night, she reads bedtime stories and sings lullabies."

Cristen raised an eyebrow at Warren, finally paying attention. "To you?"

"No, Mirabel. Can you believe it? I can't take it anymore. Anyway, let's go find some acid," he said as if it were the next logical thing to say. We can check the mercantile at King's Crossing. They have everything."

***

The general store in King's Crossing didn't sell acid. Furthermore, the shopkeeper told them he'd never give any to Warren if they did carry it.

"My pa will be having words with you, mister," Warren threatened indignantly. "He's on the Council, you know."

"I'm well aware," said the shopkeeper. "I know your pa, and he'll be shaking my hand for saving the town."

Stepping back onto the busy boardwalk, Cristen teased, "Sounds like your reputation precedes you around here."

"I've never laid eyes on him in my life!" Warren objected hotly.

"My point exactly," Cristen chuckled. "But don't worry, you're still young. It's not too late for you."

Pushing through the foot traffic, a girl about Cristen's age squeezed between him and a young couple with a baby pram. "Pardon me," she murmured, glancing at Cristen. She quickly returned as Cristen and Warren continued on their way. "Excuse me, but do I know you from somewhere?" she asked Cristen curiously.

Something about her red hair and freckled face did seem familiar, but Cristen couldn't place her.

"Maybe from boarding school?" she suggested uncertainly.

"I never went to..." Cristen trailed off mid-sentence, sudden recognition hitting him. He remembered their first encounter vividly as if it had happened yesterday. He had witnessed the result of her being shifted at Burning Mountain. With heightened emotion, she had explained to Cristen how her brother had suffered a terrible accident, delaying her return to boarding school. She'd grown a little taller since then, her vibrant hair longer, but he knew it was her.

His blood ran cold. She absolutely should not be here. "Caralee?" he rasped in dismay.

"That's right!" she said, flashing a friendly smile. "Sorry, my memory is clearly not as sharp as yours."

"Cristen," he responded distractedly, his mind racing. The idea that Sefilar brought her back to Harmony just as she did Hanna highly disturbed him. But it didn't make sense. Cristen had seen Sefilar take her northward at the time of her departure. Had it all been a ruse to deceive him?

Another chilling thought occurred to him. What if...what if the Oasis didn't exist at all? But without the northern sanctuary, what could the dragon possibly offer water dreamers besides replacing their identities with lies? Suddenly, the bigger picture clicked into place, the enormity of it all hitting Cristen like a sledgehammer.

If Sefilar were the wizard's sworn enemy, she only needed to prevent dreamers from ever learning of the wizard's existence. The cunning dragon foiled the wizard's plan with every dreamer she shifted, preventing them from experiencing his power. Even worse, they might remain forever lost in Harmony, unable to fulfill their quests as they made Harmony their permanent home. They would never return to their actual homes and families who loved them.

Sefilar's promises were merely a sham, her interference with the wizard's work malice of the worst kind. But why did the supposedly all-powerful wizard allow this mass deception to continue unchecked?

"I'm sorry...you're busy," Caralee said. "Maybe I'll see you around."

Distracted by his devastating epiphany, Warren waved goodbye for them as she left. As they continued along the boardwalk, Warren remarked, "When I'm older, I'm going to go about things differently to catch a girl. You don't have to worry about me asking for advice."

Cristen wondered how many other shifted dreamers Sefilar had returned over the years, now hiding in plain sight. "There's no Oasis," he muttered in a daze, half to himself.

"What's an oasis?" Warren asked.

"The dragon has taken over Harmony. She's a complete fraud." Cristen said.

"She is?"

"We don't stand a chance."

"We don't?"

"Anyone could be a water dreamer. Even you."

"I could?" Warren exclaimed excitedly as if he'd won a prize.

"Never mind, you're too young."

Warren's face fell into a disappointed scowl.

"But what about him?" Cristen said, indicating a man jumping from the back of a cart. "Or her?" he added, nodding toward a woman entering a nearby shop.

"Um, I'm starting to think you've gone a bit funny in the head like Ma and Pa," Warren said seriously. "Maybe it's something in the water."

"I mean...every single person could potentially be a shifted water dreamer," Cristen said, glancing around. "At least descended from one. I knew that girl. The dragon brings them right back to where they started after giving them a false identity. What if she's been doing it for hundreds of years? Or thousands?"

He could scarcely comprehend the staggering thought. It felt as if his whole world had turned upside down.

"Now that would be hilarious," Warren said.

Cristen turned on him in disbelief. "Why hilarious?" Nothing about this felt remotely funny. If true, it felt earth-shattering, overwhelming.

"Because regular folk despise water dreamers," Warren snickered. "They'd all be hating themselves."

The notion left Cristen astonished. Warren was right—the irony would be unbelievable. What if even Lora and her dreamer-hating father were dreamers, having originated elsewhere beyond the sea? Cristen shook his head, grappling with this line of thinking. He then remembered Sefilar's excuse for delivering Hanna back to Harmony. If someone bought and paid for her soul, it could only have been done by the dragon herself. In reality, Sefilar had bought the soul of every shifted dreamer.

The endless lies exhausted him. What he wouldn't give for a reprieve from everything, a chance to finally return home and leave the nightmare of Harmony behind forever. But any hopes of bringing Hanna back with him looked bleaker than ever, and he still fretted over her safety.

A thought occurred to him. "When's the wedding again?" he asked Warren.

"It was supposed to be in two days," Warren said. "But Ma never got an invitation, which was lucky for me. She'd force me to wear my straight jacket and drag me along."

The rapidly approaching date gave Cristen a fresh sense of dread. How could he possibly get through it—assuming Hanna showed up and the event still happened as planned? In truth, he had recently hoped that Hanna got cold feet and ran away. Unfortunately, it felt out of character for her to abandon everyone without explanation. He needed to get to the bottom of what happened. He didn't care if a search for her already failed. He planned to conduct his own investigation to track her down.

A window display of lace and silk caught his eye across the street, reminding him of the fabrics he'd seen draped across Hanna's bed until their disastrous prank ruined all of it. The sign above read "The Lace Factory: Tailoring to a T." Cristen pointed it out, and they crossed over to enter the cluttered little shop. The noisy clatter of sewing machines, operated by two women busily pumping their treadles, greeted them from the rear. The nearer one peered at Cristen over her spectacles when he cleared his throat to get their attention.

"Fresh client for you, Berta," she called over the din, and the other seamstress glanced up from her work.

"The date of your event, please?" Berta inquired, releasing her treadle.

"Oh, I just wanted to ask—" Cristen began before Warren cut him off.

Warren jumped in. "The wedding's in two days. He needs something for the Beacon Hill wedding."

Cristen scowled. He would never attend. He only wanted to ask if they'd recently sold fabric to a Hanna Myers.

"You might just need it if we're going to sneak you in," Warren whispered.

"We can't craft you anything in two days," Berta informed him bluntly.

"Don't you have anything already made that could be altered to fit properly?" Warren pushed.

The first seamstress laughed aloud. "Beacon Hill, Berta," she said with a knowing smirk to her companion.

"Secondhand castoffs won't do," Berta told Cristen patronizingly. "I'm afraid you're out of luck, young man. They'll never grant you entry at this late hour. Have you seen the bride's gown? Why did you delay so long?"

"Because he just got the invitation!" Warren said defensively. "It's his brother getting married, you see."

The two women exchanged surprised looks tinged with skepticism.

"And he's in love with the bride," Warren added.

Now, the women glanced between Warren and Cristen, wearing matching looks of horror and disapproval. Mortified, Cristen wanted to hide behind the bolts of fabric.

"I'm just concerned for her well-being," Cristen mumbled, his face burning. If I leave my contact information, could you please send word if you happen to see her?"

"No need, I can update you now," Berta replied crisply. "She'll be here early tomorrow morning for her final gown fitting. You can explain to her then why you won't be attending."

Cristen stared in surprise. "You mean she's been here recently?"

"A few days ago, yes. We hit a minor snag during that last session. Literally." She gave a small chuckle. "But nothing The Lace Factory can't handle. We always deliver quality Tailoring to a T."

"What about her being missing?" Cristen pressed, confused.

The seamstress waved a hand dismissively. "Of course, she's hard to pin down. What bride doesn't have endless errands to run?"

Cristen glanced at Warren.

"Told you she isn't lost," Warren muttered matter-of-factly.

Cristen fumed as he stalked out of the shop, Warren chasing after him. Could Damon have fabricated the missing person scenario only to keep Cristen away, even shutting down construction and putting the community on alert?

Cristen fumed as he stalked out of the shop, with Warren chasing him. He couldn't help but wonder if Damon had fabricated the entire story of Hanna's disappearance to keep him away from her. The idea that Damon would go to such extreme lengths, even shutting down construction and putting the community on alert, seemed outrageous.

It seemed that Damon felt no qualms about deceiving her parents either, perhaps given his knowledge that they and Hanna weren't actually related and that they held no real claim over her. Still, his extreme actions exposed a blatant disregard for others in general.

Cristen wondered what Hanna made of all this. She must have consented to remain hidden...unless Damon somehow forced her cooperation? But willingly visiting her dress fittings didn't imply coercion to Cristen. He needed to confront her directly and get the full story once and for all.

"I'm going to see Hanna," Cristen told Warren decisively.

"To ask about the late wedding invite?" Warren asked.

Cristen rolled his eyes. "You made that up. But what if I did confess my feelings, assuming I find her at Beacon Hill?"

"Well then, I'm definitely tagging along! Wouldn't miss that for the world."

"Why, so you can tell her for me?" Cristen didn't put it past him to take control of the situation.

"We have to make sure Damon's not around," Warren said, already strategizing. "Remind me why we didn't buy that telescope."

Cristen suppressed a groan. He needed to devise some excuse to ditch Warren. Cristen's risky visit would be challenging enough without the added hindrance of a rambunctious tagalong.

38

Cristen gaped at the monumental progress of Damon's grand building. The scaffolding and lumber framework had grown five full stories high, and the white bricks extended nearly halfway up, with a sprinkling of brown accent bricks throughout. The roof hadn't begun yet, but all the windows and doors seemed to be installed based on the openings. Although the crusty grounds still resembled the miserable quagmire from the day of Cristen's tragic loss of Sunfire, at least things had dried up.

However, he didn't come to admire the architecture. Cristen needed to speak with Hanna without Damon's meddling. He'd even left Moonshine in town so Damon wouldn't recognize them together. Dressed in nondescript clothing and a wide-brimmed hat obscuring his face, Cristen hoped to blend into the visitors wandering the site.

Cristen didn't spot Damon among the laborers and onlookers and hoped he was away on some errand. Skirting the east perimeter, he heard Damon's office door opening behind him—the same door he had entered previously. Damon's voice carried as he conversed with someone. Not daring to glance back, Cristen picked up his pace and slipped around the corner out of view.

Wanting to appear part of the wandering public, Cristen drifted closer to a middle-aged couple admiring the emerging grand façade ahead. He positioned them between himself and the corner where Damon might appear any second. With its grand arched entryway, this side of the mammoth structure looked shockingly imposing and stately. In comparison, Cristen's family manor would look humble and out of place.

"Imagine the view from up there," the man nearest Cristen remarked wistfully to his wife, both craning their necks to gaze at the upper floor windows. Cristen felt similarly awed by the dizzying height and expansive outlook such upper rooms would provide. One could view all of King's Crossing and beyond from that vantage. Cristen could never hope to compete with Damon's glory and wealth. He felt tiny in his shadow.

"No tours inside yet, ma'am," a guard apologized to a woman attempting to approach the entrance. Other visitors were likewise turned away.

Noticing a small side door tucked unobtrusively behind a ladder toward the far end, Cristen made his way over, pretending to admire the house. Once near the door, he checked to ensure no one, including the guard, was paying attention to him. He sidled into the narrow gap between the wall and scaffolding and slipped quickly through the plain door.

The vast interior opened to the sky, as the floors, like the roof, had yet to be tackled. Cristen carefully picked his way through the wood scraps and mortar littering the bare concrete floors. Reaching the far end of the space, he passed through another nondescript door, where a cheerful garden greeted him. Instead of finishing the concrete floor, they had planted grass and young trees, creating a courtyard—the future wedding venue.

"Pardon me, but this isn't open to the public." Cristen knew Hanna's voice immediately. He removed his hat and turned to find her cradling a tray of tiny potted plants, their stems topped with new pink buds. She never looked so beautiful, even with rich soil smudged across one cheek. Her lavender eyes sparkled like amethysts in the dappled sunlight. Barefoot in the grass, she wore a belted white tunic and gray leggings, her hair tied up with a gold and red scarf. Every emotion Cristen ever felt for her flooded back full force as if they'd never been apart.

"Oh, it's you," she said in surprise. "You came to the house before. You thought I was...someone else."

Cristen remembered that painful morning when she became Evelyn like it was yesterday. "It was a...very confusing day. Pretty flowers," he said, though he meant the compliment for her.

Glancing down, she shrugged. "I suppose. I couldn't find the tulips I wanted, but these will do. The nursery didn't know about tulips, if you can believe it."

It didn't surprise Cristen to learn tulips didn't exist here. The climate stayed too warm. Yet somehow, the memory of her gardener father and his prized tulips crossed over with her. "The gardener for my father's estate knows his tulips," he hinted. "They're displayed at celebrations a lot."

"Are there any guards out there?" Hanna asked as she glanced at the door, seemingly wondering how he managed to enter undetected. She set the plant tray on a decorative iron table. "Are you touring the site?"

A tour? Was she completely oblivious then to recent events? "Don't you know people are looking for you?" Cristen asked, unable to completely mask his frustration.

Hanna blinked in surprise. "Why would you know that?"

"I'm friends with Warren."

Hanna looked amused and baffled, a familiar expression that made his heart flutter. "Warren...my brother Warren?"

Cristen nodded. "Your parents are worried about you."

With a weary sigh, Hanna turned away, busying herself with picking off the dead parts of the plants. "It's complicated. They don't know that I know stuff. They're not good for me right now."

Cristen's frustration mounted. "So you staged your disappearance?"

Hanna glared at him, offended. "I didn't have a choice after my pa..." She trailed off evasively before adding more firmly, "Either way, it's really not your concern. Is there something else? I should get these planted." She picked up the tray.

"You don't think they deserve to know?" Cristen asked.

The distant sound of a closing door drew Hanna's gaze in its direction.

"Damon put it into your head, didn't he? He's keeping you isolated here."

"I have my freedom!" she argued defensively.

"Do you?" Cristen challenged. The mere thought of Damon exerting any control over her put him on edge. Even if she agreed to the scheme, given Damon's treatment of *him*, did she truly know the man she'd pledged her life to?

"I need to ask you to leave. I'm not sure how you bypassed the guards," She said, shaking her head as she headed toward the inside door Cristen had entered.

"You don't need to go," Cristen said. "I only want you to know one thing. I came to your house to see *you* that day. I was never confused. I knew exactly who you were."

Hanna paused for a moment before turning back to face him.

Having caught her attention, Cristen pressed, "Damon swore I would never lay eyes on you again."

"What are you doing?" Hanna cried.

It pained Cristen to witness her distress, but she needed to hear the truth. "What has he told you about your parents? Are you sure it's true?"

"How do I even respond to that?" she said. "Stop acting like you know what's going on."

"I know more than you think," Cristen said.

"He's done nothing but treat me like royalty," Hanna said. "And since you seem to know so much, you might have heard the council is questioning our new home. My father's leading the charge, if you can believe it. They say the manor is unlawful and should be destroyed. Can you imagine, after everything Damon has sacrificed? There, you have your answers. Now please go," she said, stepping aside to clear his path.

Cristen heard nothing of the sort, though he could easily verify it. He stepped hesitantly past her with a resigned sigh to take his leave. But suddenly, he realized this was their final goodbye. He had nothing left to lose by telling her everything, so he pivoted to face her.

Feeling emboldened, he began, "You have no reason to believe anything I say. But humor me one last time, and you'll never see me again. I only want you to be happy. It's all I've ever wanted, even though I thought I would be a part of that happiness." He continued even as she stared at him in disbelief. "I'm a water dreamer, " he confessed. "And so is Damon."

"Ridiculous," she breathed, crossing her arms over her chest.

"I'm guessing you've never met his parents."

"Of course not. They died years ago. How can you be so insensitive?"

Cristen shook his head, keeping his gaze fixed on hers. "It's because here in Harmony, they don't exist. If you're brave enough to consider it, you're a dreamer too, Hanna."

She gasped. "I'm Evelyn, and how dare you!" she cried, utterly offended.

"It's the truth," Cristen insisted gently. "It's just not what everyone thinks. We lived before we came from the sea. Also, Damon is...is my brother." His voice quivered with emotion, everything getting to him. "You were meant to be mine, and he knows it."

Utter shock rooted her in place, tanned cheeks flushing crimson.

Cristen continued quickly, "I learned from a dragon that I'm here on some mission. Maybe we all are. You and I flew across Harmony on that dragon, where she delivered you to a new family after erasing your memories."

"Well, that certainly clarifies everything," Hanna said, though her troubling thoughts seemed to seep through her sarcastic words.

"You, of all people. It was the worst day of my life." Cristen paused to watch her looking so vulnerable, feeling the pain of never seeing her again. He nodded, understanding her refusal to believe, but he wasn't finished.

"The dragon became dangerous when I opposed her schemes and wanted out. Then she wanted you because of me and changed you from Hanna to Evelyn. Damon also wishes me harm. They both want me out of the picture, and I guess you do too now."

It dawned on Cristen then that forsaking his quest and leaving Harmony prematurely would only hand Sefilar the same victory she sought by shifting him. By ignoring the wizard, he was only serving the dragon since that's exactly what she wanted. He still didn't know much about his purpose here, but the stark truth provided reason enough to stay.

He swallowed a lump in his throat as tears stung his eyes. After today, he saw only one way forward. "There's a wizard," he confessed. "He gave me a home and feeds me—every day. Ask Warren about my magical house sometime. Even after all the wizard does for me, I turned away from him because he asked the impossible of me. But with you lost to me now, he's all I have left. My mission is all I have to live for. Or die for, if necessary." Cristen wiped the wetness from his eyes with a sleeve. "I'm ready to answer the call."

Hanna shook her head in utter disbelief.

It was time for Cristen to look past his fears and face his destiny. He now knew he couldn't triumph over Harmony without the master's help, nor did he want to. Only the master had remained faithful all this time, never letting him down. He only needed to lose everything to finally understand.

"Bye, Hanna," Cristen said. He walked away, leaving her speechless in the garden.

39

The roar of rushing water reached Cristen's ears, and moisture had already collected on him and Moonshine before they cleared the last of the trees. His heart dropped when the chasm and suspension bridge stretched before him in the waning light. Moonshine grew restless, so Cristen dismounted and let him go.

Again, fear and doubt made him wonder if he could do this. Coming so late in the day might have been a mistake, making things feel more difficult, but he'd come immediately once he'd made up his mind.

Approaching the bridge and precipice, he peered over to glimpse the distant river and shuddered. Overcome with vertigo, he grabbed the cable and closed his eyes until the feeling passed. Gripping both handrails, he stepped carefully out onto the bridge's slippery planks and forced himself forward just far enough to keep earth beneath his feet.

Returning to solid ground, Cristen settled on the grass to think, parchment in hand. The wizard felt worlds away. Could a simple written apology ever make amends? Would the master even acknowledge him still? He took a stiff blade of tall grass as his quill, but doubt paralyzed him. His thoughts drifted again to Hanna with her flowers, and a new idea came to him instead of an apology. He scratched a few lines to make sure the parchment still worked. When the lines of light appeared and faded under the shadow of his hand, he carefully wrote:

Wizard

It didn't feel right anymore. He let the word fade and began again.

Master
Can you locate a pink tulip to send to Hanna?

He smiled wistfully, imagining her delight at such a mysterious gift. But the words faded unanswered, his message unreceived. Cristen crumpled the parchment in his fist. Resting his head in his hands, despair threatened to overwhelm him. Perhaps it was too late already.

"No!" he shouted, jumping to his feet. "Where are you?" he said wildly toward the darkening sky. "It's my destiny, and I'm here to claim it! I'll jump with or without your blessing!" A lone pigeon's silhouette circled overhead, and Cristen laughed with relief, feeling overwhelmingly seen by the wizard. He sat to scratch out a new message:

Master,
Will you command me again? I am yours.

After his bird winged away with the parchment, Cristen let out a whoop that echoed throughout the chasm—the master hadn't forgotten him! The return message read:

You know what you must do.
I am here.

Cristen knew he must take this chance to prove himself to the wizard no matter the cost, though he couldn't shake the feeling of nausea. After removing his boots, he stepped onto the bridge again. Taking a deep breath, he started across the slippery planks, his heart nearly beating out of his chest. His bird did not accompany him this time. Step by careful step, he reached midway over the churning abyss, the bridge moving up and down in slow waves from the updraft of the raging rapids.

Pausing, Cristen drank in the magnificent vista surrounding him. He felt infinitesimal poised at the heart of this ancient yawning chasm. Peering over the edge, he cautiously eyed the giant boulders disrupting the river's flow. He could scarcely believe what he was about to do. At that moment, he realized that this act of submission tested the wizard as much as the wizard was testing him. Without intervention, Cristen would never survive the fall.

Forcing a leg over the railing, he watched in awe as the water directly beneath him suddenly churned more violently, frothing in rebellion against the surrounding tumult. The chaotic surface fought to redirect itself, heaving into a tremendous whirlpool nearly half the river's width. The swirling vortex gradually calmed, though still spinning with great force. The river waters divided to rush past on either side, crashing and foaming against the rocky walls.

"I love you, Hanna," Cristen whispered. With her sweet face filling his mind, he leaned forward against the railing and lifted his other leg up and over. Eyes closed, he pushed off from the bridge into space.

The alarming freefall caused his whole body to tense up with his breath caught in his throat. Braving a glimpse downward, he snapped his eyes shut once more as the foaming water raced up to meet him. He felt no surface impact as the water engulfed him in its warm embrace. Sinking fast into the depths, he thrashed in blind panic, but his plunge halted just as quickly, stopped short by an invisible cushion.

Cristen's eyes flew open, and he found himself surrounded by an otherworldly realm of color and light, more glorious than he could have conceived. The water glowed a luminescent turquoise, dancing with a thousand golden rays crisscrossing down to the colorful riverbed from the distant surface. Twenty feet beneath him, vibrant green flora and tubular orange coral swayed over glimmering white sand dotted with blossoms in every vivid hue.

Needing air, Cristen glanced upward, but the rippling mirror of the surface appeared too far away. *Breathe*, came the familiar voice that saved him before—how could he doubt it now? Having no choice but to trust again, Cristen inhaled deeply, flooding his lungs with the liquid. But it felt as insubstantial as air, leaving him tranquil and at peace as he exhaled.

Without air, he didn't buoy upward or sink but floated effortlessly in place. Delighted by his newfound freedom of movement, Cristen leisurely swam about, taking in the breathtaking garden paradise surrounding him. Schools of jewel-toned fish wove through the undulating aquatic foliage.

It seemed incredible that such a sanctuary existed here, unknown to anyone in Harmony. Yet its raging façade cleverly concealed this hidden world of wonders. Cristen's heart swelled to know that the master deemed him worthy to witness it after testing his faith. If beholding all this were the sole reason Cristen had come to Harmony, he would repeat the journey in a heartbeat.

Something glittered among the flora where a sunbeam touched the white sand. Drifting down, Cristen gently pushed aside a wispy frond to uncover a bronze medallion three inches across on a chain meant to be worn. He picked up the medallion from the sand, and as he did so, he noticed that the sunbeam remained fixed on it no matter which way he moved it. The beam bent upward from the sand where the medallion had lain.

Cristen grinned when he saw the crown insignia within a small circle at the medallion's center. Battle emblems—a shield, helmet, sword, and breastplate—divided the surrounding space into four quarters. A flowing ribbon across the bottom read HOPE. The reverse held an engraving of Revival Park's statue of the master, unicorn, and bird bath.

Try as he might, the chain refused to slip over his head. It writhed obstinately from his grasp until it broke free completely, then sank back to its sunlit patch of sand.

Beside it lay another medallion, likewise tethered by its unique sunbeam. Cristen could see each light ray anchored to its medallion through the vibrant seascape. The name BENJAMIN marked the ribbon of the next one he retrieved, where HOPE read on the first. Checking several more, he found each bore a different name: BERTA, CARTER, SVEN, ROSITA. So Hope didn't offer some concept, but someone's very identity. Did each medallion await its rightful owner? Tragically, with the dragon hoarding every water dreamer, perhaps the medallions would linger here forever unclaimed.

Cristen thought of the endless stolen waterskins at Sefilar's lair. Yet, surrounded by such beauty, he felt full of hope instead of despair, just as the girl's name foretold. If his medallion waited for him too, he must find it. Scouring the undulating aquatic garden, Cristen didn't need to search long.

From afar, a medallion twisted gracefully toward him, swimming above the floral fronds as if alive, chain trailing like a tail. Cristen seized the chain as it reached him, but it didn't stop, tugging him powerfully through the water.

The ride afforded him a stunning tour of what felt like a mile through the hidden sanctuary, an exhilarating ride he would treasure. At last, the medallion slowed and dropped to hang from its chain. Seeing his name engraved across its ribbon, this time, the chain slid easily over his head to rest against his chest. The anchoring sunbeam released its hold, piercing through Cristen's heart instead with such searing intensity that he felt consumed by feverish heat throughout his body and racing images within his mind.

In mere seconds, everything came flooding back to him. Cristen remembered it all.

40

Cristen's lost memories came like a whirlwind: Hanna, Mother, Father, Damon, the sprawling estate, their horses, running errands, mealtimes, chores, and his summer job riding for the general.

Focusing on one vivid scene at a time slowed the onslaught, allowing each cherished recollection space to imprint before the next swept in. He welcomed the joyous images one by one. Some he didn't want to let go of, others he clung to only briefly.

He relived long-ago days exploring the estate on foot with playmate Hanna, their realm expanding on horseback to the far reaches of the estate as they grew older. His love for her ran deeper than the fragmented dreams conveyed. If only she could remember too.

Cristen immersed himself in recollections of his parents interacting with various servants—the cook, stable hands, and Hanna's father, their chief gardener. He'd roamed the grounds running errands for Mother and doing chores like sweeping the drive and weeding her flower beds. He recalled more of his rocky relationship with Damon and his father's constant traveling, yet he never missed important events. The profound relief and contentment from regaining his identity felt indescribable. At long last, Cristen inhabited his true self unquestionably, no longer an outsider in his own skin.

Lord Whitaker!

Cristen relived the pivotal day of Lord Whitaker's fateful arrival, now understanding with piercing clarity the reason behind his willingness to come to Harmony. He remembered Lord Whitaker solemnly unrolling the scroll and feeling the energized hush filling the room. He relived his indignant outburst upon hearing the scroll's summons to leave behind all he loved to voyage to some wretched-sounding land in service of some unknown king. His poor mother. No wonder she's been so distraught.

Cristen's resentment had vanished with the scroll's lavish promise in exchange for such sacrifice. The first glimpse of real magic sealed his cooperation. Everything changed in that moment.

***

Father rarely raised his voice, but now it lashed out like a whip. "Cristen, you hold the complete right to decline this proposition. However, you will hear the man out before we send him on his way."

Temper flaring, Cristen shouted back, "Fine! I'll listen, but I'm not going!"

Lord Whitaker discreetly cleared his throat and continued at Father's approving nod.

"*The land of Harmony swarms with hidden treasure and magic.*"

Magic? That got Cristen's attention. He only knew of the magic within fanciful myths and legends. "What do you mean...magic?" he blurted out. But Lord Whitaker carried on.

"*As you embark on your journey to discern the king's will, seek not only his favor but also a gift of rare beauty, something to adorn his palaces and befit His Eminence.*

"*Deliver this treasure into the hand of his statue within the hallowed grounds of Revival Park. Should your offering meet his approval, your quest shall be deemed complete, a triumph in his eyes. As a reward for your commitment and sacrifice, you shall immediately be granted a single wish, a boon of your choosing.*

"Upon returning home, you will be assigned to your regiment and serve in the king's battalion for a year's term. Understand that the power to shape your destiny lies within your control."

The scroll levitated, rolled up, and burst into flames, vanishing with its glowing embers. The room fell silent. Cristen felt frozen in place, scarcely believing what he'd just witnessed.

Mother finally shattered the stunned silence, voice quavering. "That...is the magic he refers to, my darling boy. Which is why I must let you go."

Cristen rose slowly to his feet, mind reeling. "Mother...how long have you known?"

"Your leaving has haunted me since the day you were born. Please, you must forgive me."

Still dazed, Cristen nodded. A wish-granting quest? Any wish he desired? No wonder Damon vanished—ever obsessed with exceeding their father's wealth. Cristen's eyes met his father's thoughtful gaze. He realized he knew very little of Father's success. Had he himself once walked this very path in his youth? Now that he thought about it, had he sold so much produce to be able to support an entire estate? Of course, as a traveling merchant, he likely facilitated other ventures. But perhaps the residual blessing of a wish granted long ago secretly explained his thriving success and lavish lifestyle.

Yes, Cristen would accept this quest. But first, he must speak with Hanna and bind them together. He needed her sworn devotion as he pledged his own. "I'll be right back," he announced to the watching faces.

Cristen hurried from the study, down the long hall, past the kitchens and the second hall to exit the front door. As he shut the door, he halted abruptly. *Why did I come outside?* Bewildered, he reentered the house. What just happened? He urgently wanted to talk to Hanna about leaving. Again, he stepped outside. *Why am I out here?* Did Mother send him on an errand? Flustered over his lapse in memory, he went back in.

At last, he clued into what was happening. Striding resolutely back to the study, he arrived breathless. "So she can't know about any of this?"

Father shook his head gravely. "The king prevents you. None may know of Harmony until they are summoned."

"I can't go without saying goodbye. She won't know what happened to me," he said, remembering how Damon's abrupt disappearance had baffled him.

"I'm so sorry, son."

Cristen turned to Mother beseechingly. "Tell her I love her, Mama." The childhood name slipped out.

Mother nodded, wiping away more tears.

Despite the disappointment, excitement still fluttered inside Cristen. With a wish, his and Hanna's future would be secured.

41

As Cristen clutched the medallion, the gravity of his quest bore down upon him. He had sworn to seek out the will of the king of the entire world—his beloved wizard—and serve him and his cause with unwavering loyalty. He felt great relief to know that his time in Harmony was only supposed to last until he discovered the perfect treasure. Although he would still need to complete his year of service upon returning home, it seemed a small price to pay for such a generous reward, and he would finally return to the real world.

A wish! His mind raced through possibilities. If only he could make it right then and there before it was too late, he would wish for Hanna's love. However, he immediately dismissed the notion. The cautionary tales of youth warned that no wish could compel one heart toward another, and the relationship could never be genuine.

Cristen now understood why his parents closely guarded his and Hanna's relationship. They always knew that separation—possibly permanently—loomed in their futures and did what they could to spare them unnecessary anguish. Cristen forgave them for prioritizing what they believed to be in their best interest.

He wondered if his parents fully grasped the hazards of the quest when they agreed to send him and his brother out. With Damon deserting his duty and Hanna lost, having been shifted, hadn't they been cut off from home? They might enjoy the luxuries Harmony provided them through Sefilar, but at what cost? If they remained trapped here, they would forfeit home and family. They may be oblivious to their tragic loss, but their loved ones would still grieve. It gutted Cristen to think he could have prevented Hanna's tragedy by simply keeping her away from Burning Mountain. But he couldn't even do that. He'd utterly failed her.

An unexpected exhibit amid the river garden redirected his attention. A garden fence enclosed a podium with a gem-encrusted book resting atop it. Swimming over the fence, Cristen drifted down and planted his feet before the podium. Immediately, the opulent tome came to life, the covers opening, pages fluttering until they settled on an inscription.

Cristen read: "To don this medallion, I solemnly pledge my allegiance to the king of Phaeton—to aid him in his noble pursuit of global peace. I vow to present a worthy gift in exchange for a single wish. Upon signing my name, I hereby formally accept service in the king's battalion for a term of one year."

The opposite page held a blank space headed:

NAME OF APPRENTICE.

He took a gold quill from its stand to proudly sign his full name: Cristen Stronghold. Again, the page turned on its own volition, and he read in scrolling letters:

CRISTEN STRONGHOLD, *Son of the New Dawn.*

Cristen perceived within his heart something that felt like a cheer of celebration from a throng of people. He closed his eyes to take it in, imagining his parents among the jubilant crowd. When his heart quieted, he opened his eyes to the book again. Curious to see who else might have signed it, he tried turning the page, but the pages fluttered closed, followed by the cover.

The water churned above his head, but before he could gaze up, an explosion of bubbles enveloped him. As the churning froth lifted and carried him away, he couldn't tell if he moved upright, sideways, or upside down. However, it didn't last long before his feet landed on solid ground. He easily coughed the water from his lungs and opened his eyes to the early night. He stood within the crystal clear waters of the pool beneath the wizard's statue and his outstretched hand, the one that hopefully would accept his future offering.

Cristen wiped the water from his eyes and pushed back his sopping hair, struggling to believe what just happened. Glancing around Revival Park, his gaze returned to the wizard—his broad shoulders, flowing cloak, and the hood obscuring his face.

And the statue's donned medallion—he hadn't noticed before. He placed his hand on his own.

He finally understood what Simon had searched for on his chest when he grabbed his tunic. He realized he'd been missing his medallion, a symbol of truth and knowledge. He no longer hungered and thirsted for answers with it finally in place. Though he intuitively sensed he still had much work to do, that same inner wisdom told him he'd sifted much of the truth from the lies, which set him on a clear path to his destiny.

He shook his head in awe that the master still considered him worthy of apprenticeship. Gazing into the shadowed hood, he wondered if he would ever have the chance to meet his generous benefactor face-to-face and that he wouldn't be required to Cross Old Surge to do so.

Cristen waded past the bowed unicorn to leave the pool but paused to inspect the short ladder again, with its ancient symbols etched on each of the four rungs. As he studied the carvings, a familiar warble drew his attention. Turning towards the sound, he spotted his bird perched on the fluted edge of the giant birdbath, partially obscured by the spraying water, but the scarlet mark on its breast gave it away.

Laughing, Cristen greeted it warmly. "What are you doing here? I didn't send any message." He extended his arm, and the devoted bird fluttered down to land gently on his shoulder. A small scroll was tied to its leg, and Cristen removed it carefully to read the note aloud:

As you serve me, FERRIN has served you since you arrived in Harmony. Now that you have passed through the River of Redemption, I gift him to you as your own.

With joy, Cristen kissed the bird's downy blue head. "Looks like you're coming home with me! Why didn't you tell me you were a boy, silly? Ferrin. You finally have a name." Already friends, he now accepted his faithful avian companion as family. As Cristen stepped from the pool, he laughed, realizing his predicament. "I have no shoes." He'd left them on the bridge.

He left the little green oasis barefoot, but the next moment, he sensed someone following him. Glancing over his shoulder, he saw his boots marching through the grass to meet him. Chuckling at his magical world, Cristen waited for them, then sat to tug them on. He headed home with Ferrin cradled in his arm, content to know that the wizard remained steadfastly by his side—as he always had. He no longer yearned to flee Harmony. His quest would be the passage home, not the impenetrable winter storm.

Although Harmony might forever brand him a water dreamer, Cristen didn't need to embrace the misguided designation. He was simply a man on a mission. With his memory and identity restored, even the ache of missing family faded. They weren't lost, and neither was he. Although he looked forward to their reunion, he now understood this to be a temporary separation.

As eager as Cristen felt to begin his long-awaited service to his wizard king, he needed to attend to some personal business first. A family needed to make amends.

✶✶✶

Ferrin flew up to roost on the roof before Warren answered the door, looking a little cross. "Doozy, where have you been?"

Stepping inside, Cristen asked, "Is your mother still awake?"

"Of course, fussing over her new pet as usual," Warren grumbled.

"New pet?"

"Mirabel, obviously," Warren huffed.

"Oh, right. Well, I spoke with Evelyn today. You were right about her staying at Beacon Hill all this time."

"Told you so." Warren bellowed toward the ceiling, "Ma, Cristen found Evelyn!"

Cristen frowned. "You didn't mention it to her yet?"

"I told her she's alive. But Ma won't believe anything I say about it since I haven't seen her."

Mrs. Myers hurried in scolding, "What did I say about disturbing Mary's rest? She was nearly asleep, poor dear."

"Ma'am, Evelyn is perfectly alright," Cristen reassured her.

"Hmph. If she's fine, why isn't she here?"

"I spoke with her myself," Cristen explained.

"Indeed," Mrs. Myers huffed. "Is she on her way home then?"

Cristen tried a different angle. "Ma'am, have you heard talk of the Council shutting down Beacon Hill?"

She looked baffled. "What are you going on about? Of course not, why would they?"

"I'm afraid Evelyn believed the rumors. It's why she stayed away."

"Preposterous. That project has brought a fortune into King's Crossing and benefited the Council immensely."

Mr. Myers descended the stairs in a night robe. "She speaks truthfully," he affirmed. "A few of us initially opposed it, fearing so many dragon scales would curse the land. But with the influx of gold into our coffers, we were quickly accused of superstition and outvoted."

He added, "Forgive me, darling, for not confiding in you. I didn't think it consequential when we dropped the matter."

Mrs. Myers pursed her lips. "Nor should it have arisen. How distasteful."

Mr. Myers said, "We shall set her mind at ease about such foolish gossip."

"Of course. How dreadful to be subjected to such nonsense." Mrs. Myers fretted, "Where is the afflicted child?"

"I already told you—at Damon's place!" Warren insisted.

"Then Damon found her," Mrs. Myers concluded satisfactorily. "I knew that boy was good through and through."

"No, Cristen found her!" Warren nearly shouted in frustration. "Damon hid her away!"

Mrs. Myers waved a hand dismissively. "Don't be absurd, dear. Take me to her at once. Let me fetch a shawl. The poor child must desperately need me."

Cristen worried about how awkward such a meetup would be, but Warren must have sensed the same thing.

"It's too late to travel to King's Crossing tonight," Warren pointed out. He shot Cristen a smug, knowing look that suggested he took pride in his secret ability to travel instantly. "And what about poor Mary?" Warren added in feigned concern. "You can't just abandon the poor girl."

Mr. Myers stepped in. "We'll send word first thing in the morning approving Damon's manor. I still don't understand the need for such extravagance, but no matter."

Cristen's step felt lighter as he left the Myers' home that night.

42

Mirabel pointed past a row of shrubs. "There's the Lace Factory booth," she said, her shyness having lessened after dealing with Mrs. Myers.

Cristen, Warren, and Mirabel traveled by house to King's Crossing the evening before the wedding. They were on a mission to retrieve a dress for Mrs. Myers that needed last-minute alterations from the shop owner's booth at the Rendezvous marketplace.

Mrs. Myers requested that Mr. Myers make the four-hour round trip, but Warren had insisted he could find a ride into town and run the errand himself. Somehow, she had agreed.

Just the previous day, after a courier delivered a message to Evelyn at Beacon Hill, the Myers received their belated wedding invitation, which included a brief apology note from her. She explained that her puzzling absence had all been a misunderstanding and bore them no ill will.

"Do you have a dress for Mrs. Luinda Myers?" Warren asked the vendor importantly.

"You must be Freddy Junior," said the man, pulling a wrapped bundle from a basket and handing it over.

As the shopkeeper began expounding on the extravagant wedding preparations, including the breathtaking bride's gown he had meticulously crafted, Cristen discreetly slipped away.

A few booths down, another vendor with bare shelves caught his eye—not Simon, but a younger luminary sporting a bow tie in his place. Still, he needed to speak with him to find out what was wrong with his bird. It had refused to deliver messages since taking ownership of him.

"What happened to Simon?" Cristen asked the man as he approached the booth.

"Good morning to you!" exclaimed the man cheerfully. "And who might I have the pleasure of addressing?"

"I'm Cristen."

"Cristen Stronghold, son of Gabriel and Lena! Such an honor," he said, shaking Cristen's hand with both of his. "Call me Pete."

The luminary knew his parents!

"I'm friends with Simon," Cristen said. "Do you know where I can find him? My bird isn't working, and I need to speak with the master."

The man's gaze traveled across the way. "Yet your winged friend follows you."

Cristen looked up to spot his bird perched atop a tent. "But he won't carry my parchment anymore."

Grinning, the man asked, "Might you have acquired something new?"

Cristen withdrew his medallion. "I have this now. Please tell Simon I'm a son of the new dawn."

"Then you've entered the gate!" the man said happily.

Cristen nodded uncertainly, only recalling the small fenced area around the podium.

"You've come remarkably far," the man praised. "But what is your course from here?"

"That's just it. I'm not sure where to go next."

"All will become clear, so have faith. The king does not abandon loyal subjects, so do not lose heart."

Cristen wanted to tell him that the king didn't abandon disloyal subjects either. But reassured, he inquired, "May I ask why you're here instead of Simon?"

"I await on another. Thanks to your warning, she knows the enemy."

"Mirabel," Cristen realized aloud. "I'll protect her if I can. Does she have a medallion too?" A fellow quester could prove a valuable ally.

"In due time, if she desires it, she will find hers."

Cristen offered, "I can tell her about them...and the river's beauty."

"By all means. But until she hears the master's call herself, she is not prepared."

Cristen understood, recalling his own extensive journey to arrive at this place. "I'll go get her then," he offered. He assumed the man had a parchment for her. Cristen would distract Warren to allow them privacy.

***

Later, trudging home alone, Cristen's heart felt as heavy as lead. He couldn't help feeling betrayed by everyone. Had they all forgotten he was about to lose his girl? And to his brother? Would any of them spare a sympathetic thought for him during the ceremony? He imagined Hanna and Damon pledging eternal devotion, gazing into each other's eyes, oblivious to Cristen's shattered hopes.

With a sigh, he recognized his dismal thoughts only deepened his gloom. Redirecting his energy, he recalled the change in Mirabel after receiving her parchment and key for

335

her very own house from the luminary Pete. She had been so pleased to be shown such care and attention. Pete also spoke highly of Cristen, telling her she couldn't be luckier. Cristen had paved the way by warning her about the dragon and Burning Mountain. He felt satisfied knowing he had made a difference.

Halfway home, he automatically reached to check for dragon scales, only to realize they hadn't plagued him for some time. Now that he thought about it, he felt sure none had appeared since his immersion in the river. River of Redemption, Ferrin's note had called it. Its restorative waters must have broken their curse over him. He laughed aloud in surprised relief—the river was the very cure Simon had spoken of. Cristen felt more free than he had in ages, liberated from the dragon's relentless harassment. "Thank you," he whispered gratefully.

Arriving home, Cristen sat at the table, staring blankly at his and Warren's map still covering the table. The smudged, inky notes obscuring much of their progress caught his attention. He decided to work on the map without Warren, exploring and recording more unfamiliar towns. It would provide the perfect distraction for the day.

Flipping it over, he carefully recreated the known towns, meticulously copying names in his best penmanship, wholly absorbed in his map-making task.

Hours later, an unexpected knock at the door interrupted him just as he prepared to visit the first unlabeled town. He opened the door to find Warren, his parents, and Mirabel waiting on the porch. Mr. Myers acted oddly fascinated by the house's architecture, and Mrs. Myers looked frazzled. Cristen wondered to what lengths Mrs. Myers had gone to get Warren so neatly groomed for the occasion. Mirabel looked nice in another of Hanna's dresses.

"Please accept our apologies," Frederick offered politely. "A mile from home, and our carriage seats come loose. Nearly tossed onto the road—all of us! Every screw missing."

Cristen struggled to keep it together when he looked at guilt-stricken Warren.

"We'll never make it now," Mrs. Myers despaired. "Warren insists this house of yours can...well, I dare not repeat such nonsense."

"Just get inside," Warren said brusquely, herding his parents through the door.

With the formal attire severely constricting his movement, Warren hurried to the clock but couldn't lift his arm high enough to work it properly.

"I've got it," Cristen offered, aligning the hand and clicking them back to King's Crossing as seen through the window.

"Let's go!" shouted Warren as he opened the door again. "What are we waiting for?"

His baffled parents cautiously followed him back outside. Mrs. Myers yelped in shock at the changed surroundings. They hurried off down Sion Street before Cristen could utter a word, providing quite a whimsical spectacle. He chuckled, imagining their utter bewilderment.

43

After exploring two unremarkable towns—a sleepy seaside village of retirees that watched him suspiciously from their porches and another nearly devoid of greenery—Cristen prepared to visit a third when the clock hand suddenly stopped moving. Gently, he tried to force it back into action, and it worked, but only briefly. As the hand rounded the clock again, it froze in the same spot. Tracing the line of the hand, Cristen discovered it crossed directly over a town.

He wondered if the clock had broken from overuse or if the master wanted him to see something. With his curiosity piqued and knowing he needed the town's name anyway, he decided to investigate. He turned the gear and stepped through the door.

Cristen found himself pleasantly surprised by the charming town of Thistle. Stately oak trees lined Main Street, their leafy canopies providing welcomed shade to the quaint shops nestled cozily between them.

At the town's heart lay a charming park with only a few distant visitors wandering the grounds. A gurgling creek wound through rolling hills dotted with quaking aspens. Sleepy from his solitary adventures, Cristen settled onto his back on a park bench, listening to the birds sing while Ferrin pecked nearby in the grass. Wispy clouds drifted across the brilliant blue sky, reminding Cristen of carefree days cloud-gazing with Hanna.

He dozed in and out, enjoying the respite, until a haunting melody eventually roused him from his nap, wafting intermittently on the breeze. Initially ignoring it, he rose when it woke him again, setting off to trace the alluring music to its source. He followed the babbling creek to a footbridge where an exquisitely dressed bride leaned gracefully over the opposite side, watching the water pass beneath her. Her shimmering silks and satins seemed fit for royalty, the roses and ribbons of her headdress cascading down her back. A solitary white horse grazed on the far bank. Approaching silently, Cristen noticed a drooping pink tulip dangling limply in the woman's hand past her sheer sleeve.

Sensing his presence, she turned abruptly. "Oh. Forgive me, I thought...oh, it's you again," she exclaimed, clutching the wilted tulip to her lace-adorned bosom. Cream-colored ties crisscrossed down to a low waist. "I didn't expect anyone to find me here. Who sent you?"

Cristen froze in disbelief, barely recognizing Hanna's face within earthy tones of paint and glitter and beneath the exquisitely embroidered headpiece that covered her hair. Swallowing the lump in his throat, he rasped, "No one. The clock, it...is everything...alright? Why are you here?"

Hanna turned away to lean on the bridge again, her silence stretching out, tormenting Cristen with the wait.

Finally, she spoke. "You think you know someone. You think you'll have the happily ever after every girl dreams of. You do anything he asks because you believe your happiness is his priority, just like he promised."

Cristen edged nervously closer to the bridge. "I'm so very sorry. I wish I could..." He wanted to offer comforting words, but his uncertainty about whether she had gone through with the wedding held him back.

"You tried warning me," Hanna acknowledged softly.

Sudden fury at Damon welled up in Cristen. "Tell me what he's done. I'll kill him."

"Honestly, I'd rather he hurt me than lie to me like he did."

"No, Hanna," Cristen said, taking a step closer. "You deserve only the best." He desperately wanted to go to her.

She turned her head slightly toward him. "Of all the things he could have done to push me away, do you know what tiny thing severed my faith in him?"

Cristen shook his head.

She paused again before answering. "He called me Hanna as we exchanged vows. Just like you call me Hanna."

Cristen grasped the first knob of the bridge railing for support. "I'm so sorry. I swear I'll only call you Evelyn from now on. Please forgive me."

Hanna sighed deeply, eyes cast downward at the water again. "That's just it," she said. "That one slip told me everything I needed to know. For him to also think that I'm Hanna means that he knows what you know. How could I go through with it?"

Cristen's heart pounded as the weight of relief washed over him like a tidal wave. Hanna wasn't married. With disbelief and overwhelming gratitude, he tried to regain his composure.

A passing couple eyed Hanna in her exquisite gown, then Cristen as if to witness the lucky groom who'd won her affections.

Hanna gave a brittle laugh, glancing down at herself. "Look at me. What a spectacle I'm making in this garish thing." She fumbled with her elaborate headdress, searching for pins while holding the tulip.

Cristen rushed onto the bridge and to her side, gently turning her to face him. "Hardly a spectacle," he assured her. He carefully removed each of the four pins that anchored the weighty headpiece with deliberate slowness, savoring each moment as if time paused to witness the act. His fingers grazed three faint scars on the nape of her neck, reminding him of the day a wasp stung her because of him.

As Cristen lifted the headdress free, her lavender-gray eyes, accentuated by vivid paint, transfixed him. When his knuckle accidentally brushed her cheek, she drew in a sharp breath, and their eyes locked.

Taking the headdress from his hands, Hanna gently dropped it over the bridge rail. It drifted slowly away on the current, the veil of ribbons and roses trailing behind.

"Please...tell me about my family," she implored, gazing up at him again. "Do I have siblings?"

"I can't," Cristen whispered, overcome by her beauty again. He leaned closer, murmuring, "You hardly know me, but promise you'll forgive me for this."

Hanna's eyes softened with unspoken understanding. "But you know me," she breathed. "I don't know why, but I trust you."

Cupping her face in both hands, Cristen kissed her softly...tentatively. When she didn't resist, he slid a hand around the small of her back, pulled her close, and kissed her passionately while the world spun around them.

Epilogue

T he blissful two weeks with Hanna felt like a dream. She returned to live with the Myers, referring to them by their first names now that she knew that her true parents, Joseph and Gloria Milner, waited for her back home in the kingdom of Wennix.

Cristen treasured every small reminder that she was still the same girl he'd always known—her playful pokes to his ribs while teasing him, her annoyed eye-rolls at some injustice, her arms wrapped around her knees while sitting, and her nervous hiccups when flustered.

Hanna seemed happy too, especially when they'd curl up on the Myers' sofa to whisper endlessly about life back home. Hanna hung to Cristen's every word, not letting him skip even the smallest detail as he transported them back home—the floral scents from her father's garden, the croaking frogs by the pond, their first exhilarating rides on horseback across the sprawling estate. He told her of her younger sister, Sarah, and two-year-old brother, Thomas.

He shared his encounter with the wolf the night he escaped into the yard as a toddler. After his Mother returned him to his bed, he heard his parents' heated discussion behind closed doors, their raised voices unsettling to his young ears.

Occasionally, they heard one of the Myers pause in the hallway to listen, undoubtedly curious over their endless hushed conversations.

Eventually, Cristen filled Hanna in on the harrowing trials he'd faced since arriving in Harmony—being captured and forced into the Array, his chilling encounters with the dragon, and his narrow escape thanks to the seer crystal and glowing orb. He chose not to mention her betrayal under Sefilar's influence since she had been the ultimate victim of the dragon's deception, and he refused to allow anything more to come between them.

Tears welled up in Hanna's eyes as she listened to Cristen recount Damon's treacherous attempt on his life, an act that had cost Cristen his beloved horse. The revelation only solidified her belief that Damon was not the honorable and virtuous man he portrayed himself to be.

They laughed together every time Warren's name came up as Cristen relayed their escapades, especially the ill-conceived details of Operation Sabotage. Cristen profusely apologized for his reckless role in the matter, admitting he should have handled the situation more maturely. But Hanna assured him she found it amusing and felt flattered that he fought for her affections against such impossible odds.

With wide-eyed wonder, Hanna soaked up Cristen's displays of the wizard's sorcery, enthused by each revelation. She couldn't get enough of the glowing orb and how they could travel from town to town in the blink of an eye. However, whenever he mentioned the River of Redemption and the wonders he witnessed there, her expression clouded over with uncertainty.

Beneath the joy of having Hanna back in his life, a shadow of uncertainty persisted, knowing their entire future depended on both of them returning home. Hanna needed the wizard's guidance to complete her quest. Yet Hanna said she'd never seen the brown and white bird Cristen remembered, so how could a parchment help? Cristen figured she needed to start dreaming again or retrieve her medallion to regain her full memories.

Furthermore, her lost memories sometimes felt like a gulf between them since she didn't know him like he knew her. Nevertheless, Hanna's trust in Cristen remained steadfast, and he hoped that, given time, she would remember home and him so their connection could blossom in a whole new way.

Mirabel left to live in her new house, greatly offending Mrs. Myers. But she sent word that she found a job as a seamstress, learning quickly under the tutelage of the Lace Factory's owner. With her departure, Hanna was glad to have her own room again, even though she and Mirabel had become friends.

Cristen and Hanna had just returned to Mulberry after a visit to Revival Park, which was sparked by Hanna's interest in the statue engraved on his medallion. They strolled hand in hand across the yard together to check in on Moonshine.

"Your mother's song again?" Hanna asked.

Cristen smiled when he realized he'd been humming. "I don't know why I remembered her music, but it's helped me through the worst."

"But you didn't know it was hers."

"Not for a while," Cristen said.

"What I wouldn't give to hear my mother somehow," Hanna said wistfully. "It might ease my heart when it weeps."

She'd mentioned her heart in such a way before. Cristen wished he better understood what she meant, but the sensation went beyond description for her.

They heard the gate open and turned to see Mirabel entering. She looked sharp in a shapely belted tunic and high-laced boots. She also seemed to have gained more confidence in herself.

"There you are," Mirabel said, smiling as she joined them. "I thought I'd never see you two again."

"You've been busy," Hanna said, clearly happy to see her.

"So have you," Mirabel said knowingly. "You've both been staying with the Myers?"

"Mostly," Cristen said bashfully, putting a supportive arm around Hanna's shoulders. "I'm here overnight, of course."

Mirabel's expression changed to one of humored suspicion. "You do know I've been here for a while—since my fabrics and spools of thread are everywhere."

Hanna looked questioningly at Cristen, and he adamantly shook his head to indicate he didn't know what she meant.

"Hey, look!" Cristen exclaimed when he noticed Mirabel's white pigeon circling above them.

Hanna glanced up at the bird, a flicker of envy passing over her face. She quickly masked it with a smile, but Cristen knew she was thinking about her own lost bird.

"I hardly see it anymore," Mirabel mused as she watched it. "I don't think it's forgiven me."

"Then why is it here?" Cristen pointed out. "Come on, hold out your hand."

When she did, the white bird fluttered down to perch on her arm, cooing softly.

Mirabel smiled, gently stroking its feathers. "I guess it just needed an invitation."

"He'll be a good companion for you," said Cristen. "That bird is your connection to the master."

"Simon mentioned a master," Mirabel said, intrigued.

"It's what your parchment is for," Cristen explained. "There's a lot to tell you."

"Good, because I have a lot to learn...which will have to wait since I'm on a time crunch," she said. "Catch up with you later?"

Cristen and Hanna gawked in bewilderment as Mirabel walked up Cristen's front steps and right through his open door, which they hadn't bothered to close. But Mirabel stopped short at the entrance, turning to look back at them in confusion. "Where did you put everything?"

"What do you mean?" Cristen asked.

"Where's my stuff?" she asked, her face flushing. "I spent my own money on it and need it for work."

"But Mirabel, this isn't your house," Cristen said gently, trying to understand her behavior.

"You didn't know I was living here?" Mirabel asked, now near tears.

Cristen and Hanna exchanged glances.

"We haven't seen you since you left the Myers," Hanna said, hurrying up the steps to give her a supportive hug. "What's going on, Mary? Don't fret. We'll help you find your things."

Cristen offered, "Just show me your key, and we can help you find the right address."

"But it's for your house," Mirabel insisted, taking it from her pocket to show him. "I figured we were supposed to be roommates."

Cristen felt confused seeing 1208 Sion Street engraved along the silvery threads, which again matched his key. "You're...right," he said carefully. It seemed improbable that they were intended to share such confined quarters and a lone bed, and Cristen wondered about the wizard's motives.

Cristen closed the front door to confirm that her key fit his lock. When he opened the door again, Hanna gasped in surprise while Mirabel stared wide-eyed. Bolts of fabric now lay across his bed in disarray, while spools of thread cluttered the bureau top.

"My fabrics," Mirabel cried in relief. "But how?"

Cristen stared dumbfounded to see his house transformed. Handing Mirabel's key back to her, he closed them inside to try his own key again. Instantly, he found himself back home. Somehow, they did share the same house after all...only not the same space. As odd as it felt, Cristen grew fascinated with the possibilities. How many other dreamers would end up at the same address?

The revelation brought another unsettling thought to mind. Cristen remembered the warden claiming the house belonged to him too. Though he never saw him around, did the warden share the house too? If so, either the warden was a dreamer, or he stole a key from a past sanitarium inmate.

Wanting to return to Hanna and Mirabel, Cristen knocked tentatively on his front door after closing it again. Thankfully, Hanna opened it, welcoming him back inside Mirabel's version of the house.

Mirabel still seemed puzzled by the mysterious appearance and disappearance of her belongings, but her confusion quickly gave way to admiration as she gazed around the room.

"Who could have predicted little old me getting her very own place?" she said. Finding an open spot to perch on the edge of the bed, she added, "I guess I'll have to celebrate alone with my stitches, though. I have a big project to finish by tomorrow."

"Then we'll leave you to it," Hanna said, giving her a quick cheek kiss.

"See you soon?" Cristen said. "As long as we knock on the right door."

Mirabel paused to consider the idea. "Yes, it seems there may be complications," she said, furrowing her brow in concern.

Cristen agreed, his head spinning at the possibilities as he followed Hanna outside.

"Not sure how I feel about you two essentially living together," Hanna teased after shutting the door.

Cristen grinned, enjoying the hint of jealousy in her tone. "The question is, how will we ever know whose door to knock on? How do we get ahold of the right person?" he asked.

Hanna laughed, shaking her head as they used the key to return to Cristen's familiar room. Sitting on the edge of the bed, she looked around. "How weird is it that Mirabel might be sitting in this same spot?" she asked.

"Or we're somewhere else entirely," Cristen hypothesized. "Maybe it's like different dimensions."

"I just can't wrap my head around it." Hanna laughed again at the strangeness of it all. "I guess I should believe anything after what you've shown me already."

Cristen smiled. He put his arm around her and kissed the corner of her mouth. "Here's the real magic," he said playfully.

"I might have to agree," Hanna said with a smirk and glint in her eye. "Speaking of magic, when are you going to show me your snow fort?" She glanced at the mirror.

"Make a picnic of it?" Cristen suggested as he went to gather the remainder of his food ration.

"I'm definitely ready for a bite of something," Hanna said, following him to the table.

But Cristen paused, struck by a startling new thought.

"What is it?" Hanna asked, noticing his hesitation.

"I just remembered—I have another key."

"Another key? To this house?"

Cristen nodded. "We found it lost in the snow a while back. I'd forgotten about it, thinking I'd only found a copy."

"Whose is it then? Why do you have it?" Hanna pressed curiously.

"I have no idea," Cristen said. "But the wizard led me to it for some reason." A smile spread across his face. You said you wished we shared my quest."

Hanna's eyes lit up. "But I'm not a dreamer anymore."

"Neither am I, remember?" he said teasingly. He avoided using the term for the most part, but leaving it behind altogether proved challenging. "Anyway, who says we can't make our own quest? There's at least one other person out there with a key to this house. Should we find out who?"

A mischievous grin lit up her face. "How utterly intriguing," she replied dramatically. "Sounds like some detective work is in order."

Cristen impulsively kissed her again, buzzing with excitement. He hurried to fetch the mysterious key from his drawer, nervously anticipating what they might discover. Whose house were they going to invade? Would the occupant be home?

Cristen didn't doubt the wizard meant for their paths to cross, though he couldn't fathom why. At least he didn't have to investigate alone.

With the key in hand, they stood outside the front door together. "Are you ready for this?" Cristen asked.

Hanna took a deep breath and placed her hand over his on the doorknob as Cristen inserted the key. "Ready as I'll ever be."

They held their breath and turned the key.

About the Author

Though Dana never dreamed of being an author, a burst of inspiration compelled her to write. What started as a short tale to inspire her children sparked an expansive saga within the literary world of Water Dreamers that would consume the following chapters of her life.

With four children at home and no formal training, she immersed herself in the study of writing and finding daily inspiration from authors like David Wolverton. Through tireless effort and countless revisions, her work evolved into an enthralling fantasy adventure for readers of all ages.

Now, with the support of her husband, grown children, and six grandchildren, Dana is excited to present the second book in her Water Dreamer series—Unsuspecting World. Originally from Canada, Dana currently resides in Salt Lake City, Utah.

Made in the USA
Middletown, DE
19 April 2024